THE
ORIGIN
OF MAN

ALSO BY CHRISTINE MONTALBETTI IN ENGLISH TRANSLATION:

Western

THE ORIGIN OF MAN

CHRISTINE
MONTALBETTI

TRANSLATED
BY BETSY WING

DALKEY ARCHIVE PRESS
CHAMPAIGN / DUBLIN / LONDON

Originally published in French as *L'Origine de l'homme* by Editions P.O.L, Paris, 2002
Copyright © 2002 by Editions P.O.L
Translation copyright © 2012 by Betsy Wing
First edition, 2012
All rights reserved

Library of Congress Cataloging-in-Publication Data

Montalbetti, Christine.
  [Origine de l'homme. English]
  The origin of man / Christine Montalbetti ; translated by Betsy Wing. -- 1st ed.
    p. cm.
  "Originally published in French as L'Origine de l'homme by Editions P.O.L, Paris, 2002"
--T.p. verso.
  ISBN 978-1-56478-737-8 (pbk. : alk. paper)
  I. Wing, Betsy. II. Title.
  PQ2713.O576O7513 2012
  843'.92--dc23
                    2012013729
Partially funded by a grant from the National Endowment for the Arts, a federal agency, and the Illinois Arts Council, a state agency

Cet ouvrage a bénéficié du soutien des Programmes d'aide à la publication de l'Institut français/ministère français des affaires étrangères et européennes

This work, published as part of a program of aid for publication, received support from the Istitut Français

Cet ouvrage publié dans le cadre du programme d'aide à la publication bénéficie du soutien du Ministère des Affaires Etrangères et du Service Culturel de l'Ambassade de France représenté aux Etats-Unis.

This work received support from the French Ministry of Foreign Affairs and the Cultural Services of the French Embassy in the United States through their publishing assistance program.

www.dalkeyarchive.com

Cover: design and composition by Sarah French, illustration by Nicholas Motte

Printed on permanent/durable acid-free paper and bound in the United States of America

CONTENTS

I
THE FRIEND'S HOUSE

I

Splish splash goes our man, delightedly watching half a dozen dragonflies fly past him in the bitter breeze and not in the least reluctant to splatter a few, sending some very local showers into the October chill in which he's taking his daily swim in the river this Picardy morning, splish splash, and every spatter originating from his spot (nobody else in the vicinity, except possibly for a big, huge, gigantic fish of the large, aquatic, pisciform mammalian category—example: whale; you just don't see what else could stir up so much water in the river to make it spin and fly like that) provides him a chance to warm up a bit, even though the effort involved is modest, flapping his arms, rolling his shoulders with his palms flat as rackets or spatulas coming down to strike the water while his feet and even his legs are moving underneath for the sake of keeping our man up and at more or less the same depth all around.

Splashes rise in pearly droplets over the fields of the Somme toward the gray-blue sky where, for the time being, the cloud shapes are rather static, as if poised and waiting for the starting whistle, then in perhaps even finer drops, skumbling the smooth green of the rhubarb fields, and the prettiness of the whole scene (adorned with these *Arthropoda*, insects whose four veined wings filter it like tracings of watercolor landscapes) makes the swimmer feel quite cheerful, though, mind you, he wasn't feeling extremely sad, just, you know, sort of melancholy all over, a muffled sort of melancholy, if that exists (here's proof), connected to some vague thoughts back over how days had gone by and how little had gotten done in them, but I said "vague," right, nothing like an examination of conscience with, let's say, two columns listing things done and things not done that when subtracted one from the other leaves a not exactly brilliant sum and the result is remorse— not that at all, just the sort of rather dull feeling you usually carry around without its bothering you much, and then one morning you wake up not exactly feeling like a lot of laughs so it takes up a little more space than usual and splish splash you chase it away with drops of water shot into the landscape, and there you have it, la di dah!

Our hero's unstinting efforts cause some real aquatic disorder here, a sort of—to take it further—watery fireworks, so you'd almost say, Look! Versailles! And really that's a remark good old Constantin might very well make if he were passing by, waving a friendly greeting from the shore, though he'd have to cup his hands into a megaphone and stand right on the river's edge in order to reach the swimmer's ears, then use his body like a spring,

slipsliding on the muddy bank he lurches back and forth, forming a sort of rolling *S* moving against the landscape, Hey look!
Versailles! But just now, while our man is splashing around as
described, Constantin is combing his mouse-gray hair with the
tortoise-shell teeth of a comb first dipped in eau de Cologne, there
you go, then pulling his cap on tight, okay, and then his entire
small person leaves home for the Café des Voyageurs.

So our swimmer splish splash genially keeps going and, despite
it all, attains something like happiness as he does so this Abbeville
morning, oooh but better not catch cold! He nimbly climbs out
of the riverbed (hats off, gentlemen, we can see he's an expert) to
where his great big cotton towel awaits him and starts wrapping
himself up in it, letting his teeth chatter like a child who hopes
such obvious shivers will convince his mother to rub his back.

Once the most obvious dampness has been pretty much sponged
away, unwrapping his body, exposing it to the cold wind just long
enough to flip, torero-style, the entire rectangle of towel behind
your back, not enveloping you as at first, no, trying hard to keep
the towel in a rectangle even if slightly twisted here or there, and
holding it like that behind yourself by the top right and bottom left
corners respectively (or the opposite if you're left-handed), moving it laterally against your back, rubbing your skin until it burns,
hmmm that warms you up delightfully, while whatever groans of
effort and satisfaction arise from you soak into the plain to lose
themselves in the spongy earth and leafy willows, and you think
back on your childhood, but hey, you stop and rub your thighs,
and then there are your calves, the top of your feet usually but not
always, because look at this wader campaigning to keep his bal-

ance on his bent left leg, which seems to be hopping under its own power (also, careful not to fall on the sharp edge of that freshwater mussel shell brought by a marsh duck from the bog nearby), while reaching his bent arm down for the lifted foot, a quick wipe on its top, it's reckless to try for the bottom but this seems like such a great morning, doing the same thing all over again for the other foot, the right leg scarcely less arrogant than the first and doing its own un-controlled dance, oh la la, for a moment we think that, but no, our man straightens up again, and having already dried the ball of his foot moves the towel to its arch, I'm holding my breath, good, it seems he's making it work, the towel tickling the bottom of his foot and removing the maximum number of drops of water stuck there, okay, let's not tempt fate any longer, the foot regains firm ground, all the force of its weight falling more comfortably onto the sus-tentative surface widened now by the slightly open compass made by his legs, there right smack between the two is where you could draw an arrow pointing to the grass, it's nice to feel comfortably positioned again, you're going to let your arms fend for themselves, just one quick swipe over the torso and then you put your clothes back on where they feel sticky against your still damp body despite all the fine technique you've been able to display. The wind, when it comes up, dries nothing, hygrometric study of the air in Abbeville showing such a high degree of humidity that there's scarcely any difference between being in the river and being out of it, and since the towel dropped onto the ground is now displaying its white folds rather beautifully against the green of the field, you stand there wearing your sticky clothes as if about to start the whole process all over again. Your foot sinks into the grass that feels just like a thick bath mat oozing water and it wouldn't be a fine morning at home in Picardy without the slight sound it makes, and if when you climb out of the river just that instant a cloudburst comes to rinse off your back, well, nature, I'm just telling you what I think, is nothing but a huge bathroom, where the clouds cheerfully turn on their great faucet in order to rid you of the wetness of surface water, which, with the addition of all your splashing around, has made your towel soaking wet and absolutely useless, to say nothing of your clothes balled up on the ground where they've obviously done a very good job of sopping it all up.

Anyhow, on the morning we're discussing it didn't rain when he got out of the river, and in this first chapter about swimming we even have to add a brief and welcome ray of sunshine so you won't feel colossally overwhelmed by the sky—the feeling that day seems never to dawn, it can happen; by air that's waterlogged but that tends to hold it all in so that the clouds don't erupt with a splash and return the blueness to the atmosphere, no; by days that are like nights, and thus like parentheses, in which you accomplish nothing worthwhile; so, therefore, this ray of sunshine taking you happily by surprise comes bursting onto the towel that had been covering the swimmer's shoulder and now is rolled up in a ball at your feet, then sort of curls quickly out in a stripe across the grassy bank and speeds cheerfully along to spread itself graciously across the countryside of Picardy.

Our fellow, having managed to button up his frock coat and commanding some movement from his dorsals in order to un-stick his shirt from his skin (once a little air gets in the dampness vanishes more quickly), looks a tiny bit more presentable, even though still slightly damp, than he did just now in the long johns he was wearing, so I think this will be a good moment, but no, our hero signals to me that I should wait, redoes his hair with the equipment he happens to have on him, four fingers do the trick, the thumb remaining straight up in the air like some improvised ornament on a comb, you run it through your hair several times, there you go, on the left, on the top, to the right, you don't bother checking your reflection in the river because, in the first place, a grayish-brown cloud is currently passing and making the water darker, which reduces its reflective capacities, and second, if you lean over it will wreck the whole thing, both forelocks so carefully pushed back to the top falling forward, whoosh, straight toward the river because the water soaking your hair doesn't work particularly well as gel. Our hero, remarking to himself that considering the rustic context he can't really do much better along the lines of personal vanity, comes out to meet the reader, Excuse me for being a bit late, I took my daily swim in the Somme, then parenthetically, quirky old bachelor that he is, he goes on to add the scientific details concerning the beneficial effects and the relationship to health of this *quotidianum balneum*: The secret of my apparent perpetual youth, I really think it's in the interest of the organism, I have my own ideas on the subject, which without hesitation he expounds in what is basically, undeniably a friendly and altruistic gesture even if, as far as you're concerned, going for a swim in the Somme in the middle of October is absolutely out of the question, or even September for that matter, and, though you don't dare admit it to yourself, even July and August, but it doesn't really make any difference, you'll never frolic in this too-cold river with the same conviction as our man demonstrates—or in any river, surrounded by grass and moss and, thank you very much, fish—pike and other *Esocidae* whose sharp teeth don't appeal to me at all (not to mention carp with their four limp and oily barbels).

He has completed his panegyric about exercises in the freezing cold and extends his hand to you, a hand perhaps stained with chlorophyll, but well kept nonetheless, not hardened, just a callus on his index finger, meaning his work is likely at a desk, writing—but what? A hand that has lines on its palm showing everything that has already come to pass, as far as the lesser orders of fate, and likewise everything that remains to be accomplished; light is falling on it and you could almost read it here and now, but patience, and he politely speaks his name into the cool, bucolic breeze, how happy he is to see you, his way of speaking sufficiently soft and slow that you can't tell if that's how he always talks, the serene reflection of a sizeable number of years spent in idleness, or if, indeed, it means he is paying particular attention to you and wants to be understood, because a name like his isn't easy to pronounce, especially with this northerly starting to blow, nor is it easily and clearly enough taken in by your ear for you to memorize and later repeat it. You take the hand he offers and which must smell like the river, the grass, maybe even the soap used to wash his towel, he shakes your hand, an honest handshake you'd call it, imparting a brief downward motion that you have to resist with your wrist, no hint of the limp rag and nothing stingy about it, not at all like a corpse's hand despite its clamminess, obviously the kind of handshake that demonstrates a real desire to welcome you, okay, you've understood, speaks it in the midst of the guttural cries of crested grebes, and the fluttering willows, beech trees, and oaks, whose leaves (those of the first) filter the river air and those of the third (I mean just the oaks) create a sort of copse at the spot where you both stopped for this introduction, he bows his head slightly as he speaks, and here comes a drop of river water running all the way down one strand of hair and gathering moisture as it goes like a snowball on the side of a mountain and then it stops at the tip to hang there in brief suspension, a translucent marble, before falling plop on the little trapezoid of your hand, you know, right between your thumb and index finger, his chin vanishing, in a manner of speaking, into the high collar of his frock coat, Jacques Boucher de Crèvecoeur de Perthes, at your service.

Ah, fine, fine, that means nothing at all to you (except, perhaps . . . ?), you act like somebody who has only vaguely taken notice of something, and in turn impart a quick downward motion to your hand, which he resists rather well, and it's your turn to pronounce your own name, in this green and rustic morning, and now that the sweetish smell spreading from beet-sugar grinding is growing stronger and stronger, the clouds overhead have begun their journey, off to a great start you'd say, and their rapid movement keeps the sky in a state of constant transformation, you think you can feel the sea nearby, remembering weather at the seashore, the changeable Channel sky, where a thousand seasons are apt to go by in a single day.

II

Craboudingue, craboudingue! That's pretty much what Orrorin Tugenensis thinks about this day, in a rather bad mood as he sticks his nose out of his tree and sees no colobus monkeys in his woody environs, nor impalas off in the distance where the landscape becomes more open, and picturing himself hidden from view, he gives the branches around him a good hard shake, displacing particles of light to spin frantically around the leaves, zzz zzz, if light particles could buzz, and if, precisely, it was a question of particles, and while you're musing a bit on the subject of the corpuscular or undulate nature of light, Orrorin races every which way, from one branch to the next, in danger (and I've warned him) of having one of these stick him in the eye, miles and miles away from worrying about whatever it might be, radiation or gas, in which you can take such a nice, dry bath if you're willing to nestle down cozily into the photons instead of stirring them up like this, doubtlessly on account of his having noticed, though not necessarily having turned it into a maxim, that a bit of physical exercise pursued stubbornly enough is capable of dispelling anger, so just look at him go on this October morning six million years before our time, somewhere near Lake Baringo, stopping from time to time to chew on a branch, despite the relatively modest size of his molars (M3 in particular), but still his teeth's thick enamel helps (P4, or the second lower premolar, just to let you know, has an ovoid shape), chewing thoughtfully as he broods over his wrath, but with something like a consciousness of his importance there too, which, at the same time as this periodic anger still seething up from underneath, gives him a sort of superior peacefulness, in contradiction to the restlessness of various particular parts, and best displayed during his contemplative pauses, because Orrorin, you'll excuse him, that's all the name he's got, means "the original man" in the Tugen language, and while continuing to move the masticatory muscles of his lower jaw and simultaneously letting the luminous stimuli excite his optic disks, he strikes the pose of ancestor, as if possessing the knowledge that within him he, the first protagonist of the great East Side Story, bears all that will come after, but then his anger grows in scale to match the sort of historical incarnation entered into by his body during the moments spent chewing attentively above the landscape, and assisted by the bent first phalanges of his hands, he swings from branch to branch, picks up the pace, and breaking all sorts of speed records, off he goes to the left of the picture, then to the right and again, again, again, you have to keep yourself from screaming watch out, he's getting all scraped up, not stopping—apparently this physical difficulty erases any moral difficulty—sweeping rapidly across the blank sky through the rustling leaves, expenditure of energy in the countryside a useful means of ridding oneself of irritations, clearly that is Orrorin's method, and gradually he becomes calmer; Orrorin stops to rest, this time longer than before, he contemplates the plain, the empty sky reflected as a little spot in his pupil, then off again, he's back racing through the branches, while our Jacques, his hair still damp from his recent swim in the cold Abbeville River, takes his morning route (home again) toward the shady streets of the city (the sun, still low, doesn't come in; an hour later the pointed gables will draw kings' crowns on the façades across the way), and today he seems especially hurried, I say that because of the look of concentration on his face and also because of how his body leans forward as if it wanted to get there sooner than his legs, look, his posterior, as a result, well yes, slightly more behind (should one be saying this about one's hero?), and his back and neck stretching toward where he wants to go, and as for his arms, they beat the air like oars in the midst of a storm; and cutting across fields toward the city walls like this, his legs' long, rapid stride always, however, behind his torso, our man breathes noisily into the scenery, it's all you hear, his footsteps in the spongy grass and his breath, creating a good deal of condensation, scatters into clouds over the fields where it moves faster than all the rest of him and, despite all his efforts, it is his breath that gets there first, colliding with the outermost city wall.

Our hero, still in that position, hurries past the octroi's office, where a rumpled guard, looking just like a drunken soldier in a hacienda, greets him with his usual silent nod, not emitting so much as a Bonjour M'sieur Jacques, and as for asking how things are going, don't even think about it (So, that swim? Not too hot, but damned if it's not invigorating!), or what about a remark about the changing sky, that would make you feel better (Hey, it's getting overcast all of a sudden, but what with all this wind the clouds will soon vanish, let's hope? Which we might translate as, "What a fine fellow, going for a swim in the river every morning, this is not just some ordinary man, if only I dared I'd pat him on the shoulder!"), no, the guard is the kind of guy whose look has the power to pass right through a body once said body has been mechanically identified, heading off to contemplate who knows what horizon, you'd think his eyes could see through stone too because he's facing the barracks building, which for an ordinary person would have to be considered something of an obstruction of the scenery.

Our man starts across the bridge, where he doesn't take the time to notice a young woman (no, it's not Margot. Who's Margot? You'll see), with a white scarf on her head, a red shawl draped over her green skirt, who holds nothing in her right hand except her left hand, no basket of any sort, who has maybe walked there with a traveler, because her face is turned toward the ferry that has stopped on the river; inside it, at the moment, there are two passengers who seem to be ignoring each other, one of the two being perhaps someone the young woman knows, hard to say, but it's easy to extrapolate.

Impervious to this melancholy scene, just an assumption, developing just a few feet away from him, our hero goes on his way, there he goes onto the rue de l'Isle, a rather long street, I'm taking you on a short tour of Abbeville and I don't have a very clear notion of what it used to look like, still you can always imagine it, on his right the uneven line of half-timbered façades (we'll make it uncomplicated), to the left the impassive rampart wall drawing its great brick-red stripe under a sky growing bluer as the morning progresses.

At the end of the rue de l'Isle you rather naturally cross the Hôtel-Dieu River. At this time of day no one is there to play a part in the scene, the grass pushed up between the stones is the only sign of life, a shutter probably blown shut by the wind half obscures a window and makes the sense of abandonment even stronger. I keep on going, plunging into the rue Saint-Wulfran (pronounce that Oulfran, if only to yourself), we're shivering now because the street is still deep in shadow, What an ice box of a street, thinks Jacques, a few birds fly off, specks in the sky, taking with them a whole mess of shrill sounds.

Without turning his head toward the Marché aux herbes on the left, he takes the pont aux Brouettes to continue; the light suddenly falls on the commercial canal where reality lies peacefully reproduced but upside down, as it should be. A man in a red shirt sits in a skiff, his torso cut by the boat beneath which his reversed twin hangs neatly making him look almost exactly like a Joker card in this otherwise still empty scene. Empty? But no, because you hadn't seen that woman in her window, she too has her torso cut though not extended by its reverse and with her arms crossed on the sill she's looking at the Joker, her tender gaze bringing, let's say, a bit of humanity to the scene.

Paying no more attention to it than he did to the story of the young woman at the ferry, Jacques enters this little theater; he must be lost in thought. Arriving at the place de la Marché (I have a map from that period to help me), he stops to wipe his forehead with the corner of a handkerchief embroidered with the letters JBCP and looks around him to check that all the brief texts listed panoramically in these signs are in the correct order: Café Saint-Georges, Café Boubert, Lottin 17, Mordy Grain (a drop of perspiration falls into his eye, he can't read the last letter very well, if there is one), Riquier-Bremard, Quincaillerie Mercerie, Epicerie-Farines, Pécourt-Renouard, Plebeau, Magnier, Porcelaines Cristaux Faïences Verrerie Bouteilles, the simple poem he rereads every morning just to get his mouth going. Everything is in its place, a quick glance at the clock above the Courthouse oh good gracious, our man feels a pang of urgency, stuffs his handkerchief into his pocket and hurries on, no more dawdling. And there, whether he takes rue Saint-Gilles to pick up the rue des Minimes on the right, or if he'd rather take the rue des Lingers to reach the rue des Minimes from the left, in either case he'll get where he's going, whew, just a few more feet, breathing the air of his own street, which always has something a little different about it.

You push open the gate to the courtyard where the borders, port and starboard, are somewhat neglected, go up three steps and find yourself *at home*. In the hallway, pushing the door shut with the sole of your right foot, checking the sound to make sure it's really closed, the wedge set, you toss the key into the glazed pottery jar from Saintonge. Oh no, you pick it up again, Actually, I usually put it in the pitcher. The ceramic pitcher, how could I forget? It has an image of a man holding a glass and a bottle and straddling a barrel, it's from Rouen. Jacques lays his frock coat on the chair where it looks like a huge, exhausted bat hanging there, no use hanging it properly when in less than an hour, What am I saying? I barely have thirty minutes, he's going to have to put it back on again and this time, with his suitcase in hand, head for the stagecoach stop.

Once back in his room, our hero suddenly feels greatly, hugely discouraged. He flops down onto the bed and imagines the scope of the task that lies ahead. Across from him on the wall at right angles to the window wall there is a painting that shows men making hay. He sinks his gaze into it.

He's not really paying attention to the path the men on horseback are taking, nor the sheaves of hay springing up behind them, nor the horizon with its undulating line of hillsides, dark against the sunlight but almost diaphanous at their summit; nor does he count, as he sometimes does when there's nothing better to do, the number of clouds sprinkled across the sky, which is not as easy as you think, because one cloud can cover up the end of another so that you no longer know which is which, and debating this can keep you busy for a long time, are there two clouds intersecting graphically but far apart in the scene, or indeed is it a single cloud elongated, stretched out somehow, that has, in short, annexed itself to the cloud in front, and in the end become so well fused with it that it shouldn't be described as more than a single cloud, I'll let you decide; instead, our man seems to be absorbed almost physically in the color, in the actual substance of the painting, as if he could take shelter in its depths, far from the material dilemmas life puts to you: because the question of which shirts to take and which jackets, not to mention which of the wide, floppy neckties, can plunge a person into a puzzlement equal to any set of questions concerning choices of a more abstract nature.

Incapable of starting the monologue in which to gauge, one piece of clothing at a time, the advantages and disadvantages of each choice, composing the contents of his suitcase so that his arms and hands have only to act upon his decision in order for reality to coincide progressively with the list decided upon and clik, when coincidence of list and contents is achieved with no remainder, the suitcase closed; our hero, rather persistently oblivious of the situation, lets himself float off so that in his mind he is swimming in color, fully clothed wallowing in warm pools of it, because when you get there, it's nothing but big, thick, creamy, apparently fluid patches and you lie lounging in them as if you're in some sort of waterslide (as I imagine it), gliding from one patch to another like riding a toboggan whhoosh, arriving in some blue or green pool where you splash a bit without a thought in your head . . .

At this rate it's a sure thing that Jacques is in danger of missing his coach. Hey! Jacques! Get a move on! I wave at him vigorously but he doesn't see me, I shout myself hoarse but in vain, I aim my watch in his direction and tap on it (I never wear a watch, well, almost never), it's doable, more than twenty minutes left but you can't just dawdle, luckily the same thought finally crosses his mind, he takes out his watch (he has a watch pocket) and glances at it, Hey, only twenty minutes, he exclaims as he becomes aware of what a sight he is—flung onto the bed like some old thing, his back rounded, legs dangling, arms spread awkwardly about, Come on! He says to himself (not proud), I'm not in some twentieth-century novel after all, with a sluggish, pensive hero borne along by events, not doing a lick of work, no, in a nineteenth-century novel you have to make sure you exert yourself a bit as far as action is concerned, he jumps to his feet, puts his hand to his head because he's slightly dizzy, then pretty abruptly (an effect of his short-lived voluntarism) plunges both arms into his wardrobe and takes out some wool clothes that unfold themselves as if they were live things who have been forced to stay in the dark closet too long and are now stretching themselves out more comfortably, a few, more independent than others, slipping from Jacques's arms and going off to pretend they're octopi on the carpet with their own arms waving like tentacles and taking up more and more room, like flowers opening to the light.

Jacques considers the new scene before him and takes in the air of the room with a deep breath, so you'll be more relaxed about all this, then slowly breathes it out, keeping the oxygen in his body as long as possible so it can mix in with his blood no doubt, though I'm not absolutely positive, and with his right forefinger our hero scratches his forehead and, at the same time, breathes out, as reported above, signaling to himself by this extra action that right now he's thinking, acting out "thinking right now" in order not to interrupt himself: Hold on, Jacques, you can see perfectly well that I'm thinking, Oh, yes, sorry Jacques, but careful not to let yourself go into some little nearby thought, how quickly that can happen; then one thing leading to another that thought takes you thousands and thousands of miles from here, into more comforting locales, but the clock is ticking, which keeps his mind from drifting off toward some more contemplative and consequently more subtle idea causing his body to go all limp and find itself once again seated like an idiot on the bed surrounded by wool clothing, and gazing distantly into imaginary landscapes instead of focusing directly on the pile of woolens on the ground seven feet in front of him, so our man picks up the recalcitrant but feeble octopi, sorts them, putting some items on the right (things I'm taking) and some on the left (things to put back in the wardrobe); until the whole process is completed in less than five minutes with the left-hand pile put back on the shelves and the one on the right in the suitcase, same for the pants, shirts, ties, and, with a quick check through the house, a final glance around each room before closing its dark paneled door, and then fade to black, leaving the house, end of chapter, dressed for travel, the full array, hat, suitcase, hatbox, what have I forgotten?

The story can thus begin, and this now is the tale it tells, as off to the stagecoach stop trots our well-equipped and humble hero, talking quietly to himself, going on and on like an old friend with nothing more to prove, just the old useless and obvious thoughts, along with anecdotal, unembroidered remarks, practical details and well-worn recollections unbothered by their cohabitation in his mind; our Jacques, otherwise determined to fulfill his program as hero when circumstances are favorable, casts an augur's glance at the sky as he hurries along, but if he sees something in all that blue-gray, he keeps it to himself.

III

Our hero, in the passenger compartment of the stagecoach, fluctuates between vague meditation (as if the padded compartment represented yes a camera obscura inside which thoughts take shape and then come apart, as if you were enclosed there in a space of pure reflection), loosely contemplating the countryside (his gaze slips off to the window, the materiality of the trees rhythmically marking the bare surface of the fields, as the clear, bright rectangle starts to project the moving ground, a lateral tracking shot catching it in action, in short, the world where one will act, once thoughts have been organized and put back in place, and the one or two that are still left dangling at the moment eventually finding their place we hope) along with a certain yearning for the picaresque that occasionally flashes through his monologue, because, good heavens, a little bandit popping up here would be welcome, it would distract Jacques from all his melancholy, would brighten his pensive countenance, and as for you, you'd be startled, you'd let yourself go in a happiness qualified at first by fear, you'd exaggerate the risk to the book because, you're no fool, when it comes to the main character, he'll tend to get out of any situation where there might be a silver-handled pistol pointed at him, especially if it's only on page 28; just imagine the obvious difficulty it would present for me if he didn't, me still prattling on alone through what comes next but with nothing further to narrate, except maybe a burial with pomp and ceremony ending with a funerary statue sculpted by Nadaud that would stand high up in the cemetery, its willow shadowing the city, an arm falling out from under your stone bedclothes no longer holding the pen that slips to the ground covered with autumnal leaves next to a stone book lying open, blank, in which no doubt his last story was supposed to be written.

Even so, you wouldn't be completely unfazed because it's always possible that he *would* die and this would occasion your being forced through a long flashback, and anyway you hate it when the hero dies, let him go do that outside the book, discreetly, that's all you ask, well after the end of the story, but not right there in front of you with pow a pistol blast, what am I saying? repeated pistol blasts from this bandit who's not a very good shot what a bloody mess, and all this hero's blood this hero's flesh, you wipe your forehead with the back of your arm, but just suppose—this flashes through your mind, quick as a swallow in a clear sky, that's how your thoughts go—that this was the thrust of the novel, my hero killed by a bandit in the third chapter with no flashback afterward,

afterward we'd move on to something else entirely, the story of the bandit, for example, his mother's story, any story, it doesn't matter which story, sort of a flashy gimmick, but people will do anything to get your attention, you're wary, Jacques is unarmed (you have a thorough knowledge of the contents of his suitcase), all he'd have at his disposal to get himself out of his predicament would be words, and well, words, we know what they are, so you wouldn't feel all that comfortable if a bandit showed his face and its gold teeth, but anyhow, that's not what's going on at the moment.

You're probably asking yourself where our hero is off to with the pensive demeanor he had just now and hasn't lost, you have a pretty good idea because of the title of this section, because the book opened with the usual swim in the Somme, and not in the house of the aforementioned friend, so that's where he must be going now, and you're right, but if that's not enough I'm entirely at your disposal for any additional information, at least to the best of my ability. The friend's name? André. The nature of the friendship? Childhood. Where is it, the friend's house? In the Eu Forest, you'll see, a rather isolated spot. Why such a pensive air? Because Jacques hasn't seen this friend since that childhood. And more than that, because the day of his departure, his own departure from Abbeville, years before, he hadn't gone to tell him good-bye. I realize that there's a lot that I haven't explained to you, you're picking things up right in the middle, not having been there at the birth of our hero, nor when he took his first steps, bowlegged as you'd expect, cowboy style, down the street located in the fine town of Rhétel where the roads called Turnip and Fruit merge, nor, it's too bad, any of what came next up until the day of this particular swim which has its own place in the list of all his other swims; I haven't told you about all of that, but what can we do? Beginning a story, believe me, is just one hell of a big, slippery mess, along with all the usual problems you can imagine, there's the specific problem that, first of all, oh la la, just beginning at all sacrifices whole chunks of life by starting at this point in the story and not at another, starting this morning with our hero letting himself be rocked by the jolting coach means leaving out so much, and that's why beginning, which is supposedly something joyous, energizing, and a potential adventure we can enjoy together, if you're willing to come along with me into the realms that will be our concern, is already losing, it's beginning by losing everything that went before, everything you won't read about, and that's why I'm suddenly feeling a little melancholy, I must not be myself today!

Sometimes this problem will be remedied by a quick look back, like now, for instance, reviewing the childhood departure scene that our hero has been contemplating from the stagecoach, how could he help but think about when he was sixteen and leaving home to work in one customs office after another.

You have to imagine a Russian novel for this scene of departure, with the house behind and the unfailing verticality of dark trees and the family members scattered around artistically—one on the doorstep, another leaning against the rough wall, the others each in front of his or her own tree, and then, slightly in front of them, two figures together, the mother and sister holding each other up, the sister a miniature version of the mother, both of them wearing dark blue with scarves on their heads, the mother's a solid color and the sister's embroidered with a scattering of hollyhocks which are all you can see from the coach when Coco (this is our Jacques, skinny like a child, only vaguely beginning to grow up) opens its door curtain, the hollyhocks on his sister's scarf suddenly take on immense importance, you latch on to them, and when you're inside the coach with your face turned toward the passing landscape you won't see, you'll still be picturing hollyhocks, they will linger, yes, fragile companions for the first miles you have to travel, concentrating on the hollyhocks, of course, in an attempt to forget the difficult scene in which you have clearly identified the father on the doorstep and the most nonchalant brother as the one leaning against the wall, with the other brothers each under his own tree, all of them, including the most nonchalant, leaning on something and forming the very picture of deep sadness, because (illusion or actual fact) it's as if they could no longer stand up unaided as they watched their son and brother go off alone to his humble fate.

Like the storybook hero sent on a mission who carries in his sack a few formulas against the dangers he must defy without knowing if they're sufficient, because already there are shameless sorcerers rubbing their hands together gleefully merely at the thought of the trick they're going to play on him, and the people watching his departure powerless to help, because the story really does have to move along—so young, how sad, says the bent figure of his mother supported by the arm of her daughter who is only holding her up in order not to collapse herself, like two cards leaning against each other on the green felt of a game table.

Our hero gives the side of the coach a good whack in order to get rid of this thought. Usually (he remembers) what's good about a coach is that several people are cooped up inside so they can scarcely move their bodies, just barely shift a foot, and though one arm may be wedged up against someone else's, they can probably, are even bound to manage a number of hand movements ranging from the trivial (scratching your cheek, shooing away a bug, tugging absentmindedly on a strand of your hair) to something with more semantic force, in which case the hand provides subtitles to the ongoing discourse and translates it, in a manner of speaking, offering a visual equivalent to the words within the dark and limited space where it's moving, a voluble bird flying in airy scrolls and volutes that are themselves a language (a bit like the way bees apparently fly in figure eights to indicate the proximity of something edible), providing a choreographic version of what's going on, and so conversation almost always gets started eventually, because lips, even backed by avian hands, are still easier to move, along with your vocal cords, which you pluck invisibly like a harp inside you.

All kinds of tales are routinely born in this manner, a series of minor legends that pleasantly while away your traveling time, or pleasantly so long as they don't introduce any suspenseful elements capable of shaking up our wonderful serenity, because, you know, you might have heard tell, did you ever think of the fact . . . that the Eu Forest harbors wolves waiting to make your acquaintance, one-eyed woodcutters armed with bludgeons, plus two or three supernatural phenomena that nobody understands; but this morning Jacques, as you understand it, is the only passenger in the coach and its dark cabin is clearly a sort of dark box conducive to reflection and the very picture of solitary, interior rumination, driving our hero to an introspection only if often distracted by gentle contemplation of the landscape that, presented in this rectangular and mobile fashion, forms a luminous geometric design standing, quite naturally, for the existence of the outside world symbolized for the time being by this two-color image: blue and green, sky above fields.

Then later the hills come and Jacques becomes absorbed in contemplating their sine curves, fixing his attention there as much as possible, the way you read a graph, endeavoring to interpret the lows and highs of the recorded curve before returning to egotistical daydreams and questioning himself about what he is feeling, What are you feeling, Jacques? well, Jacques, I'll tell you, talking as honestly as possible to himself and counting off firstly a sense of sweetness, I think (he takes his left thumb and squeezes it between his right thumb and index finger in the time it takes to say the word "sweetness"), along with some apprehension (it's now the left index finger's turn to be squeezed between the same right thumb and index fingers), That makes two feelings, and, now captor of his left forefinger, he remains stuck there for a bit, then lets them all go, I can't find any more, and these two things seem to him concomitant, merging rather than alternating, suddenly materializing together, hand in hand, Me, I'm Sweetness and she's Apprehension, Apprehension agrees nodding her head to signal that yes, that is certainly who she is, somewhere between affirming (Yes yes) and greeting (Hello Jacques), and in his heart they start doing a sweet little dance, unpleasant in part because of some very uncomfortable tickling by Apprehension, who regularly, between two entrechats, stops dancing to shoot off a few arrows, tiny ones but they get under his skin, and partly pleasant, because

Sweetness is leading the dance and his influence subtly wins out over Apprehension's, and also because there's an acute consciousness within Apprehension itself that some important event is imminent and this consciousness transforms the pale days in which the present so weighed you down that it kept you from imagining what lay ahead.

Looking off toward the encephalographic line of the hills, our man lets himself go a bit, and, for example, with these mixed feelings, he becomes less and less preoccupied with the fear that he won't recognize André, climbing down from the stagecoach, which would not be a trivial matter, and as a result, hey, going toward not at all the right person, that could certainly happen, the man in a checked frock coat stepping aside when he sees Jacques bearing down on him, But really, sir, whereas the Real André a few feet away would be contemplating what's going on, conscious on the one hand of the comical nature of the situation and trying not to laugh, but then, on the other hand, stricken by great regret that hurts all over ouch, So you don't recognize your old friend, extending his hand toward Jacques and striding over to him in a friendly manner without a reproach in the world, which saves the situation and then that's that, whereas inside himself this mistake would risk jeopardizing everything, André taking Jacques home with him and retaining this slight rancor, this sadness, the hurt over not having been recognized as if, rather than his silhouette—obviously changed, though not his facial features—something subtler had not been recognized: the sum of the days they had shared that should have, somehow or other, served as a recognizable sign. I didn't write you that I'd wear a green silk sash decorated with deer chased by huntsmen on horseback with gun-barrels shining in the autumnal light while bits of sky are clearly reflected in the curves of the hunting horns, nor that I'd be carrying the *Eu Gazette* under my arm, it's my fault, André would conclude out loud so that Jacques, who was his guest after all, would feel all right, but inside, well all in all you can see perfectly well it was a catastrophe and had messed things up and it would hang over the entire visit, an ever-present black bird, sometimes off to the side, but a draw on your thoughts regardless, passive but ready to spread its wings again, sometimes flying right there over their conversations, circling over the two dazed friends in their arm-chairs who are trying to connect something that one of them has said to something the other just said, and so forth, but always having the tricky raven in sight sculling overhead and occasionally coming down to hit André in the temple with the tip of its wing, or bringing that same wing flapping and rustling right next to his ear and then, up! Flying back up to the ceiling as if nothing had happened and settling on a beam, there to start building a nest as it watches the disastrous scene taking place down below, seeing only the tops of the two men's heads, their noses, their thighs, and their hands which are pausing for a moment on those thighs, rubbing the cloth of their pants, sweating, while on the big town clock the hour hand completes its tour.

So, not just some trivial lack of recognition, because one would certainly hope *something* would be there, some indicator, something about the face that was still the same, André you old devil, Jacques you old devil, or even just the fact that Jacques, climbing down in his traveling clothes, has the look of someone coming to find his old friend and searching for him among the few people there, so that André, recognizing him by his attitude, walks quickly toward him to avoid mistakes, Dear Jacques, did you have a good trip, and Jacques quite naturally concluding If he's saying that to me it's because he's André, and, overjoyed by the obviousness of it all, returning his handshake, which, as they leave in concert for the house and take the path through the Eu Forest, welds together the two portions of time separated by the intervening years.

So, not some trivial lack of recognition but, how shall I put it, one on a deeper level, you'd certainly think you couldn't possibly make a mistake in recognizing André when he headed in your direction, but later on when they are sitting in their blue armchairs and Jacques has had plenty of time to contemplate André in person, he won't be able to make the memory from the old days coincide with this present-day body, it just doesn't stack up (this is still our Jacques daydreaming), they feel at once discouraged and lazy about their acquaintance and wonder vaguely whether or not they really want to get back to work on the great project of friendship, I mean supposing I was meeting André today for the first time and same for André, perhaps, confronted with him, André who has retreated to his house in the woods and has made an exception for Jacques, inviting him over for the sake of their old friendship, So come on, we'll be just like in the old days, André might not have enough energy either to get things going again, catching up on the muddle of his history, the puzzle of his opinions and feelings, face to face like two animals in the savanna when the species to which one belongs doesn't usually eat the species of the other, and vice versa, so that they aren't really sure what to do with this encounter, standing there motionless except for their breath which regularly stretches and relaxes their skin of neatly fitted scales, two lost saurians watching each other in a sort of calm terror, neither one daring to go on his way.

Bam! Apprehension strikes a hard blow to Sweetness who falls to the ground and faints, the dance is over, Apprehension stands, hand on her hip, doing a ten count over the lifeless body of Sweetness while the other hand flings the seconds of her countdown into the air, Sweetness is down and out, KO, Apprehension turns arrogantly back to Jacques (mouth half open, hair in his eyes, just look at him), she puts the piece of lemon back in front of her teeth, okay okay says Jacques, but it's not okay at all: André and Jacques stay stuck in this imagined image, face to face, each on his side of the time trench that separates them, each wishing to make some signal from his side to the other, uh . . . uh . . . , and then not succeeding, sticking his handkerchief back in his pocket, deciding not to wave it or his arms either or to make a megaphone with his hands, just preferring to look at the sky and wait for time to go by, each on his own shore, head up, ignoring the other.

But the stagecoach, as far as I can tell, has just missed hitting a big rock laying in the middle of the road and has to stop (the coachman is getting ready to climb down from his seat to go take the stone to the ditch at the side) so, because stones like that don't get there all by themselves, no, Jacques drops his difficult forecast to make up a bandit episode, *at last*, and surely any minute now he's going to see a toothless face at his window along with a silver-handled pistol, then there'll be a dangerous dialogue with this other character demanding his money, And your jewels too, I don't have any, Come on come on, consider it your toll, and the bandit takes off laughing, a thundering laugh, yes, now you're really into it, he rolls his eyes, that's what he does, and taps Jacques in the belly, tap tap, to bring him into line, Oh you frightened me, Jacques is startled to see the coachman's curly head coming in through the door frame to announce Nothing broken. The coachman, whose body, essentially his legs and rear end, remains outside, extricates his head from the coach so you can see him whole again as he returns to his seat where he sits down with his back to us like every coachman in the world, shouting Giddy up, oh so picaresque.

Our hero goes back to his somber dreams, André and he are face to face and the trench between them from earlier is now filled by a table on which André constantly rearranges three knick-knacks: the sugar bowl, his cup, the spoons; each time reconfiguring the whole as if seeking the answer to some puzzle. Large drops of sweat fall into Jacques's teacup, it's not very attractive, he picks up a napkin to wipe his temples, he's ashamed about repaying André's hospitality so poorly, and the what-ifs escalate in the enclosure of the stagecoach cabin, André growing weary of such silence, such awkwardness, would like to take out a stick and begin beating Jacques on his shoulders and back, calling him an ass, in Italian if possible. Knocking his chair over, Jacques escapes and runs off into the kitchen (Sorry, Camille. Who's Camille? You'll see soon enough) followed by André who hits him every chance he gets, yelling in the language of Arlecchino. Jacques, taking advantage of a brief moment of inattention on André's part, jumps into the bread bag, a bag made of grayish-brown cloth, but which alas leaves the human, curled-up shape of Jacques perfectly visible, so that an exultant André, redoubling his invective, hits him now through the cloth, and finally André, tying a knot in the bag, throws it into the stagecoach that's now passing by once again. Jacques manages to untie the knot, sticks one hand out, then the other, and then his head, frightened, he recognizes the cushioned passenger compartment where he finally extricates himself entirely, stiff and aching he rubs his shoulders and turns his eyes toward the landscape painting in motion, its diversity framed by the window bit by changing bit and its luminosity contrasting sharply with the darkness of the coach's interior, how pleasant, these paintings divided in two: earth and sky, sometimes with a scattering of a few figurative elements like a house, a farm, a chateau, cattle, clumps of trees, and that's enough of that, until, look, it's the town hall of Eu.

Once you're involved in the action you're definitely obliged to get yourself out of whatever situation happens to arise, something often more easily done in life than in the dreams you've constructed and, in any case, you can't avoid the issue, no trembling like a leaf beneath the yoke of a victorious Apprehension nor huddling under the stagecoach's seat, you can't stay shut up inside any longer and risk the ridicule of the reader who's saying to him or herself that, if this is all there is to it, then anybody in the world could be a character in a novel, it seems that these days we're not all that particular, and no matter how small and white as snow you've become, you're going to have to get yourself out, the reader doesn't expect to stay cooped up with you in this stagecoach all day, he'd like to see André, and then his house, settle in a bit, breathe in the scenery, that's what he's there for, to encourage you, Come on Jacques, he moves his head side to side, repeatedly, just a little shake meaning Jacques, old man, you're not in the best shape, Come on let's go, he says again.

Jacques goes, puts his foot on the ground, catches in his arms the bag the coachman throws him, and then the body of his friend, Good old André, there you are. We're going that way, says André, and, as the stagecoach struggles through the carpet of leaves to get under way again, they walk off through the undergrowth.

Being so happy makes you speechless, thinks Jacques, suddenly affected by the earthy smell of the leaves on the ground, the awe-inspiring dampness of the forest, the branches' breathing constantly changing the lacy contours of the pale-blue sky, almost trembling, he thinks to himself, at my glance, almost quivering, just the way he is, and casting long rays of light for them to walk through, while *Ardipithecus ramidus*, in the middle Awash, forty kilometers upstream from Hadar, tests the flexibility of the branches, bong bong, jumping into the middle of them, wondering what the chances are that they'll break, in which case he'd dangle there like a fool, having lost all his panache, but an experiment is an experiment, bong bong. Conversely, André, garrulous André, is stringing one sentence after another, saying everything and nothing and also that you have to watch out for fallen branches underfoot, they like to trip you up, and the others treacherously at eye level, duck here or there, step over a root sticking out of the ground, forests with their downed tree trunks sometimes seem like giant games of pick-up sticks, and avoid that clump of slippery mushrooms that would kill an entire family including all the second cousins if you took it into your head to serve them up for dinner, says André who is obviously exaggerating, but after all these decades, And isolated because I practically never leave my house in the woods, where I live with my servant, you'll see her, her name is Camille, everything else is pine trees, right from the outset you're in the forest, no other human beings except for hunters whom you don't see but you figure are there from the bit of olive jacket hanging from a prickly tree trunk, a stray cartridge the tip of your toe sends flying when you take a walk later, you deduce their presence from the sound of a gun that makes you think that danger is lurking in the depths that lie offstage, on your terrace it's like being in a Chekhov play, that special sort of boredom while, simultaneously, you're always on the lookout. One vaguely expects the arrival of a messenger who will tell us about the disasters in the outside world, it spices up our days and raises your heartbeat slightly, to say nothing of the real danger of being shot by mistake, the hunter being distracted enough to think you were a deer (or a boar, that would hurt), and there you are on the ground in your death throes, your antlers stuck in the mud, your nostrils breathing in twigs and torn leaves along with the air, and the hunter's coming. Damn, but it's too late, your flanks are stained with misunderstood deer blood, Damn, Mr. André, but what can I do, the hunter weeps beside you in nervous exhaustion, you try to find some last words to say, something they'll be able to repeat when they remember you, tears in their eyes and a vague feeling of admiration in their hearts, I'll never bell again in the moonlight, you'll end up saying, and pretty content with yourself, you'll breathe your last sigh onto the messy autumnal soil.

IV

The curtain rises on our hero taking his first tentative steps in his host's living room, and his awkwardness tells us that this, indeed, is our Jacques, an inexact character who does his best but whose silhouette and way of walking always tend to run into a few, well, hitches, and we remember the great strides he took rushing back home with his posterior well behind him and his face stuck out in front, hoping to make himself all the more aerodynamic, that's science for you, though we can't say he actually knows anything scientific about this because his experience had not yet confirmed it, because even if our Jacques held himself perfectly upright, with his buttocks tucked under and his face naturally upturned as a slightly raised terminal point topping the dorsal line (like an upside-down exclamation mark at the beginning of a sentence in Spanish), he would have arrived no later at home (at least that's what I think, check your stopwatches), also we remember his body collapsed and untidy in front of the open wardrobe where there was so much to choose from that he just stood there, his mouth open and back bent, completely floored by the size of the task awaiting him. So we begin with the feeling that we're rather familiar with his hesitant steps, the slight displacement of his body, the way one arm swings while the other bends and straightens, looking for the right position, with his hand at the end of it wanting to hang onto something, a strand of hair, a cheekbone now being scratched by its cooperative forefinger offering some plausibility to the matter, the cloth on his pants, we can smooth out the creases or pinch it, like that, or inside his pocket, hmmm, where the hand settles in nice and cozy, curled up like the body of a hunting dog under a down comforter, and pretends to be content, in any case it's doing a lot better than the other hand dangling at the end of the other arm which is doing nothing.

And yet, along with this sort of recognition, because that is definitely Jacques, good old Jacques, about to make yes a line moving so imperfectly, so wavily through the room, a slender line but buckling slightly the way smoke does, left then right then who knows where, a thin baroque column twisting around itself, a cable you might say, a piece of yarn so soft that it won't stay straight but comes and goes in the air like so, making a series of waves, what am I saying, wavelets, wanting to shrink, to vanish, if he could, not happy with the way André is looking at him in astonishment watching him flounder from one end of the room to the other with such disturbing contours to his outline; and yet we are now seeing something new, something absent up to this point, which makes us think there is some contextual reason for this awkwardness, that in addition to his usual clumsiness something else is affecting Jacques and we must do our best to discover where it's coming from. This new thing is apparent, for example, if we consider the extent to which the shape of his body is really abnormally metamorphic (in earlier instances, his gait transforming him into a sort of asymmetrical sigma against the landscape—his upper, horizontal leg way ahead of the lower leg forming its base— you were struck by the fact, if nothing else, that this seemed his natural state; even the way his back when he was seated on his bed and contemplating his wardrobe curved to form the arc of a circle, yes, he must always be like that), and are thus attentive to the additional fragility that his variable shape has brought into the room, wondering what's going on in our man's heart of hearts, what's making him so distressed that he zigzags like a gnat in the light.

Well, I'm about to tell you. It's something I'll have to explain and that, if you delve into your own memories, you'll quickly understand, I think, and be proud of the agility with which you have almost always triumphed when tested in this manner, when nothing, practically no indication of this distress could be seen in the eyes of even your close relations, something you solved in a minimal amount of time, maybe a few fractions of a second and you had it all figured out, really, you're pretty quick. And this is why, in passing, you let in a little thought that has occurred to you, and then you get rid of it like any other: it would have been better if he were in your place, reading your adventures, and you in his, because you're far better at getting out of these sorts of situations than he, but thoughts like this are made for coming and going. So here's what it's all about.

Whenever you visit someplace for the first time, right at first there are two spaces that coexist, tremulously facing one another, the real one that has just begun to reflect on your retina and inscribe its reflection within you, its stubbornness more and more effective but still attenuated at the moment by the second, earlier image that had taken shape in your mind at the very moment you had decided to go visit this childhood friend, when you learned that it was Eu that he had chosen as his residence and that he was living there in a house, so completely isolated that you hadn't even known it existed and while you didn't bother to imagine the scenery outside the window you pictured, very clearly, the living room in which you're presently moving back and forth; it looks completely upended, upside down, as after a burglary, or even as if in your ardor, yes, your joy at seeing André again, whoosh, you came swooping into the house, but it wasn't the right one at all, in your haste to be inside his house yes you took the first door, the first portal presenting itself and now have no idea how to deal with your mistake. But André, standing right there, gives the impression that this is indeed his house, he's not dragging you by the collar of your frock coat, Hey we have no business being here it's not my house what if the owners see us we're going to get shot, hurry, no not at all, he remains calm, congratulations if he's afraid of getting hit by buckshot because there's not a quiver in his face, and he doesn't seem the least bit likely to show his heels, they're firmly planted in the carpet there, also he gives no sign of being curious about his surroundings, the décor, he isn't glancing about just to see if it gives him any ideas about his personal furniture arrangements, for example, look, that corner cupboard it's not bad

45

I should get myself one, he doesn't seem to be running any minor commentary through his head, that's not very functional, beautiful either, making fun of some juxtaposition or choice or whatever ridiculous knickknack, and so, I think, you're just going to have to get used to the idea that this is indeed André's house, different in every aspect from the one you pictured, if not necessarily in the spirit emanating from it, besides, you're not particularly surprised as far as the major choices underlying the furnishings are concerned (except maybe—but we'll get back to that), it's more the way things are presented, their configuration, their arrangement, you see, the respective locations of the sofa, the armchairs, the side table, the room's orientation, where the window is located in relation to the fireplace, and then the colors entering into it all, and the fabric choices.

And it's not that you're amazed, faced with the extent to which the very firm notion you had of the room and its actual appearance are at odds, quite the opposite, in fact, because if your expectations and André's real living room had coincided you'd have begun asking yourself some very serious questions concerning your abilities as a clairvoyant (beginning to picture the caravan where you'd tell fortunes), it would have made you sort of uneasy, and then wouldn't I be piloting a gothic novel and that being true who knows what could happen, right? monsters might come out of the walls and dreadful ghosts thanks a lot, no, you're just feeling a little uncomfortable and you'll stay that way for the first few hours you're there, which will give you, excuse me, give him this somewhat haggard look as he goes from room to room, Here's the dining room, there's the living room, I'm taking you to your bedroom now, then back to the living room where he does his pink flamingo dance, left foot coming up to scratch the back of his right knee, or vice versa, staying in that position a moment, just like that, the rest of his body leaning off to the side opposite the back of the knee in question, forming an incomplete arched column that, when all is said and done, holds nothing up because it's off to the left in a fragile curve, whereas André has a body that seems basically uninterrupted, a nice straight column with a slightly larger perimeter (though not so you'd notice, particularly).

Our man holds his bird position and dreams of being teletransported thousands of miles away from this place where it's so hard to regain his composure because of the setting's still flickering nature, retaining the memory of the other, incompatible, inadaptable, the single idea your imagination had provided without giving much thought to its elaboration, it had seemed so obvious to you from the beginning, the first time you heard the house in Eu mentioned, so that every time you thought about your visit to the house you had seen the same layout, the same sofa (why had you thought it would be red?) set in front of the window so that you had to sit there with the light behind you always, backlit by a lovely glowing background, your face dulled by the lighting on your back, so the few not very serious wrinkles on it would be erased and there would be a thin veil in the grayish tones of modesty conveniently cast over your emotions; or else it was midday, and the sunlight made two large parallel bands that struck the back of the armchair diagonally and so brought the solid curve of your arm into relief— the other one dropping stalactically onto your thigh where its extremity, meaning basically the hand, including the wrist, lay.

That's why you see our man, seemingly unaware of his body's contours, bumping into things, somehow surprised to find himself still there, all loose edges as if he were unraveling right in front of you. His gaze, briefly bogging down in one knickknack then another, always winds up in the moving details of the landscape, where tree branches on the other side of the window are scratching at the sky in fits and starts under the influence of the wind whose minuscule tempest resembles the one at work in his heart and it doesn't help that the behavior of the outside world is conforming to that of our hero's reeling soul, no, it makes things worse, it keeps the latter sort of stuck in this doubly disordered situation, both internal and external, the trembling the forest shares with Jacques's unsettled, clumsy, reedy body provides a sort of visual backup to his confusion.

On the contrary, the forest mantle from which Anamensis is emerging right now is perfectly calm, the vegetation softened by the hot damp air seems to abandon itself to a great siesta enveloping both flora and fauna, except not our Australopithecus, who, in top form, has taken a few steps forward with his robust tibia, who is walking toward the eastern shore of the lake on the Koobi Fora headland where he contemplates the orange waters of the Omo descending into Lake Turkana where they slowly merge with its blue-green over where it meets the delta.

Sandspits make fingerlike marks in the water, it's very pretty is the gist of what Anamensis is thinking, with his rugged face he breathes in the fragrance of the acacias, and that of the wild figs, he picks up a soft fig that's fallen and carries it to his mouth by articulating his elbow (his fossa olecrani is not very deep), he looks at the hippopotami grazing in the delta's alluvium, the pelicans slightly behind them who are accumulating all sorts of things to eat in their membranous, expandable pockets, turns his eyes from the flat Omo valley toward the Rift Valley; he's feeling a kind of peacefulness that is completely out of reach for our hero, given his worries.

André, for his part, stares at Jacques as if he's never seen him before. He looks at him with new eyes that suddenly have no memory and are no longer searching for anything comparable in the past, eyes in which the other looms in all his opacity, emphasized certainly by the back lighting that makes him into a dull, dark silhouette, same for his face, eyes staring with no ulterior motive and struck head-on by Jacques's novelty, bam, so that his guest's characteristics are initially of a material nature, the wool of his jacket particularly absorbs André's attention: its stitches, when our hero turns his profile to you in his tentative dance, catch the light unevenly from the side and show the slight volume of its ribs, its knit jersey surface, knit one purl one, your eyes get a bit lost in the wooly relief as if in a rocky landscape, its tan color reinforces this fiction of a Western landscape, you can imagine traveling through it, slowly riding horseback toward the rivers. André feels rather charmed by Jacques's material nature. It's a very pleasant materiality, a nice change from abstract thinking, your gaze coils up in the wool then goes on to the fine silk weave of his flowing tie, making André happy at first just to be in the presence of so much that is concrete, then progressively it takes on meaning, the friendship André feels for Jacques comes now to fill up every detail of the visible textures, as if these weren't merely the embodiment of Jacques but Jacques the Friend, Jacques the childhood friend, and certainly it's your intention for this new, grownup body that has turned a little white and, too bad, been adorned with sideburns, to become also the body of the present-day friend, recreating a bond that André felt was not only viable but authorized simply by the concreteness of Jacques's presence in his living room, no need to discuss it, no need to fill each other in, they'd do this later on, about the years between, telling stories that would provide an impalpable, fragile, and no doubt erroneous access to them.

Yes but obviously Jacques has no idea what to do with this materiality that André finds so charming, André has to help him out by doing something, he stops his dithering by showing him to an armchair rather than the sofa, the chair on the right rather than the one to the left where André himself will sit as soon as his guest is seated, squish squish the sound of velvet being compressed beneath this new weight, there, that's done. Each one in his own chair, the two of them present a nice picture of the thought behind the initial invitation: our city man is paying a visit to his country friend. Between André and Jacques there is neither continuity nor clear contrast but rather a visible dividing up of functions, André's back fits perfectly into the armchair's curves, his forearms seem to be the precise size of the armrests, his feet are flat on the floor the way they should be, everything indicates that he is the host in this furniture made to his exact measurements; whereas the same cannot be said for Jacques, whose arms overflow, elbows are generously bestowed on the sides of the chair, legs stick out thoughtlessly, and who leaves one foot resting on its heel, creating a short diagonal that is in sharp contrast with the harmony of the rest, an unwelcome segment, which, moreover, from time to time, doesn't hesitate to swing from side to side in a motion that, in addition to being in bad taste visually, makes an unpleasant sound, a slight crunching, Jacques, then, though he has adopted a position in the chair that is more credible than his earlier posture in that one-legged ballet, easily represents by the inappropriateness of his body's measurements to the living-room space the person passing through, the one with no choice as to the shapes or volumes through which he must maneuver, the one who'll need a bit of time in order to pace the rug in the center of the room flawlessly and to sit nonchalantly down on the sofa as if he'd been doing this forever.

His two hands consequently perfectly secured to the ends of his armrests, André, to the best of his abilities, puts himself in Jacques's position and looks around his living room as if, just supposing, it belonged to someone else and he'd never looked at it before, the knickknacks artificially detach themselves from the backlog of memories they represent on their shelves or side tables, André looks at them as if they were new to him, silent, opaque, and with no stories, or rather endowed with some story that you can only imagine in your ignorance, as if they are spreading vaguely into the room and maybe I could take advantage of this to slip in a few descriptive elements, things to help you see what's going on, the living room, its striped wallpaper, the particular way things look, apparently furnished with all the ingredients necessary to a scene in some bourgeois play depicting the comedic political machinations of city officials, all up to no good, quickly entering and exiting and, by means of considerable treachery, the story's naïve but not particularly scrupulous protagonist triumphing in the end, whereas, not at all, you're in the middle of the forest, there's probably nobody, neither the potbellied mayor of Eu nor any more distant authorities, who'll pass through this illusion of a city living room, its décor in sharp contrast to the solitude and isolation of the house and the thick, deep vegetation surrounding it. Just seeing, for example, the round mahogany table covered with its lace cloth, which, you realize, is in no danger of flying off—Camille, her head in the clouds, opening first one then the other of the two living-room windows and letting a breeze in, Oh, the tablecloth, it would just take off like a dove on very breezy days, going right out the window to fly over the terrace, then ending up, damn, stuck on a pine branch where it would be held by the huge tear down its middle, and Camille on tiptoe, her head back, reaching up with the broom handle as if it were a pole for picking fruit, would have a hard time retrieving the tablecloth all bunched up and backlit on the end of its branch, the effort and motion of tilting her head would make the entire celestial landscape pour in, the foliage and baby-blue sky, and then finally, you know, the abovementioned tablecloth, too dirty, with too many holes in it, something dead at the end of its branch, the tablecloth that you really have to get out of sight, perfectly useless now; though on days with just an average amount of wind, the tablecloth, despite its first impulses, would only collapse softly onto the rug, plouf, after spinning uncertainly closer and closer to the floor, hedgehopping but not in very good shape this dove, you'd pick it back up with one hand, shake it, partly in retaliation and partly to get rid of the dust, you'd put it back in place, smoothing it out carefully with the palms of both hands so it would look the way it usually does, erasing quick as a flash any trace of its regrettable escapade. Anyhow you see that this is something that simply can't happen because the table-cloth is held down by the base of a pretty heavy statuette on which André, pretending to be surprised, sees a stag in flight, dodging a tree that's half pictured, its one gnarly branch reaching for the center of the scene; in fact, the stag seems to be leaping for the top of the secretary where, here's the problem, a china pen set is likely to be knocked over if he manages the jump, with the result that, hour after hour, the stag plans his leap, weighing his chances to reach the top of the desk, safe and sound and without breaking the ink bottle, slim hope considering his hesitation and the lengthy persistence of this suspended action, anyhow, the imperturbable pen set occupies the heights all alone where it has a panoramic view of everything else: the two (this is what made Jacques's choice so complicated earlier) sofas set on a diagonal, one sky blue and the other a grayish brown, one velvet and the second one toile; the two armchairs that will frequently hold our protagonists' two bodies on either side of the fireplace; the bellows, with its accordion-pleated red belly set up against its right side, the tongs for picking up logs looking puny but symmetrical on the left, heterogeneous sentinels on both sides of the hearth, one not full at all and the other showing off its belly; the side table where you can usually find a newspaper discretely representing the concepts of action and politics, of some collective outside world, that's something André finds important, or so Jacques must be saying to himself as André imagines Jacques's own monologue, the paper always containing within its folds some news of the world beyond, so that when you unfold it on your bent knee (your legs are crossed), once it's nighttime and there's nothing but the evening's dark, opaque blue out there, no outlines behind the windowpanes, which seem just a series of blind compartments (except on those occasional moonlit nights when the light isn't hindered by the thick trees and the tight filter of their canopy, but on the contrary traces a shadow theater of the branches' arabesques), so you can feel invisibly connected, over forests and plains, and going beyond the deeper isolation induced by the dark blue Canson paper of the windows, ignoring the vanished landscape, you suddenly feel caught up in the chain of yes humanity, not a metaphysical humanity, dreaming away by the fire and asking yourself a few general questions on the subject of existence thank you very much, but a historical humanity, constructed of facts and actions, finally you're getting word of it, your eyes fixed on the unstable ink that smears copiously all over your hands as if you were yourself part of this undertaking.

André's little game can't go on for long; any amount of switching roles and imagining what Jacques is feeling is quickly contradicted by the clear way André's body occupies space here, for his back can't help but be familiar with the exact concavity of his chair, which seems to adapt itself to him, an ergonomic welcome that leaves nothing out, the same way his fingers don't feel their way out to the end of those armrests but settle onto them as if they'd been made to measure, expressly to welcome this particular body and no other, with the result that our André can always tell himself his little story, developing a whimsical hypothesis just like in childhood games, What if? What if I were the guest, and What if I knew nothing about this room before I sat down in it? But there he sits, perfectly adapted to the furniture, fitting into it in a way that shows how many days he's spent here. In spite of

himself, despite his voluntary fiction, despite his desire to understand Jacques better, assuming Jacques's role in his mind, despite
his inner efforts and good will, he embodies in the presence of
Jacques the fact that he belongs to this house to the extent that he
melts into it, yes, there in his armchair he's not all that different,
for example, from the bronze statuette on the side table, the rug
on the floor, the curtain at the window, shrinking back in narrow
folds like the petals on a tulip to its tieback.

Camille comes into the room, slipping in on tiptoe with a slight
scuffing sound, like that of a jazz percussionist's brush. Lucy, with
her broad pelvis and endowed with a lumbar lordosis arcing her
silhouette, her long arms dangling, her sturdy scapula well clad
(the pectoral girdle equipped with powerful muscles), her knees
loosely jointed and kept bent as she walks, the tibial plate slightly
convex, comes along with Camille, and her australopithecene
hand (afarensis), with its long, narrow thumb, its curved index
fingers, its strong carpal bones, its long metacarpal bones, picks
up the other side of the tablecloth that she is going to shake out
with Camille on the wooden porch.

More light spreads across the room as the hours go by, it projects larger and larger rectangles that are more and more numerous, marking the scene off into square slabs. Our two men, one of
them perfectly melted into the décor and the other one still not or
not completely despite the progress he made when he sat down,
are thus in the center of a gigantic, moving hopscotch that gets
bigger and shifts around throughout the day. They don't talk. They
sit there with their pasts floating overhead, haloing them like a
delicate, glowing aureole, and it's clear that as pasts go these aren't

too impressive, or at least that's what they fear as they each conduct their parts of a vague, unmethodical census of the intervening years, to each his own, each thinking that their stories don't have much weight to them all told, André counting up his days in Abbeville, his decision to withdraw to Eu and then the process of moving, the succession of solitary days, it all seems to have the same pale, constant consistency, and our hero for his part compares his ambitions with their meager results, they each get lost in their flimsy accounts, follow frail lines of thought like dust in the air, dandelion fluff, light and fickle, flitting here and there without a plan. They let the light creep over them, with only the shadow of a mullion crossing a shoulder, a tibia, their eyes—mildly sore from the luminosity in which their bodies are bathing—close willingly, and beneath their eyelids the atmosphere is more red than black, almost pink, as if light were still coming through. The translucent skin thus forms a kind of screen with a blood supply that their eyes peacefully contemplate, soaking in all that rosy color and beginning to feel content.

V

A day in a house situated in the forest is not like a day in the country.

Country days, remember, are rather long, drawn out in a sort of downy inaction, simultaneously longwinded and sweet, you sit inside and engage in uninterrupted small talk, and expressionless phrases you've used before get strung together like a century of maxims you've divided among yourselves, so that, having spouted in unequivocal terms a profusion of extremely forgettable remarks rather like priceless fake pearls, at the end of the day not one of them can be distinguished from the others. It's a way of distancing yourself from the words you use, not a question of saying anything but simply of occupying the aural space to cover up the thick silence of places set in the middle of fields, the trivial buzzing of the occasional fly passing through. Between yourself and the others you weave a middle ground of flat fabric, each in turn sending the shuttle back across to the other side of the loom. And then, as night falls, you get up, stretch, attend to the materiality of kitchens, moving, thus, from general discussion to a specific commentary relating to ingredients, even using the injunctive mode, Hey how about handing me that big platter there, you manipulate vegetables, transform them, turn them into tiny pieces, you're afraid you're doing it wrong, Is that okay like that or do you want them smaller, we have lots and lots and you rinse and dry them on cotton towels you unfold a bit to study their motifs, seasonal or floral, or sometimes a row of pale blue chickens with big bows around their necks, and once you've finished the meal, during which voices grew louder and you went on to tell all sorts of jokes, digging through your repertoire of funny stories and exchanging them for those of the others the same way you used to trade pictures you had two of or cards from sets you're not collecting for some you want, and, speaking of cards, you end up playing parlor games, playing heatedly and all the suppressed energy of the day gets loose and spreads around, you've come to the physical part of things, arms explosively descending on a checker to move it, bodies fidgeting on their chairs because they're impatient for their turns, and sometimes a burst of sound when one hand claps the other or when the palm of a hand hits the table to express satisfaction at the victory apparently taking shape.

Sylvan days, on the contrary, I mean the part of them you spend indoors, are subject to a sort of disorderly pressure from the forest. There are no longer endless meadows to imagine from the house, a varied countryside, paths ready for you to take or others you'd improvise through the fields, descending grassy slopes in a little breeze that, combined with the air stirred up as you run would give you a sense of freedom, who knows why, that's how it is with friction between a body and oxygen, all sorts of merely potential things that, though you won't necessarily enjoy them, give the place a way to breathe, making it larger, turning the existence of the outside into something benevolent and elastic. The forest, the knowledge that the forest is there, its heavy mass all around, the acres and acres involved, the enormity it takes on, growing straight up the hills, turning everything into woodland, creating dense, rather tangled shade, this forest that, as soon as you go out onto the terrace, turns into scenery, a place where you can rest your eyes or move them about, like that, from one branch to another, and then up a tree trunk landing plop right in the middle of the foliage, then onto a specific leaf, an oak leaf with a speck of light on it like a bead, blink and the eye continues to stroll along, and at the same time the mind, a reflection of the gaze but in another place, less easily described, also dawdles along, passing from one idea to the next the same way the eyes are moving from plant to plant and it's happy as can be, sometimes spotting the silhouette of Abel, he of the River of Gazelles, who is chewing, with his parabolic mandible, front chin subplane, typical of *Australopithecus bahrelghazali*, one of the leaves he has found precisely there; this forest, therefore, when you think about it from inside the house, is ever so dark and heavy, bearing down on the backs of our two protagonists' necks and rendering them speechless, its ballast making them slump further and further down in their armchairs, one as bad as the other, reducing the earlier difference, when their backs were straight, fitting perfectly flush with the back of the chair in André's case and in Jacques's following the chair's line more roughly, less exactly parallel, their legs ditto crossed at first, André's feet neatly together and Jacques's with one slightly behind the other like something left over and of uncertain use, taken over by their increasingly collapsed position which soon has the arms dangling and legs spread wide; and the interior décor, its out of place, urban character which has already been discussed, plays no small part in the physical and mental resignation we see here: a décor that would not have been surprising in the city, where we would have looked at it with relative attention, here, paradoxically, makes itself felt, not at all as a remedy for the forest, as you might have thought, but, well, there's the tangle of the forest, its thickets, its darkness, but here inside things are familiar, the striped wallpaper, the furniture, everything makes you feel a bit at home, so you wonder, ask yourself why this striped paper, why this side table, this mahogany table, you have the impression that it's hiding something, this stubborn desire to seem a city house, whereas you could have easily seen rough white plaster on the walls and a rustic table, an oak sideboard, a big chest here, and then over there a crude but very convenient cabinet calmly embodying, with its visible screws, the notion of rusticity. In this rather citylike arrangement, the contradiction between the room's design and the forest landscape looming if you glance out any window and always at the back of your mind, the solitude of the house seems even more obvious, as if it were lost, misplaced, brought to this reclusive setting where its interior can only seem jarring, brought from the city who knows how, brought from where it must have looked contented, on the strength of its knickknacks, the design of its wallpaper, even the furniture scattered around, asserting social ties on every side; and so, stuck in this contradiction, caused by one of our men consciously or perhaps unconsciously (sincerely believing that he wanted to create the conditions for a humble, misanthropic existence in the depths of the Eu Forest but then hanging things on the wall and placing all around the room everything that could in one way or another reconnect him to the world) and now endured by the other, our two protagonists sit there, lifelessly collapsed in silence beneath the pressure of the forest.

It looks like they're taking the whole weight of the surrounding forest onto their shoulders, weight in the abstract, of course, nothing to do with tree trunks torn up by storms and bam falling onto the house, right through the tile roof and rafters and pinning their poor little bodies now stuck in those armchairs and futilely waving their arms like upside-down insects on their backs who are trying to get back on their feet, waving them in the void with very little chance of being successful. You imagine how it would be, they'd begin thrashing their legs around as well, feet in the air, top appendages then bottom, the uprooted tree trunks like the bar across a high chair for a wriggling child would keep them sitting there permanently, unable to extricate themselves, and you, well you, no, you can't think of any way to get them out of this situation, and their daring to call you for help this way makes you pretty uncomfortable, you get out of bed (or your armchair, etc.) and even go to your living-room doorway, you contemplate the disaster, the heavy tree limbs and branches you'd have to get past to reach them and then the considerable weight of the two trees holding them prisoner, the Herculean strength you'd need, no, frankly, you just can't help them, you climb back into bed (or your armchair, etc.), except now with our heroes stuck there how can the story possibly continue, pages and pages of this business about characters trapped in chairs like insects won't do at all, and besides there's no way to be sure they'll get out in the end, perhaps if there were an incursion of all sorts of rescuers wearing every kind of helmet, yes, that you could imagine but, now that I'm telling you the weight is abstract, you calm down, you breathe, nobody's asking you to undertake some heroic intervention into this closed room where our two men slip more and more visibly into drowsiness while occasionally some large birds fly past the window.

When, however, they decide to go spend some time on the porch, everything is reversed.

It's a modest porch, crude you might even say, constructed out of wooden planks, basic, and it drops suddenly without transition into the forest, no railings, no line of bamboo, the woods you can almost touch right there in front of you. There they talk a blue streak and the nature of their silences is different.

In this case you see them seated side by side and usually on the floor on either side of the French doors opening onto the porch, positioned like two symmetrical sphinxes guarding the entrance, their faces turned not toward each other but deeply absorbed in the forest, penetrating its foliage, digging through the tangle of branches, the chaotic leaves of which, stalks weakened, some few have already fallen (requiring no more than a little cooperation from a gust of wind, since the process was already well underway), frequently getting stuck, held between two branches, to pile up there in a limbo where the oldest leaves that weave the underpinnings to the pile are beginning, let's face it, to rot and turn ochre and that color soon reaches those that are more recent, the pile gets damper and damper, heavier and heavier, and shrinks until it collapses and falls to the already cluttered ground bristling with brown needles and previously fallen, waterlogged leaves.

Yet despite all this, something alive emerges, especially in the event that Little Foot, Miss Ples, and the Taung Child happen to walk through, with their divergent big toes, and the way they land on their varuses (that is to say they place their weight on the outsides of their feet as they walk). With their fluid gait this little group of *Australopithecus africanus* clears a path between the branches, their astragalus bones being well adapted to favor an action of flexion-extension that is most pleasing to the eye.

Tongues relax in this setting and that's why the account of the next four days spent at Jacques's friend's home, I might as well tell you right now, will progress in four conversations, each held at a different time of day, some in the afternoon, others at nightfall—night coming early as winter approaches, taking you by surprise at tea time—and always here on this porch where they look like two Robinson Crusoes, very happy to be able to sit on its organized surface, its hard, bare wood consistent with the rest of the forest. Because of the various times of day when they go outside to talk, all sorts of changes in the light will come into play, a clear sky, blank as an empty page, pale blue, a sky colored halfway between a ripe fig and grapes in those long transitional moments, a dark blue sky graced (or not) with a moon, round or crescent, with some possible intermediate stages, and veiled (or not) with a long cirrus cloud. Sometimes the night will be so dark that you'll set out candles and insects will spin around the flame (but it won't be a serious problem, you won't get bitten).

The self-containment of the setting (now you've already seen André's living room, gone through the several hundred yards of forest separating his house from where the stagecoach stops; you're acquainted with Abbeville, our hero's residence, the streets plunged in darkness, the spongy fields cut in two by the flowing river), which would make it easy, moreover, to adapt these pages for the theater (a scene recommended for amateurs), mustn't put you off: it's an airy place, breezy, even windy, it affords vivid variations of sky up over the tops of trees of many different species; and then, bear in mind that in the next section you'll be going to the seashore.

So, while we wait for the sea breeze where we can lose ourselves in the invigorating shades of blue spread across the landscape, let's take advantage of the earthy fragrance of damp leaves as our two friends converse on the rustic wood planks, recounting a few ancient events, shared or independent, occasionally interrupting each other to follow some thought of their own that arrives in the mind like an unsettled butterfly, look, how it quakes and moves in fits and starts, nothing to hold it down in its broken flight, panicked against the green and brown background of foliage at the end of fall.

Thus, the first day (meaning, if you count correctly, the second day of the visit, the very first having been marked by the arrival of the stagecoach, the passage through the forest, the long hours becoming acquainted with the premises during which our hero's body became less and less uncomfortable in his host's living room; but first in the series of four conversations conducted in the damp air on the porch, that's what I meant by first) was devoted to recalling memories from the years they'd spent together. Those memories—belonging to their communal legend and cementing the fragile bond between their two bodies—must be invoked once again to provide the foundation for conversations to come, they'll provide a sort of concrete slab or, if you prefer, a stonework platform upon which to construct their future relationship, which, for the moment, is still pending, awaiting the reaffirmation of the connection between the two men: an episode that might be entitled "An Abbeville Childhood," necessary for their reunion not to be a failure, yes, but primarily a celebration of their youth, this brief foundation narrative, this tale that will form a basis for contemplating everything else.

They also know that this first act, indispensable to reviving their friendship, will have to be repeated in some lesser fashion each time they meet again. Unlike this first recalling wherein they will, at least, learn what memories each even has of the other and what they have retained in the great sieve of years, each of them having, no doubt, gathered his own memories so each can show the other his collection and vice versa and still, in the end, keep his own little mixed bag of nuggets and pebbles, but having come to know the other's (because it's always a surprise to see how the shared days of friendship and particularly events that took place outside that friendship have been differently interpreted), the next times they meet they won't discover anything new on the subject, only recite a text of friendly litanies, one composed of identical, agreed-upon tidbits, passing certain paragraphs back and forth, André telling, one day to the next, what Jacques said the time before and vice versa, each one agreeing with his friend's account and taking it further, filling in an omitted detail, combining words with a few physical signs of complicity, a tap on the shoulder always works, laughing out loud, and a few onomatopoeic words of confirmation, and the faithfulness with which they'll tell each other about the old days again and again will demonstrate their goodwill, making a secure ritual of meeting up like this from time to time, promising each other on this cool morning at the end of October, But we won't wait so long, will we, let's say in a few months, we'll keep in touch, they contemplate the practicalities of these more frequent encounters, Jacques might come back to Eu, why not, or André might make an exception by traveling, accepting the bother of an occasional return to Abbeville, In my house says Jacques, it won't be the same exactly, but it'll be like in the old days, we won't bother to go by your family's house, now sold, lived in differently, we don't need to see that, we'll just sit in my place surrounded by my father's bric-a-brac, and we'll just talk without getting all worked up about things, that's what I suggest, or else, why not meet halfway, If you prefer, at Renard's inn, hey, a nice meal at the big table, a real spread, pheasants, good strong wine, dishes with pictures on them, and then we could get two rooms where you'd open the blinds in the morning to a view of the hills, what do you say, anyhow, somehow or other, in the house in the forest, the bric-a-brac at Abbeville, or the inn with its big windows open to the countryside, they'd bolster every get-together with a new version of their story, the inaugural myth forming the basis for their connection, passionately repeating it to each other so they wouldn't lose touch again.

VI

Eyes staring toward the piles of trapped leaves still hanging there, caught by the fig traps of forking branches, our friends have placed their hands on the planks on either side of their bodies as if on the lookout, not relaxed the way they were in the armchairs, so weighed down by the weight of the surrounding forest that it was better just to go along with the wild, exhausted silence, but with muscles tense, quivering, all in all like wild animals, taking part in nature and understanding perfectly that it's a good idea always to be vigilant, ready to hup! seize the memory as it goes by and triumphantly show it to your friend, Hey, look here, see what I've caught, Not bad, show me, closer, yes, No, wait, don't touch! don't touch! I'm not touching, just looking, come on, closer, ah yes, I see, I see perfectly.

André thus is the one who begins by randomly catching the memory of snowy winters in Abbeville in the strings of his net, particularly the one, snowier than others, when you couldn't even walk, so they'd made sleds, riding through a white Abbeville on their sleds, the idea seems to flutter overhead in its cartoon bubble with more bubbles growing and rising toward the main big one, the same for both, floating above them and in it are the sled and the two of them getting on it, sliding, turning over, getting it right-side up again, starting over, nothing to it, this memory, the snow's consistency, falling off, skin stinging, the joy of new sensations, the outside world turned into something like a big auditorium with delicate soundproofing where their whoops and shouts are absorbed by the snow muffling the world of sound, and the slightly Russian aspect of the city, perhaps, the short capes flapping like great crows' wings, hats with earflaps, faces furrowed by the painful, biting wind, mouths eating the flakes of snow that hurl themselves courageously inside, covering lips with bits of fluff, colliding with the wall of teeth.

As for Jacques, in the vegetation facing them he catches two memories. The first is a memory that often flickers through his mind, slipping between reality and himself, keeping him from seeing very well what's going on behind its big gray filter, and keeping him, above all, from acting, yes, because how can you do anything when this memory has inserted itself, I'm talking about when they fished for carp. The two boys squat on the riverbank, and each pushes one sleeve up, ready for action. In the muddiest water, if you work at it, you can manage to make out the rippling bodies of cyprinidae, plop, in goes a hand and you try hard to catch the creature, which however left that spot in the river long ago, having shot itself way out ahead of you and is now living its life over there in complete peace, slowly sucking in bits of food that have turned up on the surface just a few yards away, its truly dreadful mouth mocking you with its filaments. Sometimes it even shows half its body to you, or its whole body, jumping out into the open air, hup! signaling your complete defeat. So then off it goes, disappearing once again, circles inside circles widening on the water's surface, more and more eccentrically, the final outside circle may even come as far as you and flip! break against your wrist, as if the creature had thrown a lasso at you, as if, yes, your wrist had been in danger of getting caught in the wave's loop, as if the wake farthest away from the carp's leap had threatened, in response to your failed fishing, to encircle with its snare your defeated hand, which, luckily, got free because of the fragility of the slight liquid disturbance caused by the carp's motion, a snare that the least obstacle, including even your hand, breaks as though it were nothing, leaving behind in the water only a great hullabaloo of short, conflicting waves.

If you were quicker you'd have managed to feel the animal's scaly body with the palm of your hand, oily and rough at the same time, but even then it wouldn't have lasted for long because the carp vloof! would have literally slipped between your fingers, escaping the useless vice you'd thought would confine him, and this was the worst feeling of all, because a moment ago you could always have said to yourself that it was a matter of speed and practice, you would improve, thinking well maybe another time, and practice getting faster, promise yourself all sorts of happy endings in the future when you'd naturally get better and better at it and finally end up extracting from the river an annoyed example of *Cyprinus carpio* that would thrash around in the air, whereas now there was no getting around the fact that you'd never catch a thing, you didn't even know how to hold onto what you'd actually grasped, and right then and there Jacques developed a bitterness disproportionate to his age and drew from it a meager general philosophy that was no help when circumstances required resolute action.

This bitterness had been reinforced by the fact that André, after a few days, using his hand like a pincer and no doubt squeezing very hard with it, had managed to pull a cyprinid from the river and then, day after day, others, holding them above the water and shouting like a warrior, holding their heads up to his face and delivering brief sermons, swearing to them that he was master and that it was only out of extreme kindness he was letting them go on with their lives unharmed despite how ugly they were, after which he would throw them, essentially now his subjects, back into the river. Sometimes André would say it was always the same carp he caught, Maybe, who knows? One who'd been caught once by mistake because she was particularly absentminded, perhaps distracted the first time by something that she coveted, something good to eat floating in the water, unaware of the danger lurking, and then from there on in she just let it happen, knowing henceforth that he would turn her loose, getting caught just to please him, a carp in love with André (André supposed), yielding to his whim and then going back to her own problems in the river, maybe even a princess turned into a carp at birth and who, when André would dare, when he'd bring his lips to her barbelled mouth and kiss her, would be transformed into a splendid young girl; I doubt it, said Jacques grumpily in those days.

Anyhow, André couldn't have cared less about any princess, he preferred carp and his little victories one after the other, Not, let me remind you, something we shared, Jacques today says to André on this sylvan porch where they are recalling things, and that I couldn't do it was extremely painful to me, he confesses in substance, because I came away with the idea that I'd never catch anything in my life, not carp, who cares, but also not anything I really wished for, nothing, and certainly not Margot.

Ah yes, Margot, André follows up, a glint in his eye, a particular glint in the transparent, refractive, anterior tunica of his eye, a ray of light that hasn't come from outside this time, reflecting back outside, a physical phenomenon with no special significance that might occasionally light up a friend's brown iris, making it easier to see in its forest-wood color the concentric streaks or rayed fibers of the iris, and lighter, parallel and incomplete circular lines not covering the entire circumference but distributed unevenly over a third of it, perhaps even less, that make it look exactly like the trunk of a tree; no, a light that seems to come from inside and is aimed directly at his interlocutor, And what's become of Margot?

Jacques shuts his face like a book, clack, like you would saying that's enough when you're reading out loud, with both hands or even just one you close the chunk of pages on the right (the ones yet to be taken into account) against the chunk of left-hand pages, and there's our man just as undecipherable as a closed book without a title on its cover. A foolish bunch of starlings fly through the leaves, spin around just over the pines, and fill the acoustic space in a way that's welcome. André registers Jacques's rebuff, and then becomes swallowed up in thoughts of how sad Jacques must have felt, his dismay as a child, realizing how he, André, had seen nothing, cheerfully returning from the river with his fable of the Carp in Love, that's all it took for him to be happy, whereas beside him, Jacques must be mulling over his little theory, Come on, come on André thinks, with an abrupt wave of his hands as if there were gnats around, hoping to get rid of what he's now seen.

Luckily diversion is at hand, the flat-faced man of Kenya makes a quick appearance. Not looking too awake, bristly hair, vaguely yawning, you can see his rather large incisors, his smaller canines, his medium-sized molars, his premolars with their three roots. His yawns stop and stretching takes over, mixed with twisting and spinning, until *Kenyanthropus platyops* turns once again in our direction, see how the nasoalveolar clivus, the vertical walls of the nasal opening, and the molars (he's yawning again) are situated on the same vertical plane. He shakes his head, as if he were having trouble getting rid of his dreams, as if he were shaking off his vivid memories of dinofelis or giant leopards chasing him in the forests arching over the streams where soon they were joined yikes by lots of the scariest saber-toothed tigers. He had ended up near the mouth of the river surrounded by giraffidae and three-toed horses and was wondering if he'd be discovered.

The second memory coming to mind for Jacques was likewise about the days when they'd been friends, but not about a shared experience, because Jacques was the lone hero of it, and when it was over and done couldn't wait to tell André; they stretched out in the grass and André plucked a piece of it that he chewed while he imagined what had gone on while Jacques, all excited, filled the landscape with his shouts, starting to wave his hands wildly then soon standing up to act out his adventure.

So here's Jacques, maybe eight maybe ten years old, his arms up in the air and running back and forth in the meadow, telling about his incredible adventures at sea.

A tale of the sea, fine, hoist the sails, let yourself be carried along in a great rush of vocabulary and wind, come get your hands in there, rigging, pulleys, lines, breathe hard work hard, you plunge in with both hands, doing your best to get into the rhythm, you sheet the sail in, your aim is to yes keep the sail parallel to the wind that's good like that, everything, you name it, skysails, stay-sails, the lower studding sails and mainsails, mizzens that slide along a cable, gaffs, square sails (that actually form a trapezoid, I don't want you to get the wrong idea) attached on booms like crosses to the square mast (which is cylindrical, what were you thinking), the topping lift keeping them at the correct angle, you wipe your forehead with the back of your arm, sweating gladly over your share of the work, you're a happy link in the chain making this enormous boat go, let's continue, triangular lateen sails, gaff-rigged trapezoidal sails attached perpendicular to the mast on booms that are, more or less, long, horizontal, wooden spars, spritsails, the storm trysail we'll find useful in heavy weather, a glance confirms that your peers are no more stinting in their efforts than you, you look up at the mizzen topgallant flapping in the wind on the mizzenmast just above the topgallant, against the blue of an oil-painting sky with white cumulus clouds that for now lie motionless in layers way up in the air, you untie the reef knots to let out the reefs, you really feel the excitement of departure, and a sort of correspondence with, face it, the rather technical, material nature of everything around you, this joy in the physical handling of rigging and watching sails harmoniously unfurling, trapezoidal shapes proliferating against the blue, the three staysails (spritsail and big and little jibs in that order), the extra sails (by which I mean the studding sails) rigged on a raked mast, more staysails, the spanker (the trapezoidal sail at the stern), I almost forgot the forestaysail, and reigning over it all the mainsail, stoic, white, and lethargic as a termite queen, but soon taking charge of the whole thing for you, demonstrating her precedence in the hierarchy of geometric white or tan shapes deployed on the masts. Or else, hands in your pockets, you're standing up in the bow and taking the sea spray as you look off at the vast crumpled fabric of the sea, hearing the long litany of orders like something that doesn't concern you in the least (passenger = someone passing through), you assume a pose that is more contemplative but also exhilarated by the air and salt, somewhere between a state of passivity (picking up information from a distance, some word or other collected in the hollow of your ear remains for a while and if it gets explained moves into the lexicon of things you know somewhere in a corner of your mind, things you'll be able to reel off at the dinner table) and a post-romantic reverie, involving soaring meditations on the subject of vast spaces, the watery immensity of the sea, then returning to the actual and getting back to the actual sky and likewise its vastness, both specific and even broader as a concept, and finally to the question of long voyages, how the incredible sense of time they induce is a break from the small time frame of Abbeville, which you consider in some detail while the seagulls flying in the blue sky add a pleasant touch to your reverie. You have no idea that in a few hours it's going to be a totally different story, when the lookout in the crow's nest spies the enemy

ship pitching scurrilously on the horizon in the ring of his telescope, and definitely approaching. Enemy ship on the horizon!
the lookout calls out, telescope still glued to his eye up there, and
a single shivering wave runs through the crew passing from one to
the other, the sailors yes look to you like a large sheet undulating
in fear, they're thinking about what's going to happen, how everything, shivering sails, topsails large and small, royals large and
small, everything will be ransacked, talking in a sort of grumbling
choir that rivals the growling sound of the sea, and you, from the
height of your ten years, what are you going to do, you spot a
trunk nearby, you climb inside, sitting there surrounded by nets,
you keep the top open with one hand over your head (soon with
both hands, because it's beginning to feel heavy and even more so
because of your uncomfortable position), and you look through
the opening you've made, sort of like peeking through a transom
except that you are definitely not in your own house and the landscape you're looking at isn't one with peaceful hills but instead
panicked sailors, the watch continuing to provide a commentary
as the other boat draws nearer, in a sort of voice-over (from here
and with the reduced visibility afforded by the half-open trunk
you can't see the top of the mast) he undertakes an informative
description of the situation, so that you are kept perfectly up to
the minute concerning the progress of the opposing boat, until,
Holy Smoke, two hands appear holding on tightly just over the
edge there at the stern, I'm not dreaming, then a pirate's head with
its eye-patch, there's no mistaking it.

Damn, thinks Jacques, Damn Damn and Doubledamn, and he
pulls the top of the trunk shut.

So he'll see none of the battle, remaining in total darkness, at first imagining the confrontation in a realistic version based on the sounds he's hearing, a little translation turning them into mental images, shout after shout, the sound of someone falling, then someone else, and pretty soon he has no need for the sound-track to imagine the massacre, picturing more and more terrifying scenes before remembering that he himself, little Coco, is also in the thick of it, there in his trunk a thousand miles from terra firma, shedding a few tears that turn into sobs as he thinks first about life in general and how he has fit into this life till now, a humble runaway, by which he means that, as he's conceived of himself in his life thus far, he's seen himself, above all, as running, through fields and meadows, fleeing, what exactly? The words of his mother, dismayed by the child's lack of talents, the mother unhappy because of him, Jacques, her idiot son a shame to the family, said his mother as she sewed by the light of a lamp, no fame in sight for silly little Coco, his mother far preferred to look at her work, he remembers her with her eyelids lowered, yes, only when he came home would she open them upon him again, if he had the good luck to return, if he escaped alive from this awful battle taking place around him on the decks where the sea now rises in salty puddles, slosh slosh, splashing around the ankles of the men fighting and the trunk where the tired child is hiding, hair on end, shirt torn at the elbow, would he find some little place for himself reflected there finally in the pupils of his mother's eyes, Finally!, and they would shout at the same time Finally, mother! Finally, my child! (at which thought he sobs all the harder); then next imagining the reasons he is now where he is, seeing the back of a large silhouette looking out the window at the garden and the child who has been summoned waiting for this shape to utter some word, I had an idea, says the father, the child wonders just what this idea might be, he looks at his father's hands crossed behind his back, the left hand holding the back of the right in its palm, closing tight like pincers as if it were about to escape, the other no longer even resisting, but soft, fingers relaxed, conquered, sweating a bit in the dampness of the plump cushions lining the palm like in a padded room, I thought, what do you think of this? How about a nice expedition at sea?

VII

It's the precise hour when day turns into night, and takes some time doing it—a blend where watercolor blue, having dominated all day with, occasionally, some room left for zinc-white or grayish or yellowish (there are skies stained with nicotine) trails, now darkens in contact with navy blue and dilutes it early in the struggle, until yes the navy takes over. All our two men's energy is now concentrated on battling the evening damp rapidly weighing their clothing down; the cold, saturated air flouf comes in through the bottom of their pants and flouf again up their sleeves, its current provoking the rise of tiny dermal hills that in a microscope would resemble an exhausting landscape to climb through, all ups and downs and ups again is what the bug venturing onto it must be thinking, tickling André somewhere on his calf, tap, he jerkily extends his leg again and again tap tap tap, before finally outright scratching himself through the fabric, which action we have to fear is in the process of erasing a life, one oh so humble but still, the ant, according to scientific authorities, having a solid carapace, one that I've heard people say is impervious to nuclear radiation, but not so impervious that this shielding allows him to emerge the winner against pressure driven by a muscle as singularly large as André's brachial triceps, which, though its proportions are reasonable and quite ordinary, is of a volume big enough to smash every organ on a good thousand ants.

Their struggle against cold becomes practically gymnastic, almost like swimming, each man in his own lane reaches a hand over to rub the opposite arm and simultaneously kicks his feet, it's a complex stroke, almost a breaststroke crawl in fact, hands swirling and legs doing scissor kicks in the air. André soon switches into more of a sidestroke, lifting one arm toward Camille who is on her way out the French doors at the same time as he turns his head toward her and, continuing his sideways motion in this manner, he asks Camille could you bring us the candles, then starts doing his breaststroke crawl again, face once more turned toward the forest, indistinct but perceptible because of all its rustling, trembling like a mass of flesh inflating and deflating in the darkness.

Camille returns with candlesticks, she puts them on the wooden table turned grayish by rain with its two benches around it, lights the candles one by one, as in an abandoned chateau open to the sky where the candelabra have been preserved but nothing else remains, and suddenly Jacques thinks about his ancestors, about the moats where truncated ghosts might turn up, or just parts of them, yikes, the sight of them making even frogs go silent, about the pond red with blood, families' pasts are dreadful things and their genealogies, as told him by his nurse, Françoise, are terrifying, a third memory therefore, you can't always predict these things, and at the same time his own face, creased by the glow spreading from the candles, redesigned by their flicker, emerges strangely from the night.

It's a history you have a right to know, after all, and one I'm about to tell you just like everything else.

A chateau lies in ruins in the middle of the forest of the Ardennes, everything there exudes a kind of physical weakness, the prime example being sickly Lady Marguerite whose trembling silhouette sometimes appears in the courtyard, where beneath the sun of a medieval afternoon she casts her frail shadow (hardly any bigger than the cone of her hennin with its too-long veil floating from its tip like a big black aquilid) upon an idiotic osprey dying of hunger because he's not finding fish in the frothy moats anymore, either because, lacking a methodical approach and being just naturally stupid, he's hunting badly or because the moorhens have carried out their raids before him; and the Lord of the manor himself has only a hackney with an ambling walk for riding out to check on his estate; and their children are skinny, and their servants such shadows of themselves that we wonder if we're not just seeing things.

Only the moorhens behind the crosshatching reeds seem slightly prosperous. Those birds are the ones also called gallinules, small wading birds, marsh birds, and their distinctive feature is that they are carnivores, said Françoise rolling her *R*s and whenever possible her eyes too, opening them impossibly wide so you could see the iris round as a planet floating in a vast white sky, or rather it would seem white at first and then, if her eyes stayed that wide, Françoise's voice having gone silent and so leaving you to imagine the worst of the butchery enacted by those meat-eating birds that always had some scrap momentarily dangling from the corner of their beaks, scraps that would, in an approximation of mastication, sometimes end up back in the animal's mouth and sometimes fall into the water making an appalling stain, and if you kept your eyes glued to the white sky of Françoise's eyes, in the middle of which swam duplicate central planets, you would see that the vascularity of the choroid coat traced onto this blank background great red streaks, which, to the child, looked like branches of blood spread out on the snow, well, I'd be hard-pressed to make anything more of it.

The dreadful story Françoise used to tell was that, sometimes late at night, beneath the selenite rays of light spreading their milk over the moats of Chateau Crèvecoeur, a bloody head would come up out of the water (I'm not making any of this up), then fleshy fragments, and that the whole body would dance a sanguinolent ballet above the water, a kind of solitary scuffle in which pieces of flesh would beat upon its head (I'm still not making anything up), until an arm holding a sword would join in and strike out wildly all around (there's no way I'd imagine a story like this), and the waves on the moats would turn red in the milky light, the same sort of effect as adding grenadine to milk (this time it's my imagination), and then the vision would vanish the same way it came. One time Lady Marguerite's children had met up with some ill-intentioned ghosts who had given them fishing poles and hooks, so they ended up hooking a few of these bloody body parts in the moats, that was the worst part of the story, and they showed them to Lady Marguerite, which made her feel sick, you can understand why, and to the Lord of the manor who, this is the most unfair part, whipped them, poor confused fellow, his eyebrows meeting angrily to create a single hairy wave in the pale sea of his forehead.

People think that *Australopithecus garhi* had flint tools to use for cutting things. His postcanine dentition was very well developed. His maxillary dental arcade was U-shaped, the sides slightly divergent. But he also ate fruits and leaves that he pulled down from the trees, his forearm was long, sometimes he would dig in the dirt with a stick to get roots out, his femur was elongated, and his toes curved inward. He could also break open the rigid husks of certain plants.

When you're descended from something like that, from ancestors who pal around with bloody ghosts, the idea of descending from apes is really not a big leap, and the fanciful child had developed a terror of his lineage the memory of which returned full force in this sylvan landscape stuck in the dusk.

Camille has just brought them wool blankets (Thank you, Camille, you're perfect, André said; Camille has now gone back into the house taking the compliment along with her) that they've wrapped around themselves, so now they look like two old cowboys who've stopped for the night and are talking by the fire.

The candle glow creates an optical impression of incredible mobility, of fragile photons moving crazily around and being quickly absorbed into the darkness, immediately replaced by others in continual flux but of shifting intensity, so that a kind of suspense arises around the light's fragility, a general, vague anxiety, setting off all kinds of thoughts that touch our two men deeply; thoughts,

I bet, about how ephemeral things are, their physical or theoretical fragility, fearing that all this will come to an end, this light, that the glow will lose more and more ground, that the photons and their increasingly anemic replacements will finally pass away, one way of saying "die," their defeat leaving the night a completely, totally free hand in this evening where the moon, clouded over, supplies none of its enormous, white cotton sheets to hold you.

In addition to the visual flicker that plays across their faces, superimposed like undulations of a transparent scrim in front of a stage, there is also the physical shivering set in motion by the night, the slight chattering of teeth you occasionally allow yourself, shoulders quivering and sending out vibrations that have an effect even on your facial features, so our two protagonists occasionally half bury these features under their blankets and only half-faces show, their glittering skin standing out against the dull surface of the wool like half moons. At other moments, though, their faces remain whole but entirely remodeled by the changing light, metamorphic now, which isn't any better. They turn this ill-defined anxiety gripping their hearts into sadness, into a sort of sadness balloon that they have held in check, kept deep inside themselves, and that now, released from this pressure, floats freely overhead on this porch where it monopolizes their attention; they try hard to dispel it, deflate it by providing a rational interpretation of the situation, but this is my old friend Jacques, but this is my old friend André, and things begin to sort themselves out, anyhow more or less, these reciprocal identifications functioning well as minor reassurances, so they then can let their thoughts drift onto the thoroughly agreeable theme of their reunion, knees tucked up under their chins and gripped in the ring of their arms under the blankets, underneath, as in a cave, or a mini Indian tent while their foreheads and cheeks take the wind and cold head-on.

Days two and three, whsh whsh, I wave my hand like a windshield wiper, and suddenly I appear on the porch to tell you this in private, will be devoted to memories of the years they spent apart. These accounts will have a different function from that of their founding legend. Their function, if you will, is to fill the gulf of time between the last time André saw Jacques or Jacques André, the night before our hero's departure for a succession of positions as a customs officer and this reunion starting about forty-eight hours ago on the edge of the Eu Forest. They will, in short, ensure the smooth transition between these two disconnected periods in the landscape of their relationship that at the moment still form a vast crevasse that they would do well to fill in, in order to walk calmly across its once again flat surface, if I may put it that way.

Is it the cold, deep blue night that reminds him of nighttime vigils during the war, the rustling of tents in a camp on alert, how time is suspended the night before battle, when everybody is wrapped in the folds of his coat and talking to himself; unable to sleep beneath the flimsy walls of his canvas room, he wanders among groups of talkative soldiers standing guard. They're exchanging some brief ideas concerning the future, the imminent future, what action will be taken, their chances of success collectively, and the likelihood of their coming out alive individually (which is, if you think about it, not at all the same calculation); each one jumps in with his own prophecy, developing his catastrophic account in the moonlight; then there's the more distant future of what will happen next in

their lives if they do come out of this, and, pulling miniature portraits from their pockets, they sniffle and go closer to the fire to
show them around, you can see them bent over each other's hands
and looking (sometimes the man talking to himself in his coat the
color of darkness will interrupt them Excuse me gentlemen, will
come over to see how the troops are feeling, asking two or three
questions and possibly he'll be alarmed by their answers). A few
Paranthropus aethiopicus, having caught a catfish in the pond, are
setting up camp. As they dine the moon lights up their enormous
faces, their protruding cheekbones form hills in them; theirs are
faces described as saucer- or dish-shaped, because rather than being convex, they are concave. Jacques begins to speak, his voice
emerges from the checkered blanket to take aim at André's ear
only to die further on, absorbed in the damp foliage. I'll tell you
about the disastrous times first, André, my border wars, my bands
of thieves, and the wolves I had to avoid, and André keeps silent
in the darkness, he doesn't know anything about wars, it was because of my position in Customs, says Jacques, informing the
reader at the same time, we constantly had to defend the invisible
frontier, roughly reestablish its line, I actually didn't have many
troops, I had with me an army of henhouse-raiding rogues who
just wanted to get something different to eat. Jacques, surrounded
by the night forest of the Eu, describes looking for battlefields
they couldn't find, circling around them with no firm notion of
where they were, the trees look like Indian arrows that fell into
the landscape and stuck, or a scattering of watchmen frozen in
place, but everything's hidden, the armies your eyes can't make
out in the fabric of the plains, and those thick veils in the depths

of the valley won't reveal whether they're stagnant fog imprisoned by the hills or a whirlwind of dust from enemies who'll shortly disappear. The Customs bayonets encounter nothing, unstable armies, quick to vanish like optical illusions, quick to appear in the distant landscape and then, before you're able to catch your breath, there's nothing to see other than the splashes of light on the edge of their own blades, their nonsensical horse brigades led by a drummer and surrounded by flies driving the horses crazy (we never remember these other dangers). André hears how the men hurtle off, unseated by stinging dipterans, their bodies moving in semicircles against the background of almond-colored plains, thud thud, while thicker and thicker clouds of *Muscae domesticae* attack the eyes of horses rearing with appropriate neighs. And then there's the whole collection of Jacques's tribulations in the wooded mountains, the caves in which he occasionally had to make his men sleep, the camp (would you like a bit of catfish, a *Paranthropus aethiopicus* inquires, chewing noisily in his temporary encampment; somewhat egocentric, he's elbowing in to get a second mention), the mud, the storms, how they slip and slide, skidding the whole way, twisting their ankles, the horses no longer proud, the war is a huge puddle of mud from which you emerge like a clay doll that keeps on marching with only your eyes hollowed into the soft clay covering you, like creatures born of the soil, as if it were the soil itself advancing, until the next rains wash you off and restore your human face, soaked now, hair plastered to your head, darkened clothes sticking to you, and your poor little body inside them chilled through and through, completely uncalled for.

You really have to remember that this body is the one your mother swaddled, washed, dried in big towels, dressed and rocked, and now here it is deep in the muck of defeat, on slippery marches in a war that's invisible more often than not, the idea of it rustling like birds of prey that whirl and cast their huge shadows wherever you set foot. Sometimes you are ordered to set out on nocturnal manhunts through forests where you beat your way through thick brush and what with the noise of twigs snapping underfoot and your own breath, how could you hear the man who's lying low, holding his breath the best he can and not even quivering when the end of your stick pokes him in the ribs; that must be an old root, you say to yourself, because it hasn't budged. Those nights are the worst. Who are men if not your little brothers? You look up at the moon, which is also half absent. You hope you won't encounter one of them. Sometimes you fire off your musket or your blunderbuss, there, on the right, a branch moved, maybe that's where he is, flash, the barrels of your weapons catch a ray of light among the leaves and suddenly reflect the sky. Your shots, guns and rifles and pistols, are heard in the plain but nothing runs out of the bushes, he's already dead or maybe it was just a big breeze washing through, natural, you keep on advancing, our hero's nostrils quiver, breathing deeply (so war seemed more tangible) the smell of gunpowder mixed with the fragrance of flowering thickets.

The opposite sometimes happens as well: no longer the battle you're trying to locate and that seems to take place nowhere at all so you think it's the enemy when some branch shakes, you think it's an army when a bit of fire shows on the horizon (just a peasant burning his pile of tree limbs and grasses), but the battle you find yourself in the midst of without recognizing it, the sound of rifle fire but you think it's something else—a branch breaking, a rock sliding, you're right in the middle of the action and you don't even know it, That was truly my comic novel says Jacques, not being able to find combat and then somewhere down the road dancing around in disbelief with bullets overhead, telling my men You're imagining things, fellows, the danger is far away, and at the same time as I'm speaking, curbing my terrified horse, wheeling and taking me forward clumsily and sideways like a crab, like some ten-legged crustacean who has no business being in all that greenery. We'd come to after the pell-mell of the confrontation (you couldn't seriously call it battle), waking up in a bucolic landscape plundered by bayonets (because it's in the pleasant valleys that wars are waged), grass torn up, earth bared, two or three corpses that I'd mourn without even remembering their names and that my men dragged off to the forest where they buried them, grumbling about how hard it was to dig and the danger of getting stuck in the eye by some inconvenient branch, which would really add insult to injury considering everything they'd been through. Occasionally munching on a bitter berry, I led my men with their scrapes and scratches along a line of arbutus trees and began drafting a letter in my mind that I'd write back in barracks after bathing my body in a pike-filled lake.

On the porch, in silence, our two men smoke cigars lighted ceremoniously with a candle, crinkling their eyes, approaching the candlestick slowly, as if at the same time they were telling themselves some little story in which they appeared on stage lighting a cigar, see, as if this gesture contained a condensed version of some adventure, maybe you're familiar with this sensation, as if they were putting on a costume for just a few fractions of a second with this action, playing a cowboy or something else, an explorer, just like that, and then, the vision growing along with the flame that grows only to disappear on the tip of the cigar pouf the vision is gone with the flame, oneself as a cowboy, or something else, an explorer.

Jacques suddenly feels exhausted, the exhaustion you feel after telling a story. His muscles go soft, his back relaxes, the hand not holding the cigar is like a rag dangling at the end of his arm, and his mind is like a ballroom where lots of people got all excited only to desert it in the early morning hours, almost all at the same time, leaving only a vague streamer dragging behind, and that's it.

He says he's going in, I'm going in says Jacques, his direct style offers no additional information. He means inside the house, and that he'll probably take a hot bath or go to sleep before eating dinner, getting some fresh air, and then digging up more of these memories of ours.

Is it because of the wind sweeping the air that there aren't many insects, though a moth fluttering there, livid, white as linen, stands out in particular, slaloming above the flames. After Jacques, André remains on the porch for a bit, he watches the moth's flight, the chances it's taking in its white tutu, then he raises his right arm and swings it like a racket, biff boff, in the air, first backhand then forehand, biff boff, chasing the creature away but back it comes, Idiot, says André, he blows on the candles, one by one, until all are out.

VIII

Third day. Our two men have returned to sphinx position on either side of the French doors, a position, all in all, that is becoming habitual for them, a means of beginning to construct a present in common.

They are conscious of how this position turns them into statues, due as much to the symmetry of their two bodies, impeccably distributed on either side of the door, as to the parallel alignment of their profiles, their eyes looking straight ahead deep into the forest rather than turning from time to time toward each other to intersect, André's toward Jacques's, Jacques's toward André's; in how their thoughts unwind one on top of the other, and the words they gradually exchange, as if to loosen up their voices, as if to train them in the manipulation of vocabulary, syntax, hmmm, something I just said, a word hangs for an instant over the porch, then goes away, and then another, a cohort, a small squadron, before finally arriving, soon but not right away, at the narrative of the day, words for warming up that don't make much sense, that have a redundant relationship with the world they describe, words to connect a lot of comfortably obvious things or just for lounging around in, words in which you can relax, just letting them come; one on top the other, therefore, you feel they're vaguely enjoying this arrangement of their two custodial silhouettes, as if they were playing a game, Hey! What if we pretended to be statues! they'd have said to each other, both charging at the same time out onto the porch and, bingo, no sooner said than done, first one to move loses, this being something they know how to do together, imagining without thinking, so that something comes to both of them at once, you can't tell if it's Jacques or André behind it, neither one can claim ownership of the impulse, no, it's as if they were one man, after a fashion, whom they've divided between one sphinx and another like this, pleased with the shared invention they happily repeat day after day.

A few gnats spin in the unseasonably warm air, you can smell a sort of late summer there that takes you by surprise, it's disconcerting and fascinating at the same time, you just can't make the olfactory sensations coincide with the visual as you sit there breathing the slight sugary smell that usually comes on summer breezes, while there facing you in the forest straight ahead you scrutinize the brown patches indicating the extent to which the season, the third in the calendar year, has already thoroughly organized its task of progressive decay, having begun to weaken the deciduous leaves and turn them reddish before whoosh letting them fall. If you shut your eyes you could think this was a day derived from all the days in July combined and moved, misplaced here, an extra bit of stray summer, a sampling for the guest, since they haven't seen each other in all these years, a glimpse of what it's like in the host's home through the year, two seasons in one visit, or almost, because there's pressure from the darkness, you certainly feel it, yes, behind the thick, mellow air plunging you into a pretend summer, you can sense that it won't be long before evening plunk drops its dark blue curtain on the scene, I'd say it won't be more than, more than, what, an hour and a half before the sky turns into that early darkness of fall that makes your days so short, nothing more than little gaps in which you can get less and less done until December 21, really, that takes the cake! (afterward, things improve and it's even sort of thrilling, you're secretly enthusiastic about witnessing the delightful lengthening of days; they turn warmer and more comfortable and at the same time they're also growing longer so you can fit more and more into them, making those days richer).

In that balmy air, neither one thing nor the other, Jacques decides the time has come to recount the tale of his social life, the story, depending on how he tells it, of dinners and balls, a very nineteenth-century novel about a young man going from salon to salon where he leans casually by the fire and the engraved mirror in the mantelpiece behind him catches the reflection of his back in a dark frock coat forming a sort of trapezoid around which society with all its froufrou of dresses and twinkling necklaces is reflected, while on the painted part, over the mirror, some ragamuffin shepherds are having fun, one of them has a pipe, another a drum, and a shepherdess seated wordlessly there contemplates their dance without daring to get involved.

Dinners, well that was a different kettle of fish, especially the first ones to which he was invited, our hero remembers the silent suppers in Abbeville, where his father dreamed about which plants he might collect tomorrow, already imagining himself making his rounds as customs officer and pulling out of the jumble of ordinary vegetation some notable specimen that he would stick between the pages of his big notebook, already seeing the enormous sky hanging over the scraggly, windblown flora, and his eyes searching deep into this disorder while his body would be offered to the intensity of the outside world that had to be a contrast with the closed-in dining room under its low ceiling where the curtains, already drawn, hid the garden and as for his mother, he wasn't sure about his mother, submerged in all the clutter of things his father brought home—the decorated plates hanging on walls, too much furniture, prints and paintings right next to each other so there wasn't even a smidgen of wall between them where you could look—she used to seek in vain some fragment of white plaster to rest her eyes on so she could come up with some thought really her own, hardly too much to ask, but no, everywhere there were myths to read again, compulsory stories, his mother wore her eyes out with all these givens, all she had left was the window, the wide, smooth pleats of a curtain the material of which, at least, she had chosen.

The other children had already eaten their dinner in the kitchen between the two Delft jugs always adorning the table and in front of them there stood, first, a small Japanese pot with a painted woman and her paper parasol about which his pensive sister thought up entire novels, and second, some cows made of china from Saint-Omer whose solid build the boys studied, themselves chewing the day's offerings and imagining entire farms, stories about crops, around them. But there was a different fate in store for Jacques, the eldest, and the brother next in line, said to be more talented than he but with no more permission to speak, though no one could remember if that was by parental order or, instead, some sort of implicit, floating constraint that they had interiorized before anyone, mother or father, had even taken it into their heads to pronounce it. The two boys, thus condemned to silence in accordance with a ban that was lost to memory, were witnesses throughout the entire meal to their parents' parallel monologues, their mutually irrelevant ramblings, and occasionally one of the two would have the idea that some genie had made them mute, and then, speech really and truly being suspended, the question became if the spell would vanish when the meal ended or instead would they would all be condemned to remain that way for good, in their Abbeville house, mute mother, mute father, and the children too, getting up from the table to discover that they couldn't say a word.

Nutcracker Man, the *Paranthropus boisei* with a retreating facial plane, very large, strong molars, and thick enamel on his teeth, was used to tough food but missed the savannas full of grass; he was there beside them now gnawing on a few tubers, then he finished off with some exocarpal fruit, attacking the shell with a hard blow, crunch, and spitting it shamelessly under the table (but be glad that it wasn't right on the tablecloth), which gave Jacques and his brother a good laugh.

In the winter, their mother (or else a servant) brought in the soup tureen from Marseille with its cover topped, this is really true, by three greenish leeks and on top of them a fine mushroom sat enthroned, pretty well indicating the sort of mixture inside, and in the spring it was a tureen from Strasbourg instead whose top, still with a nature motif but no thematic connection to its contents, had a branch from an apple tree across it with an apple attached, what a stroke of luck, just right ergonomically for gripping the lid.

If something wasn't salty enough they used (Careful! It comes out fast!) the salt shaker from Nevers with its white designs dispersed against a background of lapis blue; and if they wanted to put sugar on their fruit they had a sugar bowl from Rouen with its imitation Chinese decoration, no way to imagine anything in there.

And all four of them sat there like that without saying anything, or almost nothing, here and there some edict of a practical sort, with its accompanying polite phrase, at best a comment, regretful or in praise, about the freshness of the vegetables. Sometimes, one of the boys' fingers, making its way across the tablecloth and telling itself as discretely as it could a vague story with a chase scene, would run into the duck-shaped gravy bowl that was ugly enough amid all this mealtime boredom to really get excited about.

As a result, you can pretty well imagine the difficulties our hero experienced when thrown into the verbal rush of conversation in society, when he would sit awkwardly at his place at a table where all the serving pieces were irreproachable (nothing, not the duck-shaped gravy boat in pottery from Saurus, nor the yellow porcelain pot with a swan on it, nor the dish from Palissy depicting summer to send our man off into any serious daydreams giving him, if not words, the profound look of a contemplative person), present, at best, like an umpire watching the game of lawn tennis apparently taking place in front of him, each phrase flying rapidly back and forth like a ball and landing on the racket of one participant or another in the conversation, unless someone else ran up to the net to get there first and, whup! stole his shot, while the previous player had to reestablish his position sheepishly because after two or three misses like that you risk no longer being considered one of the guests, which they all knew well. It went so fast, they were passing shots back and forth so easily, making it look like there was nothing to it, not even running, their cheeks not getting red, their breathing unhampered, not out of breath, no, as if they were just strolling along, as if this were something that didn't make them tired in the least, that there was no question of our hero entering into the fray, though it was possible that his being so absolutely vulnerable would touch the mistress of the house who would let him have a second chance by inviting him again, accompanying him into the hallway and slipping into his ear two or three sentences, making it clear by the way she said them that, next time, he could have a head start.

Our Jacques soon acquired some skill. After studying a few of these tennis matches in a number of houses, he came up with an empirical notion of the rules and threw himself into the melee. He had to weather a few shots, a few spatters of mud, which is perfectly normal, slipping on the court just when he thought he had the ball, and, in his enthusiasm, he had two or three crash landings, so he emerged from several matches with bruises on his arms and legs. But in general, his novel style, which at first put some people off or brought half-smiles to their faces, its asymmetry a painful illustration of irony, ended up by winning support, and he even had a few disciples, which just shows how much progress he made.

As for the balls, they weren't so hard for him. He was a good dancer and, as far as he was concerned, waltzes, contra-dances, and montferrines were no secret, as they say. People would often leave the room to go out on the terrace and contemplate the cardboard sky showing over the balustrades, where, against the smooth background of breezes, the moon, round or crescent, would be tracing that motif indispensible for crystallizing first conversations by way of comments on the subject at hand, its shape, its whiteness, before the participants' eyes would move down to the gardens, the gravel paths reflecting the opaline light of that moon, the clumps of box-wood or broom behind which, perhaps, really you never know, it's the sort of thing that happens on nights when there's dancing.

If Jacques were leaning there alone, a bit of music escaping through the half-open French door (re fa la la, la la fa fa) and spinning around him before vanishing into the branches of papilionaceous plants, you could be sure that there'd be a man some ten years older who'd come up behind him and begin to fire off a few maxims apropos society, what went on between men, what went on with women, and how the world was coming along, firing shot after shot until he thought he'd shown him what's wrong about everything. Then this man, whose hat was tilting off to one side, would go back into the ballroom where he'd act as if he'd said nothing at all and would become perfectly indistinguishable from everybody else. There was no need for Jacques to turn around to know this, no need to look through the wooden framework of mullions cutting the dance scene into squares like a crossword puzzle; he could keep on letting his eyes wander to the plaster fountain surrounded by the dry vegetation of summer evenings.

Paranthropus robustus, a good walker, with shorter arms and longer legs, finding that the garden was something like a wooded savanna near a watering spot, did a few steps of her own, so Jacques had a bit of company. Occasionally people would ask him to talk about where he was from and he'd launch into a lyrical description of the green fields of Abbeville, its broad river, its thousand streams; he'd tell about how Abbeville used to be just an island between the branches of the river; he'd construct his little *locus amoenus* so well that another person, even most other people, would feel inspired as they listened to his bucolic hymn, being careful not to show how astonished they were to see he had such rustic origins, and taking his words as more of a poem, an ode, an elegy.

In his room our hero secretly wrote a few sentimental stories, and freely in verse, letting himself go, and sometimes, in the course of these intimate recollections some alexandrines would come to him, an octosyllabic or so, charming, improvised. There, that's the inane novel of my youth. Salons where there were women whose game I'd play and even be taken with them but never staying till the end of the game, and all those nonentities, one in particular more annoying than the others with his green frock coat, a frock coat that he went around in for a long time in solid wool of a green so vivid that you couldn't help staring at it. Those are my years of exile. Exile, even consented to, is hard. You stand there in a sort of exalted state, excited by all the new things in a place where even the least little practical procedure becomes an adventure; and then you pull back, grab hold of an imaginary definition of yourself, and afraid of losing it you hang on with both hands and sometimes it'll feel reinforced by your surroundings (emerging all the more delineated from the differences affecting your basically heterogeneous self), and other times compromised: because it wouldn't take much effort for you to be, skillful little chameleon that you are, from Marseille, first, then from Italy, and so forth, until, dithering like a spinning top, you finally end up back in Abbeville with a memory full of roads and that's all.

Jacques and André sit there as if caught up in the persistent, diminishing sound of a fermata, as if something of their stories still hung in the air, a sort of acoustic tremor, despite being inaudible, mixing with the memory of the warm, indecisive weather in which they had been immersed for hours. André finishes picturing the scenes for himself while Jacques, on the other hand, erases them, as if things told could only disappear following this extension of their last vibration, the prolonged sound coming to die a long death in the air, like a mosquito, exhausted and shaken by being batted a few times, one you don't even try to kill because by its weakening buzz you can see and hear perfectly well that it's not going to be flitting around the scene much longer, no, after having carried on for a while, and losing its faculties one by one, like something deflating, bzeee, it ends up just letting its life fade away, ebb, bzee, and then bze and then, just barely, I don't know, maybe bz, and it's over.

IX

The fourth day on the porch they can feel a few special particles floating around, particles that hadn't been there any of the earlier days, particles, how to describe them? of some anticipated nostalgia moving back and forth between the two men as if, yes, the air our two friends' nostrils exhaled were suddenly full of this inner sadness that's beginning to get them in its grip, that stays hanging there, bursting intermittently, moving from one to the other, and as those first particles gradually become diluted in the larger mass of oxygen, the other exhales in turn a load of these melancholic particles, creating a brief whirlwind that soon scatters, and so on, with the consequence that something forms there in the air, blossoms spontaneously as it were, like a water lily, like a plant sprouting and blooming, there, fast-forward in the atmosphere, the feeling of urgency arising from the idea that tomorrow at this time they won't still be together, in their sphinx positions, twin statues, that the door will no longer be guarded or adorned by its two sentinels, that the house will go back to looking the way it did before, with an André prostrate with grief at first, wandering, as if the house were no longer his, and a Camille, true to form, taking care of everything, so flawlessly it seems like it's taking care of itself; the feeling of now or never pressing more and more on Jacques's heart, there, where he puts his hand, on the suddenly windless porch, facing the motionless fir trees, in this strange, almost eerie suspension of the wind that then, bit by bit, returns as a breeze, slight but present, making the air lighter and lighter, reviving it, the content of this urgency becomes clear, Jacques, yes, would like to tell André about his project, now that they've established contact and filled in the intervening years, an ambition he hasn't mentioned, the great undertaking he's tackling now in Abbeville, one beginning to bear fruit, oh still rather modest, minor fruit, but encouraging, even very encouraging, something after all the things he's tried that should at long last make it possible for him to become famous, Hooray, something that's taking some time but proceeding at its own pace, and he hopes he will have succeeded before the end of the book.

So, since André is still silent on his side of the doorway and no doubt ruminating over some gloomy thought relating to their imminent separation, Jacques starts to speak, quietly, in the forest air, words to get rid of the particles of melancholy and replace them with something else, the phantom of his project spreading, translucent and impalpable, over the porch, beginning to share this great thing he's imagined, This is it, says Jacques, I need to tell you.

You don't understand right away. At first it all just seems to be about various landscapes. Jacques talks about the peat in the countryside, the sandpits, the one in Portelette, the ones in Menchecourt, Saint-Acheul, and Moulin-Quignon, where, really it's true, as you go deeper and deeper through their layers you're going back in time. He describes using a pick in the quarry, with the open sky overhead like a bright dome displaying its ever-changing spectacle, and then the shovels, the wheelbarrows, all the different clothes the workers wear. He takes a photo from his pocket, Here, look, there are two workmen in the picture, one sitting on a wheelbarrow, with his face turned toward another who's standing, leaning on the quarry wall and showing him something. It's a high wall and you can easily figure out its height, clearly there could be three or four men standing on each other's shoulders like a fragile circus column before the last one, a fifth, perched on the shoulders of the highest, reached the opening, and then could see the countryside, the fields, the land descending to the first houses. In one corner a shovel handle propped against the wall at an angle. In another photo a white horse has gone down into the quarry with its cart. Ladders are up against the walls. The workmen wear all sorts of different clothing, nothing they're wearing matches; this diversity creates a realistic effect.

Jacques shakes the two photographs that he's holding in his hand like two playing cards, to emphasize their importance and in a voice over he adds, It's all been gone through, marny soil, tufa, fluviatile layers, blue sands, all of it. I don't understand, says André. Nonetheless, take a better look, Jacques puts the first photo onto the back of the pack as when you shuffle cards, There, the thing the workman is pointing at, André leans over, he's willing but no, he doesn't see a thing, a flock of starlings flies over this scene of our two men seated on either side of the French door but now with their chests and heads forming convergent arches, sort of like an ogive, toward the middle of the door where Jacques holds the photo and André is distracted by the sound they make, Those birds are stupid, like clouds of big mosquitoes always in a gang, Jacques could care less about starlings, Come on! You can easily see, there, the pad of his index finger now hides the object, Move your finger, they're both getting annoyed, one because he doesn't see anything, the other because his friend doesn't see anything and, frankly, neither do we from here, Camille makes her appearance on the porch, she was feeling a brawl brewing, their heads are nearly as nose to nose as Pulcinella's and the policeman's, Would you gentlemen care for some tea? Exactly like puppets on strings both men sit up straight, Why yes, Camille, why not, André still has the photo and peruses it the best he can, it's no good, I give up, says André finally, and Jacques who's pulled himself together, speaking each syllable separately and as calmly as possible in or-der to be understood, says, That-is-a-flint-stone. There.

Well, so what, a flint-stone, says André, who's seen plenty of other flints in the region, they're not rare, ploughshares chip against them, fields are chock-full of them, Yes but, says Jacques, the difference here is that, since I have to explain the whole thing, this is an old old old flint, dating from prehistoric times, and it's been shaped, What do you mean shaped, It's an ax, if you will, made by men, our ancestors (this time, André gasps), Jacques goes on, he takes out other photos, portraits, May I introduce Théophile Hoin, peen manufacturer who lives on the rue du Haut-Pas in Menchecourt, who saw the workmen find the flint; François Hautefeuille, cart driver and sand carrier, who also was a witness; Jacques goes on calling his gallery to the stand, ending with François Corbillon, known as the Lark, a workman living in Menchecourt, who, listen to this, brought in a shaped flint stone found amid mammoth bits and the molars of a wooly rhinoceros.

Jacques tells André about the period during which mastodons and crocodiles came into the land around Abbeville, they imagine together the large hoofed feet of proboscideans rattling the sidewalks in Abbeville, it's even better than sleds, André is beginning to get really excited, the façades crack and brown mammoths come snorting out while in a corner of the picture some furry men are seated in a circle cutting flints without lifting their heads.

These men, see, that's my project, to find the ancestors absent from our family albums, right there where we come from, among the elephant molars, among these shaped axes, to find some fragment of a skeleton proving they existed in those remote times, Well, you don't say, says André, as in a fifties film where friendships are expressed in old-fashioned phrases that have vanished over the years, well you don't say, and André in turn tries imagining this, but from inside, look, acting it out, as if it were coming back to him, he scratches an armpit with his opposite hand and then the top of his head and sticks out his lips, Houhou, he mouths. He stands up on the porch and hops up and down repeating these simultaneous actions, hand scratching and vocal cords uttering their simple cry, a phonetic emission not requiring too much effort. He sticks his foot out toward Jacques and then his hand, here we go, leading him in the dance and there they are, the two of them as evening falls acting the parts of early man, trying various moves, bumping into the table, starting all over again. When Camille comes out with her tea tray and sees them in their simian poses she almost drops the tray Oh! because her arms start shaking so badly. Come on Camille, join us says André, he tells her about Jacques's project, explains their sarabande, Camille stands there in astonishment, she sets the tray on the table, folds her hands together and watches the scene. André tries to climb the trunk of the nearest fir tree, Jacques makes up a ritual under the moon now directly overhead, André scratches himself, moans, their onomatopoeias move through her ears; she takes her right hand out of her left and twists a strand of hair, begins making up her story then and there, the one about the prehistoric woman wondering just what she's going to do while one of the men climbs a tree and the other one is starting sublunary sacrifices, the story of a woman who could join in the devotions, or climb the nearby tree, but who'd rather hang back for a moment, a woman of a contemplative nature, very happy to have this moment all to herself, Come on Camille, André insists, not seeing that she has already begun to play.

On the morning of the last day André is already outside, he pulls a few plants that were growing between the planks of the porch and tosses them into a china dish, the sort usually used for washing. Jacques stares at him through the windowpanes in his room, his valise is ready on his bed, his visit to André will come to an end at the same time as our first section.

He goes downstairs with the valise which he sets down in the living room, not at all hesitant now, he has the arrangement of the two sofas and the two armchairs mastered, and moves right through it all with no trouble out onto the porch where André is making little clouds with his breath as he continues uprooting weeds. They discuss a bit the way autumn effects things, considering that there are some trees with stamina that struggle through weeks and weeks but still retain the physiological means, which you don't understand, to resist the season or less well, some of them almost entirely bare now yet others, though of the same species, still displaying rather a decent amount of foliage compared to the others. They talk about autumn's stubborn determination to carry away every last leaf, and how much time it takes while you're anticipating the debacle ahead, and you imagine the garden with nothing there anymore except the outline of tree trunks in India ink against the frozen grass, which you dread and at the same time are impatient to see, just so it will be over with, once and for all, this great autumnal devastation, and so you can dream about what comes next, yes, what comes next.

II
WITH MARGOT AT MERS-LES-BAINS

I

The fact is, it doesn't take much, untrained though we may be in such matters, for train trips to lead us to develop great, grand syntheses—of our lives I mean, not by theme (listing, for example, all the countries we've traveled), but rather syntheses that are chronological, as if everything could be seen at once, from the first twisted tree we climbed to the very morning of the day we sat ourselves down in this seat, with the countryside going by alongside, field after field, with fences marking how far we've gone, or from time to time a line of trees doing the same thing (sometimes too a redundant line of barbed wire running from tree to tree doing its best to keep the animals in that like to break out, something that almost certainly happens).

When plain follows plain like this, a clearing turns into forest then back into a clearing, and two or three households become a hamlet, and farther along a village is heralded by one sign and ends with another, so there's no mistaking territorial boundaries, private or communal, and here and there a peasant wearing boots crosses a bare field at an angle, somewhere else there's a woman with geese, episode after episode and you can't confuse one thing with another, suddenly your own life, which up to that point had seemed something of a jumble, composed of such complexly intertwined or superimposed layers that you had given up trying to differentiate them, suddenly this life of yours seems linear, reflecting the journey you're taking, and those successive fields, those well-defined forests, those clearings, the two or three visual events introduced by the peasant going by or the woman guarding geese, seem to you to reflect the well-ordered sequences of your existence.

You begin to feel that this landscape, rolled out like this beside you, provides a model for the legibility of a life finally revealing itself to you in a tranquil sequence, finally lending itself to summary; you could represent it as a line with indentations and arrows that you'd use to indicate important episodes: here I climb my first tree, there I go to school for the first time, here I meet my tutor, very quickly (next indentation) we're making paper birds, my first time fishing for carp, there, all the other times I fished for carp, my first trip at sea, and there, at sixteen, with everybody's support, bam, I leave home, I underline this break several times, it's a decisive indentation. My trips, there they are, Marseille, the Camargue, riding horses bareback through rice fields, I make the sky blue, make the frisking spikelets of naked-seeded graminaceae springy, and then the foreign appointments, meaning the society dinners, the balls, moonlight watched too bad more than once from balustrades, then the wars, forests in wartime, beating out game, leaves rustling in the night, swish swish, other appointments, my return. I underline my return several times. Okay and off I go to visit André, I put in three fir trees, I don't bother with the needles, I use the ready-made pictogram of fat triangles that expand and decrease symmetrically on either side, and I add the wooden house. And then, music, the trip with Margot, the one starting now as I'm writing triumphantly on my line.

Margot, who is asleep across from Jacques, her head nodding, and whose presence here surprises you, because it had seemed to you, anyhow considering the very brief bits of information that had been leaked to you—Margot's reserve, which you guessed, her reticence—that any such arrangement would be in the distant future, and even though nothing has happened yet, meaning a hug, a kiss, a declaration, or any performative action or word by means of which two individuals, while keeping themselves physically separated from one another, are nonetheless bound together, invisibly, on the basis of something said, an embrace conveying precisely a sense of partnership, some sort of contract whether formulated or tacitly understood, and always reversible, let's not get too excited, still, you're a bit surprised that she's going off to the seashore and that Jacques has offered to go with her, accompanying her with motives all aboveboard, you have no reason to think the opposite, a fact what's more confirmed by the trusting sleeper.

Because there's no reason to believe that she was sleeping before getting on the train, even though we didn't see her cross the waiting room in the station at Abbeville with our own eyes, nor did we see her walk down the platform, or climb up into the car, or choose the seat she liked best, for the simple reason that we don't make her acquaintance until just now, when she's already a sleeping silhouette in the jolting train. Consequently, all told, we couldn't go before a judge and swear to anything, if by chance the assumption was made that ether-soaked cotton had been involved: Margot, for example, at the bench repeatedly throwing her arms up into the air (where the sky, the painted ceiling of the courthouse, as it happens, has secular cherubs wrapping themselves in wispy clouds plastering veils against the pink of flesh and the baby-blue air they float through), thus, with a great flurry of gestures, launching into the story about how she'd been taken by surprise, the accused, being familiar with her schedule, knew that at precisely this time every day of the week Margot used to go by the station and had run up behind her without making a sound and put his arms around her so he could hold the ether-soaked cotton against her nose and mouth, after which she didn't remember anything except waking up at Mers-les-Bains, right on the sea, where he'd slapped her because he was worried about her still somnolent state, where the slaps and salt air had brought her back around, where she'd been stunned to see Jacques's face and the row of half-timbered, painted houses, Where are we, and the dishonor which he caused her with this escapade, what were they going to think in the city. This version, which seems quite improbable to me, would still present an advantage for our hero, because this local news item would be a means, a quick one (such speed being to his advantage), and not too dangerous (it's a lot easier, less risky, to kidnap a small, young woman who isn't expecting this to happen, than to discover, God knows where and how, the remains of a prehistoric man), of becoming famous; it's easy to see how the scene would make it possible for our man to open his newspaper and find they had spared no expense to relate his story, even including a picture, what bliss, with his name prominently displayed (he's touched by the thought of the typesetter composing the type), and repeated several times on the page, and, what's more, transmitted thereafter in conversations, in the buzz of the villages this name that would burst forth, his name, clearly, and his story that they'd pass along like the baton in a relay, and which would soon take its place in all the conversations in the region, and as for Abbeville, just imagine the excitement, Our Monsieur Jacques, who seemed so, I don't know what, with his frock coat, Monsieur Jacques de Fine Family, and who's found a way to surprise us; but despite all this I wonder, without even calling the strong moral sense of our hero to the witness stand, nor even the refined sensitivity he's always shown with regard to Margot, that way he has of never forcing anything, no, rather his indecisive character, a sort of incapacity for really beginning to act, making it so that even if he'd concocted all this (to my great astonishment, and absolutely without my knowledge), he'd just have stood there, I'll give a hundred to one, at the street corner, ether-soaked cotton in hand, Well, my goodness, what are you doing there? Constantin would have asked when he suddenly turned up there by chance (or almost), Nothing special, and following close behind Constantin, Jacques would have stuffed the now dried-up piece of cotton into his pocket, Come on, since we've run into one another, let's go have a drink at the Café des Voyageurs.

I think we'd better stick with the idea of her really having gone to sleep; Margot has just put the train to a different use, as compared to Jacques's, she hasn't looked at the great tapestry of the countryside beside her, she's listened to the regular motion of the turning wheels, the pistons' unremitting labor; watching the fields go by has simply made her eyes tired. Margot, who, as they say, has let herself be cradled in the movement of the train car and who, there we go, is now asleep, without putting up a fight, only from time to time, and less and less frequently, raising the eyelid given the duty not of keeping her awake but rather tasked with some vague responsibility for oversight, she herself being pretty unclear about whatever information it provides, just wanting some sort of overall assurance that everything's fine, that the train's still going where it's supposed to, or even that there's no unfamiliar gaze landing upon her and deciphering her figure in some forgettable yet extremely disagreeable way, its owner quite prepared to say something to her that would startle her, suddenly pulling her out of her dreams voom like *Back to the Future*, or even just a reassurance that the photograph above Jacques is still there in its frame, offering a first glimpse of where they're going so that when they get off the train they'll identify it correctly, Why yes, it's Mers-les-Bains, just like in the picture, the promenade, the houses crisscrossed with timbers, so it would confirm the idea that they hadn't made a mistake and could thus walk unconcerned between the sea and the beach houses.

While shapes soften in Margot's mind, things she's thinking about jumble together, the way objects you're imagining accumulate and combine with no reason one can see, and so that, unlike your thoughts when awake, those economical thoughts that at least make a show of attempting an orderly presentation of whatever small content they might bring to bear (yes, sometimes you let yourself go in some brief procession of images that flow freely and carelessly, but there's nothing really baroque about these), here you are submerged in bizarre carryings on where the least element is subject to metamorphoses, you know how that goes, with spaces changing their shape at leisure and people drifting from one identity to another, Margot beginning her trip with Dupont turns around and, hey, no it's Durand, with complete impunity, having picked up the same gesture and then proceeding as if he'd been there all along, a few seconds later a third person of her acquaintance takes his place just as easily, the way Margot goes from a room in her house to the kitchen of an old aunt, which just happens to be adjoining, then, who knows, into Jacques's customs office, which, if she'd only known, was merely separated therefrom by a partition, for Jacques, quite the opposite, things are only becoming clearer.

I said right at the beginning that it doesn't take much because from here we can see clearly the insidious, hidden little process that's taking place. We see now that when we sat down decently, without prejudging, with no particular intention, just thinking to perform whatever physical tasks were required, something that, after all, demands minimal concentration, while we were basically preoccupied with wondering if maybe we'd left something at the snack bar back in the station, a bag or something, or the book we meant to bring, why not, to leaf through, just to fill the parenthetical time of travel where there's no other choice than to accept the principle of the contiguity of spaces and moments that results in our inhabiting real life unfortunately deprived of any hope of ellipsis, which would be very pleasant when you think about it, while maybe you stayed standing in the compartment after having lowered the window on all the racing around that accompanies departures to look at the Abbeville station and the two or three façades beyond that which you were accustomed to seeing and wouldn't see again for another week, and since Margot was still trying to find the most comfortable position on the seat, so now in passing we're reassured on the subject of Margot—in short, while we obviously understood this trip as a normal, natural necessity, in short, one that there's no sense discussing at greater length and that we'd simply be taking under the best possible conditions without paying much attention to it, Margot was growing more and more impatient because it wouldn't get going, there we go! There, it had started, and the rectangle of the window had begun its calm, continuous projection, field after field. So you let yourself be absorbed, less by the contemplation of things in the landscape considered in isolation, nor even one after the other (you could have wondered, for example, if it was all that smart to stick a corn-field and a field of beets right next to each other, because of the pollen's spreading and the possibility that in the end you might get two untidy, mixed fields, all set for salad of course but not convenient to maintain or harvest, far as I know, anyway), than by the process of succession itself that was presenting itself for your appreciation. Succession that you've less analyzed than felt, and not for its content but rather for the principle of the thing, you see, its dynamics, so that in the end you became, with no resistance on your part because how could you have known this might happen, the plaything, sad to say, of the inconspicuous processes underlying the metaphor, just seeing the fields and everything else roll past having called to mind, without your lifting so much as a finger, the notion of the years themselves rolling by.

So, without having given any thought to the subject, without, at least consciously, having agreed, you've found yourself going along with this idea and thinking about the outline of your life, which you've imagined in the contagion of this visual experience of unfurling countryside, perhaps for the first time in a somewhat linear fashion—a linearity that seems pleasant at first, even exciting, our Jacques grasping his existence all at once like a clear frieze, like the Bayeux tapestry, where events are recorded one after the other in a joyful epic.

Jacques thought about André, and his eyes—filled with the continuous series of plains going by with the passage of years superimposed—filled with friendship. He remembered their conversations on the porch, facing the forest, the two of them parallel statues on display, and remembered too the long stretches of confidences, the engrossing stories of their lives to that point, the bits and pieces, when a tiny, random anecdote chanced to cross his mind like a lone bird that has lost most of its flock in a cold sky, and consequently doesn't mean that there will be others flying by in a moment or two, no, only the loner slowly but surely making its way and then disappearing from view.

He thought how much he'd have liked to show André this new, linear, complete tapestry; he'd have liked to run unspooling from his outstretched arms the cloth that despite its weight would float in the wind behind him in a way that was absolutely medieval. Picture Jacques on horseback, riding through the countryside and holding the tapestry on the tip of his lance where it would wave in the breeze; sometimes an episode would get lost in a fold but it was always likely to reappear through the conjoined effects of the wind and speed whipping the fabric. Against a backdrop of inevitably verdant hills, the tale of the adventures of Jacques flashing across the countryside a little like the advertisements on strips of cloth or plastic that monoplanes pull through the sky at the beach (but the colors of an entirely different nature and the materials richer, a tapestry requiring wool thread, a dense texture). Look at the steam from the horse's nostrils, the sweat on its coat, the earth splattering under its hooves, look at the lance our hero proudly carries and behind him the long summary of his victories, look at the poem opening out infinitely into the countryside, while the peasants put their pitchforks down and lean on the handles, the grape pickers bent at right angles set their lower back joints in motion to stand upright again, and the shepherds sitting on their heels jump to their feet, alleyoop, all of them watching the tremendous tale that's being told them go by.

Having ridden all the way to where André has taken refuge in these isolated regions, our man dismounts and leaves his horse, tying it somehow under an oak tree. A herald blows his trumpet and André comes out of his dwelling to see who this unexpected visitor could be. Jacques bows to him and presents him with the tapestry. Here, André, here's the account of my intervening years. André, very pleased, tells him to come in, reads the thing, nods in agreement here and there, sometimes bursts out laughing, sometimes sheds a tear, and finally having had his fill serves the liqueur of concord to Jacques, who goes off again with his tapestry wrapped up tight under his arm so he'll be able to reconsider it occasionally and revise his history, so when called upon to tell it again he would be in a better position to do so.

Hmmm, but after a first moment of happiness over this complete and linear contemplation of his life, a possibility unhoped-for because up to now it had seemed to him that it was more of an inextricable collection of loose threads thrown together, there came a sort of grief at seeing the permeability of his dear self, Jacques faced with the flabbiness of Jacques's own character, which echoes our own, since it's a recurrent matter of fact that trips by train are, for us, an occasion, despite ourselves and without even giving it a thought as we climb aboard, to apply this little analogy between the landscapes rolling by and the passage of time; here we are, head against the window and letting our thoughts submit to what we're seeing, to the transformation, as you look through your mirrored face, of this visual experience into one that is temporal, concerning memory, so that, for example, when you ride facing backward in the train, looking toward its place of origin, at first simply geographical, you soon see clearly what it's all about, and the whole notion of origins makes our heads spin, it's a way of feeling the linear flight of years in the increasing distance between where you are and where you departed from, it's not at all the same thing as when you ride facing the direction the train is going, which reproduces the passage of the years in the very fact of moving forward, but with a target, the finality of the place where you're headed, which, from your viewpoint, is what is then pulling you forward.

Forward, where Jacques and Margot are going, at least that's what Jacques hopes, turning his eyes away from the window to contemplate the sleeping woman facing him with the body that she seems basically to have vacated, Excuse me I'll be back in a moment, going off into anamorphic realms and leaving behind on the seat a silent envelope that says nothing about the reasons for its presence here. Let's go back a bit and see how this all came about, says Jacques to himself, since he needs to find something to think about in order to detach himself from the dangerous contemplation of that body, it was simple and happened in two stages. Climbing down from the stagecoach on his return from the Eu forest, he runs into Constantin. So, sounding a bit jealous, how was the trip, Great, And your old friend André, Constantin is pretty casual about the way he holds his head (always just vertical enough so his cap never slips off, imagine a recalcitrant crêpe coming out of the pan and bam falling to the floor you have to start all over again, the cap tumbling down from its lofty position, bouncing off his hip and crashing wretchedly at the base of a linden tree, that would be too sad), and his coolness is sort of ostentatious, meaning, Well, we weren't bored while you were gone, you know, we played plenty of good card games too bad you missed them. They go off to the Café des Voyageurs, just to celebrate Jacques's return, the others are there, they have a few, clink their glasses, talk louder and louder, everything's terrific. Leaving the café, so this is part the second, Jacques comes upon Margot. It's winter, it's six o'clock, night comes early, faces are barely visible, it's a good time to say things to each other that you wouldn't necessarily say in the daytime. I was worried, says Margot. No need, I was with my childhood friend, André, You remember André. She knew, she'd found out in town, but at first she'd been worried, the first few days, before she found out. It's winter, night comes early, all faces are gray, there's not much moonlight tonight, I'd like to take a trip to the seashore with you, Margot. Why did she accept?

That's what her silhouette sunk into the seat isn't telling, her face against the gray curtain, eyelids shut, like the panes of a window on a door where a little handwritten notice saying Closed is dangling. You wonder, it's true, why Jacques doesn't take advantage of this to kiss her. It wouldn't be all that honorable, nor all that brave, nor all that heroic, nor even all that much easier than doing so when she's gazing at him with the sum total of her reticence. You're thinking that sometimes, at the end of an episode, you, you the viewer, get asked a question spelled out plainly and running along the bottom of the picture saying something like What was Jacques afraid he'd forgotten at the snack bar in the station, with numbered answers for you to choose from: 1) A book. 2) A box of chocolates that André gave him. 3) A package of cookies Camille made; or maybe What time was it when Jacques encountered Margot on his return from Eu: 1) Ten A.M. 2) Six P.M. 3) Ten P.M. You think this might be a good place to broaden the quiz to include some of the hero's character traits, some degree of interpretation, for example Why doesn't Jacques kiss Margot now while she has her eyes shut, and again the answers would be listed for you: the depressing version about how much time has gone by; the strategic version about how it wouldn't be an opportune moment, she'd resent his cowardice; and then the lazy, somewhat poetic version, about how there's something pleasant about putting it off, about contemplating the promised blissful moments from a distance, peacefully magnifying them, not rushing into things (while the salt air coming through the window in larger and larger quantities swirls through the train car, giving you some first notions of what's coming next, the slow transformation of agricultural land to a maritime countryside, because, this part of the novel, once we're in it, is going to be blue and gray, the gray of the pebbles at Mers, as opposed to the first part, which was, as you noticed, essentially brown and green with a touch of dark blue for the nights), just dreaming about what lies ahead.

II

The kiosk with the revolving postcard stand open to the wind and sometimes turning all by itself, spinning like a weather vane, is so close to the sea that, at least at high tide, the cards it contains could be hit by sea spray: marks of authenticity, of course, but then their surfaces would buckle and blisters would pop up here and there, not very large but still they could make it hard to see the pictures on them, just suppose there happened to be images of tiny silhouettes and one of them was hit in the face by a drop, imagine how its features would be swollen then erased, what a pity.

Our hero and his sweetheart look at the cards and point to them with their index fingers, sometimes picking one up between their thumbs and those same forefingers then putting it back behind the ferrous spike that holds it in place, the whole operation accompanied less by commentaries than by exclamations, after which Jacques chooses two cards, one for André, the other for Constantin.

There's something absolutely geometric about the card for André; it shows the casino surrounded by its white fence, two panels representing the angle of this enclosure, and the rest diminishing in a perspective emphasized on the left where the fence vanishes, the casino's façade seemingly attached to another turreted façade, and it's hard to see whether it's the continuation of that first façade or if maybe it's sticking out from some house, it's not especially clear, and on the right the line stops even sooner, runs along a lawn, below a low stone wall that begins to crop up under the fence then goes off in a triangle that grows higher in the distance, probably to make up for a depression in the ground, the slope of a broad road, there, in front of and to the right of the casino, which really looks like it was just dropped out of the sky, while the ground takes up a lot of the foreground space, grayish stippling, you can't tell if that's road or sand or even pebbles, so I'm back to all that grayish stippling occupying more than a third of the lower part of the card, then that image of the casino receding right and left, nothing else on the left after the casino except that suspicious façade with the turrets, and on the right, beyond the interruption of the low stone wall and something dark like a lawn, charcoal gray, another fence farther in the distance that has kept all its whiteness and must be drenched in sunlight to seem so clear and so white from such a distance, with little sticks indicating its successive uprights really standing out, and beyond this fence, hard to say exactly what this relatively broad band is, I look closer but no dice, another lawn possibly, the color is identical but there are white spots there that don't appear in the first lawn, uneven spots, with some black too, people maybe, you could imagine they're playing croquet, look, near the casino, which would make it a lawn, studded with wickets, with two wickets crossed in the center of the court and the *cloche*, how do I know all that, the men and women leaning on their mallets are paused there like Renaissance martyrs with their weight on one leg, while the one at play, squinting and thinking up a thousand imagined trajectories for the ball (a wooden ball with colored stripes to make it recognizable), moves his mallet nearby in a swinging motion, as if his muscles, or the clock mechanism he's imitating, don't allow him to actually touch the ball, as if he wasn't going to go that far, and then, toc, yes, anyhow there you go, the ball rolls through the grass followed by everyone's gaze, goes through the hoop phew and stops at a convenient distance from the next one, good, we'll keep going. Above the croquet court and beyond another fence, there's a white crest that looks like thin foam in the background, probably a road to cross, and a line of façades, this time seen from the front, very far away but directly facing us and standing out clearly against a background of hills that make a decrescendo toward the right-hand side of the card, or a crescendo toward the left, toward the line well in front of them that represents the edge of the casino wall and bumping into it in your imagination. After that it's sky occupying the final third of the card, practically the same gray as the band of ground in the first third, but with a less granular structure, more diffuse, just like that, so you can't tell if the weather's nice, if that's the full, generous light of a blue sky or a white sky's bitter light, whether it's morning or afternoon light, whether it's summer or winter. The wind must be blowing because the flags on the roofs of the casino stick straight out so their stretched fabric clearly shows the different colored stripes. The casino windows take the light full on, reflecting the landscape so you can't see anything inside. In the parts escaping reflection, or where there must be big white curtains flapping gaily against the masonry in all sorts of magnificent twists when they open the windows (flocks of doves, flaps of drying linen, the delicacy of wedding gowns, the creases of a priest's robe, or, in short, what have you)—or else maybe those are awnings, stiff, never deviating from their rectangular shape and making a harsh sound as they bang sideways against the poles—smaller windows in the areas forming a sort of frieze over the big ones just look like a series of black rectangles alternating with black squares, a black rectangle, a black square, a black rectangle, a pillar, a black rectangle, a black square and so forth (so that, if you've counted, there are more rectangles than squares), you can't make out any tables, or figure out if the casino's open at this time of day, you can't tell if in the anxiety of the game there are gowns rustling and ruffled shirts sticking to people's backs. The casino has an upper floor, narrower and dotted with portholes providing no more information about the interior. Marked by a nine-part emblem (the mullions inside the circle trace a central square with sides extending both up and down), they vaguely allude to the sea down below, and if a boat just happened to appear with its sailors contemplating behind their porthole the coast with its casino and its portholes, they would fit right in, while card players thinking about the next hand behind the casino portholes would glance absentmindedly at the boat, and sometimes a player less persistent than the others might even linger for a moment at the window, letting patches of the nine-part acronym splash on his clothing or his face with the drifting mullion shadows while he dreams of sea adventures, for a moment imagining himself leaving everything behind to risk storms, cut masts, scoop out holds, and the permanently sunny days, the great tedious seas that go on forever.

I cough slightly just to pull you out of your sea dreams and return to the photo and what it shows: look, there on the roof, leaning at the level of the portholes against one of the four façades, a ladder. A ladder put there with no reason given for its being there, nothing points to a workman, a toolbox, a bucket, or what have you, no paintbrush, no rag, no roofer's paraphernalia, just a lone ladder, as if forgotten, you have to admit that's strange. It goes to the roof sloping up to a large chimney, apparently decorative (there's a flag on top of it that isn't sooty in the least), you're beginning to have some serious suspicions. You're thinking a man's body can easily go down that chimney, or even several men's bodies, suddenly dropping down to show up plop in some room, the game room on the first floor, for example, or the director's office where he's alone, feet on his desk and with his back to the intruders, a position that makes him completely vulnerable, Don't move, and considering that his legs are propped up so they are at right angles to his pelvis, which is stuck in that position, how can he possibly get out of this fix. You think, the awnings lowered, all those big curtains, and the reflections all working together to make the windows mirror the facing exterior landscape rather than revealing what's inside, all that would certainly come in handy from the point of view of a burglar.

The director's office is separated from the rest by a one-way mirror so you can clearly watch the players moving around, pacing up and down the room and engaged in weighty discussions with themselves and then suddenly, driven by some impulse, placing a bet at some table, and then, torn between hoping to win and anticipating the deliciousness of loss, describing that loss in detail to themselves, hands on vests to feel the undercurrent of their hearts as they beat to bursting beneath the cloth, what a godsend this is, when its grown tired of ordinary amusements, the pain the heart can feel, the shudder, they just keep right on making up their own little abstruse novels with impunity and have no idea of the scene taking place on the other side of the glass—the director first tied up in the ridiculous angle we saw earlier, then thrown under his desk where he forms a triangle on the ground with a pistol at his neck (not all that comfortable, but anyhow, okay, we have to hurry, no time to pick him up), The combination to the safe and no dirty tricks, and the director with his cheek on the carpet can see the unsuspecting players still working on their novels, We wouldn't really shoot him, walking from table to table in their usual choreography, So you're going to spit it out, the combination to the safe, My dear casino of Mers-les-Bains, I was so proud of it, it was my pride and joy yes, I thought about it the moment I got up and went to sleep with the thought of it, the director looks so sad, he gets slapped in the face, hard, but it's the other cheek that hurts him worse, scraping against the carpet as an indirect consequence, I made it my entire world and now it's come to this, the director is in despair over the film made for television going on behind the one-way mirror, a little distorted because he's looking at it sideways and from a rather low angle but still perfectly visible, By the way, you wouldn't by any chance want to take it off my hands, would you, this crappy casino, all this razzmatazz, this abstract stuff makes me sick, the director goes on, come on, honestly, instead of the money you want to make off with but that would just be a flat amount, there wouldn't be any dividends, why not just take the whole casino then you'll have a steady income, the burglars scratch their heads, try to figure out if there's a catch, he seems sincere so okay we'll untie him and then the director takes his own pistol from the desk drawer and pushes the button that sets off an alarm directly at the police department, this having been foreseen, Oh, after all, so what, says the director, he's so depressed by this inane casino that he can do without it, No no fine, it's okay says the ringleader but you've got to sign some papers for us, I expect you're right says the director, he's familiar with the forms, I know all about that, the ringleader, a little embarrassed, looks at the others, Our heroic act, our plan, those hours we spent drawing on big sheets of paper tacked to the wall, putting pins at strategic points, timing things with a watch, we haven't exactly followed through on all that, but to be a casino director is good too, we'll settle in but still keep our pieces under our suits, how would you like that? A nice little turn toward collegiality, it's something we can imagine after all the suspicions we've all had about each other but look it's not going to happen right away. Well okay, Mac, they tell him American style, the director is very pleased, well, really, I ask you, a little ladder on a postcard and here you're telling me the story of a robbery turned into a donation, and where's our little Jacques in all this, in these romantic chapters about the seashore, Jacques is still choosing a postcard to send his friend, André, as in epistolary novels, and who, with the idea of writing this letter, has finally sat down on the café's open-air, bamboo terrace with the collar of his frock coat buttoned up to his neck, It's true says Margot, leaning over Jacques's elbow, Did you see the ladder, pretty strange, right, it looks like something's up, and Jacques looks at the ladder, Ah, he says, think so? And then he says, Look, there are three old people sitting out front, what with your burglary story we didn't even see them.

So there are three old people, first a tiny man and woman, really right in front of our noses, sitting between the fence and the casino, the man on a chair, the woman on a bench, and then beside her another woman who is showing us her silhouette in profile and who seems younger, their daughter perhaps, or a servant. So two little old people plus a woman, they are all covered up, the old man has a white hat, a black coat, he's carrying his cane like a scepter, diagonally across his chest, a white line, making a stripe across him as if he were an image on a playing card; on the other side of that line, however, it's not his upside-down figure but his two legs set wide apart. The hand not lifting the cane-scepter is resting on his thigh, against the black fabric of his trousers it seems very white. The old woman vanishes beneath a black hat that covers at least a third of her face, you can see the nose and mouth, her eyes must be there right under the edge of the brim, vlouf, about to catch a glimpse of the photographer and then dive into the camera. A dark cape is opened up over her long, light-colored skirt, which also has a line across it, but vertically, a cane or an umbrella with her two hands resting one atop the other and covering its handle. The pose of the woman in profile, or actually, three-quarters profile, facing us, is much less hieratic than the two others. The old man and the old woman, despite being some distance apart, despite the scale of their bodies, which represents nothing at all in the photo's broad expanse, sit like they're having their portrait taken. They're holding their bodies like a king and a queen, they're already thinking about the frame they'll be in, they don't often have their picture taken. They're thinking about the polished sideboard where they'll put the frame, or rather, no, on the wall, to the right of the tall chest. They're in agreement, they are looking at the camera, both with the same thought deep in their eyes, the tall chest with the white wall on its right, the picture would look good there. The younger woman, born after the invention of photography, couldn't care less about it, she's uncomfortable on the bench, she's looking at the sea just to think about something else, though she doesn't manage to think about nothing, she has both her hands on her thighs but not symmetrically, one is higher than the other, her arms are awkwardly positioned. The hood of her cape isn't squeezed between her back and the wall she's leaning on, it's covering her head, part of it, you can see her smooth hair clearly, which must be plastered flat and pulled back in a bun inside the hood. The cape is dark colored, her dress is a plain gray one. The young woman is wearing nothing with any contrast like the black and white on the old woman, her clothes are dull, black on gray, she'd rather nobody pay attention to her. She's sorry that she accompanied Madame and Monsieur and that she's sitting there in her dull dress and her dark cape, slightly closer to the camera than the others, even if coming here was still the reasonable thing to have done, I'd say that like that her body sitting down takes up five millimeters in height on the space of the card, in width two or three where it's broadest, it seems to her that even this is too much for her, the photo, she mistrusts it, sometimes those things steal your soul. She's getting tired just looking at the sea; the sea that washes over everything, cleans the beach, pulls back, returns to do its work again, the sea, a good housekeeper, with its big sponge, its big blue-gray rag lashing the pebbles, the servant watches this huge, well-executed chore, she'd like the sea to wash over her thoughts, if only, Jesus-Mary, make the sea wash over my thoughts.

Margot says, They're not the only ones there, there's somebody in front of the casino, look, in front of the steps . . . more unanswered questions . . . The man is wearing a black suit and white gloves. He looks to the right, toward the photographer, he's not sure if he should get out of there or not. His left hand, he's lifting it toward his pocket, he's already started to do this. Maybe he's left-handed. Maybe he has his pistol in that pocket. Or else he isn't left-handed but wants to stick his hand in there so he'll look casual. He's pretending to be some casual guy just leaving the casino. We can see by the hesitant way he holds his body that his heart is in his boots. Maybe he has the papers. Signed. He's taking them to a notary. Meanwhile the others are holding the director just in case there's a mix-up. They're waiting for the lawyer's seal. Good the papers are in order but it would be best to avoid any witnesses as long as we don't have the seal on them. The director phoned the notary, told him that he was sick, that he wouldn't be coming, but that the papers were valuable, please stamp them. The guy leaving the casino knows what he has to do but he knows also that he's never done this before. That he's never appeared before a lawyer like that, with papers transferring the directorship of a casino to a group of his colleagues, a collective gift, with the director still tied up in his office. I hear some people thinking that this man could simply be the casino doorman, but he's not wearing a cap. Lean and lanky, his hair slicked back, looking at the camera, you have to admit he looks nothing like a doorman, nothing like a bellboy. Or else, is he one of those abstracted gamblers, leaving empty-handed with only the gloves he brought along that morning to cover up those hands, he's gambled everything away, right down to his suitcase, container and contents both, I'll let you be the judge. On the other side of the fence, on the promenade, just about at the same level as the lean and lanky man, separated from them by the hatching of the white wooden bars (could be seen as foreshadowing, foreboding, a bad end, prison), a group of three women, mother and daughters each looking off in her own particular direction. The mother turns her head in the direction of the lean and lanky man who is looking at the photographer; one of the daughters looks at the sea; the other daughter, shading her eyes with her hand, looks off into the distance. The three women form a compact group, their dresses intersect, their gazes going off in three directions, they constitute their own little scene. A shape at their feet is perhaps a dog, sitting, looking toward some fourth point.

Wait, look, says Margot, there. She's triumphant. We're back to the burglary. In the background on the left, there where the casino stops to make room for the house with the turrets, there where it's bright now, there's a road, right up against the white fence, and a man walking rapidly. In full stride, his right leg well clear of his left. He's no more than a millimeter high and yet that's who it is.

He's the one with the papers. He's coming back from the notary's office. He has to pass them on to his accomplice waiting there on the doorsill. Left hand preparing to return to his pocket because he doesn't know where else to put it. It's hard to wait, especially with a photographer looking at you. But we're confident: at that pace the other man should be back in less than a minute.

As for Olduvai Hominid #7, pretty much shaped like a *Homo habilis*, short big toe (hallux) sturdy and right alongside the other toes, equipped with an arch in his foot, he too is standing still, not on the paving stones of the seaside promenade, where he might run into our gangsters, but on the Serengeti plain. He looks happy sniffing the air, his face rather slender, the chin region set back, he seems pretty confident about what awaits him. He's holding his rather short thumb expectantly above his hip where he wiggles it, quick little movements, as if he were looking for an imaginary pocket.

III

The third chapter really takes place outdoors. We're happy to be getting a bit of sun and air out there with our hero. Jacques is looking for two or three flat pebbles light enough to skip on the surface of the water, toc toc toc, bouncing more or less effectively, suddenly he almost squats and zip throws a projectile that sometimes sinks like a guy at a pool who climbs, proud as a peacock, onto the diving board then crashes onto the water in a magnificent bellyflop, but other times it works better and the pebble looks jolly, as if it were bouncing for joy, as if skipping gaily and under its own steam, with each bounce making splashes that give the great grayblue blanket, already rippling rather forcefully against the lumpy carpet of the beach, a new lease on life.

Jacques stands back up and blinks his eyes to look at Margot, who, in the distance, beneath the snack bar's white umbrellas, forms a little, unexpected speck in his line of sight. For the time being he's not too loath to be taking part in a minor sentimental novel. Having Margot so close to him, with him, and his heart constantly pounding wildly, his lungs all puffed up with love and sea air, and above him the vast sky, no longer chopped up by the roofs of Abbeville, no longer only half a sky that gives you a crick in the neck because of twisting every which way to try and see it out windows, but right in front of you, a clear, limitless sky making you think everything is somehow in suspension. You can stretch out in this sky as you look at it, as if it were fluffy eiderdown, a vast quilt covering the beach, a sky where you can really spread out, stretching your body, rolling around, mmmmm, delicious. Margot at the other end of the quilt, still under her white beach umbrella and shivering in the salt air, finally takes the umbrella off its base and walks with it, using it as a fragile shield against the wind, holding it with both hands; pulled off her path by its weight and the strong breeze, she walks like something between a crab and a little soldier, then finally the umbrella gets the better of her, it escapes, rolls along the beach alone, for a long time, far, nothing but a white, moving circle on the crest of the waves, all the way to the seawall against which it stops, a stray golf ball thinks Honorine who's riding in a carriage along the promenade, and that's that. Margot, empty-handed, at a loss, contemplates for a moment this collection of cloth and wood declaring its independence and recklessly marking the patches of damp sand that emerge from under the flat stones with the proof of its hesitant journey, the confusion one feels in the first moments of freedom, Come on over to this side of the quilt, shouts Jacques, waving at Margot, bare-handed now and coming toward him saying something inaudible. Come on, she's having a hard time with the sand, the pebbles, the wind, her dress sometimes violently plastered against her legs, sometimes catching a breeze underneath and turning into a hot air balloon, flying erratically in his direction however the wind blows it, fouah, fouah. Jacques exudes encouragements toward the awkward air machine approaching, There, that's good, a bit farther, Whew! says Margot, as she comes up next to him, and then, You know what? I thought I saw Honorine.

Honorine is Margot's friend from when they were children and then young girls. One day, it was June, the air sweet, Chinese lanterns, accordions playing beneath the linden trees, Julien, someone from far away, from Saint-Valéry-sur-Somme, whom they occasionally would see at the markets on Sunday, had worn his blue suit, everything in motion, not just the dancing lanterns but also the paper butterflies hung among the lanterns, butterflies made by the girls of Abbeville all week long, sitting together in the town hall on their knees, in preparation for the dance. It was the ball that signaled the beginning of summer, Midsummer's Night, when you'd best stuff cotton in your ears and go to bed early, pulling the sheet (too hot for a blanket) up over your head if you don't want your heart broken. The girls hadn't followed this advice. Just like they had spent all week making paper butterflies, they all went to the dance. The day had been long and idle, they had dozed in the grass, picked daisies, spent a long time looking at themselves in the mirror after they put on their dresses, gazing into those mirrors mounted on the big country armoires where you could adjust the door, set it just right so you wouldn't be back-lit. The mothers, full of their own memories, just let it all happen;

sometimes they'd say a little something to their daughters, about a hem to sew back up, a pleat here or there in the dress fabric, but really they were off in their own thoughts, the bodies containing those thoughts, how to express it, like great dark fortresses where they existed in a vast solitude. The absolute solitude of mothers. The big clocks had struck seven, sometimes cuckoos came out of them and sometimes a country parade appearing through one door and returning through another and sometimes just bells; the fathers had come home. The mothers had looked at the fathers, who existed not in a solitude of fathers but in a solitude of men. A solitude of husbands focused on themselves. The husbands had sat down in the comfortable chairs, they'd done better at crossing their legs than you might have expected, and glanced at their newspapers, they'd kept none of their promises and crossed their legs. I'm not talking about the things they'd actually sworn to, I'm talking about the things they'd let you expect from them. The things you could hope for from a young man in a blue suit who was dancing with you beneath the lanterns in the breeze that was too sweet, almost cloying, as summers begin. Honorine had said Goodnight Maman, Goodnight Papa, she'd gone off to get Margot, and they went to the esplanade under the linden trees, evenings in June bring such intolerable happiness. They sat down on a stone bench, breathing quickly, feeling desires full of nothing they could imagine clearly. Julien had come up to them, he smelled like lilacs, he had invited Margot to dance, then Honorine, Honorine had danced with Julien, she never came back to Abbeville.

The white umbrella, rooted to the seawall, no longer moves at all, it must be taking the wind head-on, which pins it there without making it shake. It's beginning to drizzle but so lightly that our characters don't let it worry them. Jacques looks at Margot's face with its flickering memory of the ball, the hanging lanterns, Julien's blue suit and the loss of Honorine. They wrote each other at first and then you know how things go. Their epistolary novel ended. Honorine was busy with the farm in Saint-Valéry, she got up at five in the morning, bustled around all day, did the milking at night, too active to write, never opening a book anymore, falling asleep right away against Julien's shoulder. Margot worked at the bakery where she stood all day long behind the counter with a word for everyone; Jacques had begun traveling ages ago, he had left when he was sixteen and hadn't been able to be there. He remembered Honorine when she was younger, he remembered a time when he didn't like Honorine very much, she was always clinging to Margot. We could go see her, says Jacques, in Saint-Valéry, we could go to Saint-Valéry.

Margot lets a little wind go by, a little rain, a little time, she replies Why not. How about you, would you like to take a quick trip to Saint-Valéry-sur-Somme?

While we're waiting for you two to decide, let's look at the card that Jacques is planning to send Constantin. It's a lively variation on the first one I described. There's still an ample view of the casino, occupying, let's see, about a quarter of the surface, though lengthwise, but in front of it, instead of the half-deserted esplanade we saw in the first (you'll remember that you could see several silhouettes on it but they were no bigger than midges, so you had to get extremely close to see them, and even the dog, you couldn't have guaranteed for sure that that mark depicted a canine—and not, for example, an infant sitting up, or any other thing you might guess at, which I'll leave up to you, perceptive as you are), is the beach, completely overrun by numerous figures and objects. The sea, another quarter lengthwise, right in front, the sand where the pebbles are, equally a quarter, also lengthwise, the casino as we mentioned and then the sky, another quarter, same configuration. The sky, in the space remaining above the casino's two chimneys, surrounding them, between the two, which this time no longer have flags on top, no, all the flags are gone, there's nothing nationalist about this card. Consequently, it's a quadripartite, composed of four superimposed bands, water, sand with pebbles on it, stone, and air, the whole thing, no doubt, highly iodized. Iodine acts invisibly, binding together the scattered elements, providing some harmony to the heterogeneous subjects juxtaposed there, assuring a common element to this landscape otherwise partitioned into its four bands. It swirls in the water where it stirs around, still liquid, then goes onto the sand and slips into one or another of its many cavities, squeezing between two pebbles, making another one gleam, I'm just mentioning those two and then mentioning one other, but of course it goes on forever, so volatile that it even strikes the façade of the casino, coating the stone, leaving a portion of its troops on the spot, its microscopic colonists okay you will adapt to the relative porosity of the walls, you'll set yourselves up here, you'll be no less contented here than anywhere else, while the remaining molecules keep traveling, and go off to join the sky, slaloming there between the chimneys, more nomadic than the others, sometimes when the wind is with them pushing all the way to the edges of Mers, so that someone coming from inland who walks across the border from the country where there's a sign saying MERS-LES-BAINS in dark blue letters on white, so there's no other conceivable destination (not like a crossroads in a Western where wooden signs carved like arrows offer a thousand possible choices and the hero scratches his head), just the sea, land's end, this walker is struck then head-on by the compound of oxygen and iodine entering his nostrils then his lungs and, if all goes well, coming back out again, but leaving something behind perhaps, so that iodine is at work on bodies also, the body of the walker if he comes close enough or if the breezes blow toward the land, the bodies of the figures in the photo, all salty flesh, like that of sheep fed on salt hay, though slightly less so.

Jacques must have thought the cheerful disarray depicted on this card went well with Constantin's good-natured face, ignoring all the petty annoyances of life one on top of the other, all the things he didn't know about the past, I mean all the things that must crop up suddenly at the nape of his neck in the evening when he's sitting alone before his bowl of leek soup, after swaggering with sweeping gestures all day long under the lindens lining the esplanade, the Abbevillean light filtered through the foliage into impressionistic splashes on the fabric of his suit, showing it off well, and in the harsher light of wintertime, with just an occasional stripe thrown across his body by the shadow of a branch, when he really has to work to fool you, and now here he is facing a soup bowl with homey, lace curtains in the background unfurling a row of identical ducks against the darkness, all very busy ducks, one after the other with all their heads turned toward the door, doing their best to get out of range, in short a stream of them leaving, maybe not even the same ducks one evening to the next, a possibility, escaping his gaze every time and going off as if it didn't matter, not deigning to stay, thank heavens for them and all the ducks from generation to generation ignoring the man collapsed there, his elbows on the windroses of the oilcloth, no longer dreaming about his prospects, the little gloomy part of Constantin that used to wake up when it got dark, the other side of his smiling face, the heavy load of memories and the other equally heavy load of things that never happened, but I don't want to get you down and we can just keep to the face that's visible, secondary characters work just fine without secret compartments, and when we're finally back in Abbeville we'll go and have drinks with him at the Café des Voyageurs, it's not much use to predict lonely evenings contemplating the dark spots of night between the stitches on the curtain lace, the cheerful, social part will be more than enough and will let us settle more comfortably into this fiction of a good-natured Constantin (this will always be his public epithet), something he so pleasantly, generously constructs for others so those others will feel completely at ease in his presence, reassured by his gentle nudge serenely telling you how everything is for the best, allegorizing the way to keep your feet on the ground and with his fat body, whose mass takes up most of your field of vision and thus rather deliberately hides the droves of stupid little problems that you've created for yourself, apparently on your own, countering the horde of anxieties that cross your mind; so finally it was this cheerfulness coinciding with the visible aspect of fat Constantin of Abbeville—all you had to see was his cap and you'd feel festive, all the uncertainties besetting you, all the hesitant thoughts vlouf gone—that cheerful display was what attracted Jacques, the pleasant disorder of beach tents opened wherever they happened to be, obviously no one had planned in advance, the disorder giving you the idea that this was something natural and the random result of individual initiatives after all why not, everybody setting up however he pleased and not trying to alternate between the solid-colored tents (white, no doubt, rather overexposed in a light you'd describe as summery) and the striped tents, maybe blue and white, it's hard to say with any certainty just what color they are, that are the perfect incarnation of the idea of seaside vacations, while the white tents introduce something medieval, like canopies, the fluttering tents in the skies of bygone days, while the memory of the figure of Ivanhoe emerges in the company of a woman, storklike and hieratic with her long white neck, wearing her very dark hair in braids, and looking out at the reader.

Also there's a crowd of people as poorly arranged as the tents, because in place of what we might have expected to be a number of well-organized groups whose separate fates we could have discussed, there's only a cacophony of figures and you can't tell who's with whom, except for two children in the sea in the immediate foreground and who are in all likelihood together, even though their postures show no connection, the little one with his legs set like calipers, hands together on his thighs and looking up at the photographer, his face stuck in a grimace whether its origin is psychological (slight shyness together with the pride of being there right in the center of the viewfinder) or physical (the sun may very well be more or less where we're standing out of range and so opposite the child), you can't tell, and the big one on the other hand completely involved in what he's doing, his eyes looking down at the water, and his right hand holding some sort of tool shaped like a large T and that he's holding by the middle, like a metal detector (or maybe you have another theory). To which of the seated figures, planted at the openings of their tents like watchful guardians, faces turned outward apparently less to keep an eye on the maritime scene than to defend the entrance to their space, do these two children belong? The posture of these home guards is so identical that you'd think a stamp with a seated-figure logo had been repeated there thump thump thump at the entrance to each tent (except for—a requirement of realism—one or two that definitely seem not very well guarded, but inside which some animal probably lies in wait ready to leap, anything is imaginable).

Margot lifts her head and looks at Jacques who's putting the postcard in his pocket; she's thinking two or three things, but not firm thoughts, not entirely composed syntactically or lexically, such monologues aren't always completely verbal, which is why we can't always transcribe them, concerning Jacques's physical appearance, which seems, this being all we can tell from Margot's present thoughts, to give her a certain amount of pleasure. Jacques, whom we haven't attempted to describe other than to mention the uneven lines of his awkward silhouette, yet of whom we have a certain number of physical representations (because even in his lifetime he wasn't stingy as far as reproductions of his face were concerned, in every kind of medium), medallions of painted porcelain, bronze, pewter; painted canvases, charcoal sketches, lithographs. Grèvedon's lithograph is probably the one Jacques prefers, showing him from just slightly below, which makes his form more emphatic, still wearing romantic, bushy sideburns, with a smile like the Annunciation angel's and, in his eyes, the Abbeville sky, its haze, its glow, great! The broad collar of his cape resembles the crest of a foamy wave rising above the medals on it, which are like droplets of water. The charcoal image is less flattering, face puffier, shorter sideburns, and yet the gaze pointing off into the distance reveals a picturesque melancholy, even though we sense that this pose is slightly forced, the eyes a bit weak from having stared too long at that fake distance, possibly a jar of brushes on a shelf attached to the studio wall, some more or less mundane object whose triviality, in the end, has prevailed over his expression. The painting, I don't know, I haven't had access to it, maybe it burned when Jacques's house was bombed, there's nothing left of the house and it's painful to see, the fallen stones and the statue of a woman still standing in the former garden where she contemplates the extent of the disaster on a snapshot dating from May 1940. And I didn't even take the sculpted images into account; there's one regular bust thanks to M. de Forceville's chisel, and then one that was in the vanguard of technique, during the construction of which our hero did not shrink before the needles of the physionotype invented by Frédéric Sauvage, who also thought up a way that boats could be driven by propellers (which went on to replace paddle wheels). This apparatus made it possible to obtain the face's true proportions, taking a print of it a bit like those decorative toys in fashion during the 1980s where you pushed your hand into a mat of rounded metal needles, leaving its impression in relief. So, sliding steel needles were pushed toward Jacques's face by a moveable plate, let's hope it doesn't hurt, not only for the sake of his comfort, though there's no reason for us to be insensitive to that, but also because, well, imagine the mouth getting round, imagining opening your lips for the onomatopoeia of pain and inscribing its O on your face for posterity in place of the slight, subtle smile we wanted there, what a catastrophe, anyhow all went well, the needles clamped against that tiny smile became immobilized by tallow set between their interstices so that the shape thus obtained of Jacques's forehead, his nose, his cheeks, his chin, et cetera, would remain intact, There, it's done, we'll let you go now, M'sieur Jacques, and finally the last stage, the plaster had to be poured properly, while the proportions of the bust were taken with calipers, in the end obtaining a statue that is a composite, created both by Frédéric Sauvage and one Edmond Lévèque, whom we'd like to thank here because it isn't every day that you get to go see a sculpture of your hero.

Our two characters resume their walk in the sharp light by the edge of the sea. Because of the tide the space separating them from it is ill-defined, not only because of the distance it moves going in and out as the hours go by but in the endlessly changing tempo of the waves' motion as they advance and retreat as well.

So sometimes Margot (and our Jacques along with her) will abruptly take a step sideways, sometimes with a little shriek but not always, to avoid a wave more forceful than the others and very likely to carry the water to her feet where she's happily wrecking the leather of the shoes she's wearing in the pebbles and sand.

We see them walking along like this, by and large following a straight line parallel to the sea, and sometimes, like that, off to the side just long enough for a timely swerve, and then we're back on the first track, unless, if the tide is clearly getting too high, or if the swerves are increasing because of the capacity of certain waves, their occasional ability to push things farther than the others, in which case we'll follow another parallel, slightly higher than the earlier one, slightly more to its left, closer to the line of the promenade and the one formed by the house façades, still crisscrossed by their half-timbers, and the line of windows from which we can see our strolling couple, Well, the cold doesn't bother those two.

The people of Mers turn away from their windows and go back to their business in the contrasting light of their interior spaces, where the white light wars from minute to minute with thick darkness, constantly dividing the territory anew. Or else, the opposite, the residents who had been way back inside go to the window, just to get a good bowlful of sky, and they catch sight of our little couple, who are only a couple numerically and by geographical proximity—two of the same species side by side, though hoping, anyhow Jacques is, to arrive at a more complete definition of the word. But how then does one move from a loose, distant, fragile, ephemeral conformity reserved for the length of a single walk, or of a few such walks, to an absolute, secure conformity, so that people never invite one without the other, that's what preoccupies the mind of our hero, at this point somewhat absent from the scene, slightly removed in the intensity of his enormous anxiety, and after all is said and done, finding in every moment spent in Margot's company, not the Finally, it's been so long in coming! wherein a body relaxes a bit and a happy heart lives its life frolicking without a thought in the world, but rather the opposite, a sort of fundamental annoyance not caused, far from it, by Margot, who, in Jacques's eyes, is still glittering, still endlessly special, but by the acknowledgment of his own inadequacy, clearly manifested both in comparison with Margot (Jacques considers himself dull and her witty, himself passive while she is active, himself always putting things off to tomorrow while she is impulsive) and in how obviously unsuited to the situation he is, because of the fear keeping everything in check, and it's not simply fear of its all falling flat, or that he'll be jeered at, slapped, a huge back-handed slap in which the ring the hand wears leaves its mark for several minutes on the cheek of the one being so thoroughly put down, no, it's also the fear, how best describe it, the fear that this all might be successful, that the emotion is too strong, that it will melt him, his little body disintegrating on the beach, there, in Margot's arms, the fear that she might indeed be willing to be kissed and that his body would become liquid and thus slip from her arms, spread out on the ground in a pool, a huge puddle, the huge puddle that was Jacques's body soon absorbed between the pebbles, sucked in by the sand, and there disappear.

IV

Honorine opens the door to her house on the two silhouettes of our strictly numerical couple, surrounded by a sort of halo coming from the reflection of the daylight shining directly on the light-colored façade that is their backdrop, and looking like two ghosts suddenly emerged from the very distant past, and ready, if it weren't for their spectral immobility, to dust off their shoulders with the backs of their hands to remove some of the galactic dust of their trip through time.

For Margot, Honorine represents something like the alter ego that André is for Jacques, with the difference that André is really a friend from early childhood and Honorine a friend from when Margot was somewhat older, and then again this other difference, that André has chosen a solitary life that you might consider misanthropic, whereas Honorine lives with a husband, children, and animals, or yet again that André leads a rather contemplative existence and Honorine, on the other hand, bustles about and spares no effort from sunrise to sunset, and at the end of the day, there are, as well, endless narrower differences between them, because, you see, nobody is another person even within the limits of analogy.

Honorine therefore, radiant with her newly acquired singularity, leads the two of them into her house: glazed tiles on the floor, two orthogonal windows, the third wall pierced by double doors opening into the next room, the fourth wall partially obscured by a prominent buffet and, look, above it an engraving of the square at Abbeville, That's been there right from the beginning, says Honorine, meaning since she arrived in Saint-Valéry and implying the extent to which the engraving, in its shall we say makeshift frame, must have been the recipient of many a damp gaze, the exile sitting with her elbow on the table in the middle of the room, her head raised toward the gray lindens, toward the motionless mass of their foliage, imagining a little breeze, a little breeze coming up to get them moving, an injection of chlorophyll, well, why not, into this frozen, colorless landscape, the faint impression of the other, though you could easily wonder just how, in all seriousness, it could ever claim to represent that other.

What Nono isn't telling you, says Honorine's husband, is that there was a time when the print was turned to the wall, you couldn't see anything but the back of the wooden frame, I only said it had always been there, Honorine objects, with its back showing it was still there. We're not going to squabble on that account, says Margot, and besides, at Saint-Valéry you have the sea, You talk about sea, says Honorine, there's sea half the time, the rest of the time, when the tide's out, sand and mud is all you see of the bay, a crying shame.

On their way to the house they too had seen the bay uncovered, the cove no longer a cove, full of sand, in short, rural; when they'd go back at the end of the day the bay would be full of water the way it was represented on the cards, obviously shown at high tide.

Honorine has stopped making conversation for a moment, she goes zip zip rather far back in her mind, she thinks about the walks she took those first months, when she went walking alone, she thinks about the sandy bay all emptied out, a disaster, how she'd poured her secrets into it, poor bay ugly as can be, completely deserted, completely lifeless and waiting for the tide to come back in, see, you look the way my life does, Honorine said to it in those early days, you look just like me and both of us are weary of it all, Honorine often burst into tears at the sight of the desolate bay in those days, So Nono, cat got your tongue? asks Honorine's husband.

Nono's husband takes out the brandy glasses, he carries them like big sewing thimbles on his fingers, one two three and four, puts them down on the red-and-white checked tablecloth. We'll have a little quick one so our tongues don't have to fear any cats, but from behind the double doors Toto and Titi make an appearance, soon followed by Mimi and Leo, Well here come the monsters, says Nono's husband. The monsters address a noisy greeting to the assembled company and then make their boisterous exit into the depths of the house somewhere.

Okay we're going to drink some calvados with them and then after that I'm not sure if we want to stay at Honorine's house, where the conversation is definitely frazzled, reunions are not always successful, and Margot doesn't know what to make of all this, the checkered oilcloth, the monsters who appear and disappear in the frame of the double doors, the gush of nicknames in the air, everything's changed so much, And you, Margot, still no husband? asks Nono's husband who casts a glance toward Jacques and raises his right eyebrow into an upside-down V, which is the best an eyebrow can do to resemble a question mark in the typography of physiognomy, Well, anyhow, I didn't see a wedding ring, Jacques is an old friend from Abbeville, Margot replies politely, her hands on her knees like a child being questioned. A few more cats make off with tongues and you can hear the flies buzzing; soon that's all you hear, those flies, Nono's husband abandons his conversational efforts, Honorine tries but doesn't remember the years in Abbeville anymore, she barely even recognizes Margot, well, yes, at first, her general appearance, something came together, something you can't explain emanating from her, but then after all these minutes, nothing more, she can't see anything but differences, in her facial features, her shape, Margot is entirely different, a homonym, that's all you can say about her. Jacques looks through the windowpane at the little garden at the end of which there is a vegetable garden, from here you can clearly see the beanpoles all sticking up and farther along the hedge where the leafy shrubs tremble against a watercolor sky. Margot feels her heart contract, the palms of her hands stay motionless on her thighs, and she doesn't take her eyes off the oilcloth on the table, she's engrossed in checking how straight the lines are, how regularly they cross, how many squares there are, she gets mixed up, counts again, there's no end to it.

Margot and Jacques go back to the hotel sooner than they expected. They are in the public lounge, where Margot's disappointment is bubbling up and swelling like a wave, displaced, and now affecting Jacques whose disappointment includes his relationship with Margot, insofar as it's with himself, considering himself insufficient in every situation where he's with her, and then as regards Margot, after all, if it weren't for her, he wouldn't be here—in short, the atmosphere is not unclouded. Jacques stands with one hand on the doorknob, you know what that's like, putting one hand on the doorknob and thinking about what's outside, to indicate to the other person in the discussion who's waiting behind you that you're thinking about something outside and shouldn't be interrupted because there are a thousand additional thoughts entering into your considerations, that it's far more than taking a census of the two or three passing pedestrians, far more than contemplating the size of the houses, the remarkable sky, how the clouds travel in different ways depending on the layer, so that in a moment of inner destitution you can always make a bet on how they'll do, we know just how interested Jacques can be in clouds and how he finds in them a variation on the game he plays with the picture in his room, imagining their movement as a race in which each cloud stands ready on its line, with the wind for a motor, and bang the starting pistol's fired the instant you choose to begin your predictions, I could easily see that little one there as the winner, it seems to be keeping up a pretty good pace, unless it'll be that big one farther off which is stretching and might win just by stretching, I wonder if that's illegal, stretching, up up up a third one enters the field, obviously it's gotten a somewhat later start than the others but it seems to be gaining on them so quickly that you begin to doubt your own memory, you go back to your first little cloud, which, well, has moved along nicely, a bit out of breath toward the end, on the brink of becoming, well, we may have to reconsider, somewhat sluggish, moving in fits and starts, puff puff puff, jerkily, more like a cloud of smoke from a train, your thoughts go to the station behind its façades, imagining it visually at first, so you see all the half-timbers painted blue, the glass door to the lobby, the potted plant, the things you'd noticed upon arriving, and then thematically, the departures, all that, and who knows, your own departure, so now you're deep in absent-minded daydreams alternating with a concrete consideration of the sky, and clearly it would be a mistake to interrupt you, which is the meaning of having your back turned so obviously toward the other person in the discussion, while that person sits on the sofa and wonders what position to assume, because you're certainly going to turn around sooner or later, and that person, who has no access to the sky from there, who can derive no amusement from cloud races, who has nothing to look at but, what, two prints, probably not particularly bad ones but, seen from where one is seated, not extremely distinct, so it's hard to become seriously lost in contemplation of them, hence this other person in the discussion is wondering which expression would be the most suitable to put on for the occasion of your return. That of a bored person who has spent all this time, these minutes that for you have been so intense, in a state that would register encephalographically as almost flat would annoy you no doubt, the retrospective demand contained in it that you stop turning your back like this, that this not go on so long, please, that you show some interest, a little bit, that you just say something, will cause in you a feeling of acute displeasure, because silent demands, states of expectancy, drive you completely crazy and you don't know any other way to get loose than to flee, Great God Almighty I forgot I'm supposed to meet so-and-so! probably that's not the greatest excuse (especially at Mers, who would you be going to meet?), but that's all you can think of and you leave the hotel, no sooner said than done. And yet, it's real, this boredom, this expectancy, this demand, but the other person in the discussion has a hunch that it needs to be disguised and takes stock of two other tactics, consequently, a maximum interiority (assuming a deep air of absence, hardly still in the room at all but entirely in another world, so that when you turn around you'll say, hey, you'll say to yourself, hey, what world is that, you'll want to enter it yourself, you'll come over and sit down next to the other person in the discussion, you'll ask what are you thinking about, like that, as if it were just an anecdotal question when in reality you're burning to know, to understand what it's all about, to take a little excursion inside that world and feel refreshed), or a maximum exteriority, a sort of close, sharp attention to the room, whereby everything is interesting, except for that opaque silhouette, backlit and hiding a good half of the view, thanks very much for that, and the prints that this other person gets up to see, chin in hand, taking in the details one by one, they give you something to dream about, you turn back to study the lamp, the shade, you play with its fringe, you wonder what period the low table is, so finally when he turns around you've almost forgotten him, Oh, you still there, Jacques? and then, as if it were less for the pleasure of doing something together than to expand your studies to include things outside, Shall we maybe take a walk?

So Margot, seated uncomfortably on the sofa crosses and uncrosses her legs, then holds them together, first side by side then by joining them only at the bottom, ankle-level; sometimes she forms a curved line with an arm flung casually over the sofa's back, hand dangling against the cushion and trying hard not to tap it with her fingers, no, making it stay flexible, loose, like that, comfortable, or so it seems, because, actually, the cloth of her dress is tight at her armpit and soon causes all sorts of uneasy prickles, then, bringing her arm back to her side, she'll put her hand on her thigh, there, a hand that's a little too well-behaved, she's perfectly aware of that, a patient hand, but oh poor thing, all alone on her dress and feeling nostalgic for the social pantomimes, the arabesques we make to provide subtitles for what we say, missing the fabulous ballet of hands telling stories, and its colleague, on the other thigh, is no more spirited, occasionally they meet up with each other, merge their fingers, twiddle their thumbs, then come apart, a ring finger stretches out to show the ring it's wearing to its owner, then drops with the other fingers back onto her thigh. And also, sometimes two or three fingers of one hand take hold of a finger on the other or else the ring and twist it, just a bit, like that, it doesn't help much.

Jacques offers the back of his frock coat; he's actually feeling pretty sorry for himself and inwardly praying to the clouds for a solution; he's pretending to enjoy the pleasant solitude of his thoughts but inside, holy smoke, it's Napoleon on November 27th who has to cross the Berezina in 1812 by November 29th, a total disaster, Jacques lingers over the scene for a bit, was there snow already, and the repeated shots from bayonets can't help but conjure up the little needles of this huge anxiety now piercing him, our very uneasy hero, very shy, the years haven't changed that and it's pointless to count up former mistresses, look, that cloud, the one stretching out just now has come completely apart, excluding itself from the race, I could tell Margot about this, Jacques thinks, say Look, it's fun how the clouds move at different speeds depending on what layer they're in you might even say they're racing and you could bet on one or another, Margot would get up and come to see, they would be side by side the two of them in the window's embrasure and embrasure is not far from embrace, what do you think.

Jacques leaves Margot in the hotel lounge, he waves at her on his way out (with a flutter of his hand above the wrist as if to get rid of some imaginary smoke or start a little tune in the air) and goes for a walk.

The hero's solitary walk is usually a key moment in the story, a thoughtful pause necessarily suspending the action and usually involving a weighing-up of past and future, less the one in comparison with the other than one after the other, successively, considering the things that are already good and the things that need another look (sometimes in order not to do whatever it was again and at least draw some decent principles from it, sometimes because it would be good to make it right, do it differently, in short, some work remains to be done—which naturally leads us straightaway into the future) and then the future, the series of possibilities among which one has to make a completely conscious choice, with full knowledge of the facts, because a Boucher de Perthes has never acted rashly, said the father, framed in a window with his back to the child and creating against the light a perfect silhouette cut from fine black paper as he committed Jacques to maritime adventures.

One is soon out of Mers, soon up in the low hills looking out over the sea where it will be possible to prepare a few lines to exchange with oneself in rehearsal and then, once the proper point of view has been established, possible to talk frankly with oneself, one part in accusation and the other defense with oneself the umpire, don't try to figure out how many parts you play, while the old dreamer still dozing deep inside (hey, look, a fourth!) distances himself from the battle from time to time so as to lose himself in contemplating the sky, or the sea, or where the two meet, the incredible line of the horizon going on forever.

So we have to imagine the Scotch broom, Scotch broom and bare earth alternating so they form something resembling the tufts that manage to escape alopecia, and as for the bare earth, which wouldn't seem particularly bald otherwise, no, it just looks like bare earth, black, mixed with sand, making an uneven mixture as when you put some black onto yellow on your palette and it looks like hell, the black and yellow, a really bad mix, so, it seems to me, you'd consider, even if you weren't thinking about baldness in particular, look how those tufts not covering it completely make the bare earth, where it's bare, look like it has alopecia, bad luck, and into this skinned landscape our potential hero resolutely continues on his way, climbing up like a young goat, occasionally using his hands, into this countryside, suddenly timeless, thinks Jacques, an old fixation of his, putting more and more weight on his palms, his head close to the ground risks getting scratched in the face by the broom, and beginning to make little noises, so much fun, first one or two grunts, then looking carefully all around him, checking to make sure there's nobody else out for a walk with a stick in his hand and about to greet him, our Jacques at that point having lost all notion of vocabulary answering uh, uh, out of what was left him of sociability, or maybe he wouldn't answer at all, or maybe just pounce on the person walking along, or run off without demanding his due, but no, there's no hat on the horizon of Scotch broom, Jacques's line of sight from here is definitely impeded by the bushes, but at any rate, you'd certainly see the top of a hat even from this height, no, not a trace of one, and so our Jacques begins to really enjoy himself, emitting squawks and squeals into the landscape, moving in rhythm to the sounds he's making, and *Homo rudolfensis*, Lake Rudolph Man, fat and with a rugged face and heavy-duty teeth, but definitely more assertively bipedal, hops up and down beside him, making cooing sounds and taking advantage of the way his thumb (*pollex*) is articulated to create bird images in the air, crossing his thumbs and flapping his hands for wings.

From the rock where he squats, his position half-prehistoric, half-contemporary, Jacques thinks about the hotel lounge, the soft blue stripes of its wallpaper, how the furniture is prettily placed, and about Margot sitting there, dreaming about what, exchanging a few remarks with herself, then, if someone happens by, with that person, that's easier, you only have to provide half the text, while behind the window casement you can see a sky of gouache with two or three perfectly suspended clouds, Jacques can tell this is true because he can see that the sky has stopped dead in its tracks, a huge contrast with the workings of the sea.

The brief, self-imposed absence of Margot is, at the moment, bringing a lump to his throat, there in the midst of the landscape rustling in the sea breeze, the Scotch broom tickling the edge of the sky, while the part of it that arches over our hero as he talks to himself, like a canopy as if it were borrowed from a different painting, stays there, billowy and motionless, a suspension of cirrocumulus that rather fortunately coincides with his own suspension of action, taking the time to pull back and examine the bay in solitary contemplation, and fiddling in his pocket with a last bit of tobacco though he doesn't feel like taking it out right away, considering it as a potential extra pleasure, but not necessarily, when now the top of a black felt hat is clearly coming into view, which means (since there are beginning to be too many people here) that it's time to go back.

V

Meanwhile, Margot is taking a bubble bath in the lavender-tiled bathroom adjoining her hotel room, she sings, si do mi re fa and from time to time lifts a foot with a pompom of foam from the water and tosses it at the ceiling, laughs and does it again. This all goes on for a while—the little song interspersed with laughter, and the pompoms of foam that usually don't go very far, but stop halfway in the air and fall flop back in with the other bubbles. Except perhaps this one slightly foamy patch on the ceiling, sort of like a stalactite, look, maybe one pompom reached its goal, who knows, and is disintegrating peacefully up there, torn between falling down again and evaporating and choosing, if you want my opinion, to do a bit of one and then a bit of the other.

Moments pass, the water's getting cold, Margot's done with bathing, and just because you hoped to see her get out of the tub, it was bound to happen, she shoots you a glance, draws the shower curtain, and stands up behind its cloth, so you see nothing. Her bathrobe is hanging over the curtain rod, she grabs it from behind the curtain and tries to pull it down, it slides, sort of catches on one of the rings and then completely surrenders. Margot pulls the curtain again but this time in the direction indicating the show is beginning, she makes her appearance wearing the bathrobe. Let's hope it gapes open slightly. She sets one foot down on the tiles, then the other, goes off to the bedroom with her hair soaking wet, rubbing it with a white towel. The window is wide open to the outside, the sea, the seawall, the landscape, and on the top of the cliffs the green ridge of grass that looks like their hairdo.

Nariokotome Boy, chin in hand, is thinking about how time goes by and how you're even more aware of this because it's emphasized by the contrasting seasons. Off in the distance, having renounced moving around in the trees for good, and become fully upright on their long legs ever since moving into the open spaces of the plains, a few of *Homo ergaster*'s colleagues, older than he, are sitting around and chipping away at bifaces (yes, exactly the same kind as those our hero exposed in the Saint-Acheul quarry). The child looks out upon the steppe, the stark, bare steppe that is only brought to an end, way off in the distance, by the vertical surface of the sky.

Margot, her head tilted to the right, studying the line made by vegetation between stone and sky, keeps on rubbing the hair at the back of her neck and turns back to the room's interior where the mirror reflects light from the sea; she gazes cheerfully at her image, begins talking to herself, making extravagant gestures with the hand not holding the towel, so what is she saying to herself,

Jacques wonders as he watches her with the telescope, he's now on the seawall, at the end of it, he's turned the telescope in the direction of the room, put a coin in and has two minutes to watch Margot, offering her hand to herself, pulling it back, making arabesques with her arm, looking first serious, then charming, making polite conversation with herself, perhaps she's complimenting herself, albeit without illusions, then she goes back to more abstract remarks, continuing to philosophize, with no time at all just two minutes to convince herself that she's being sensible, that she's the good little Margot she ought to be, as good as you'd wish her to be, that all her life she's taken the years as they came and now here she is at the seashore with Jacques, and we shall see, is that what she's saying to herself, fluttering her hand like a telltale on a sail, like a bird, and twisting her wrist in a manner that might very well mean we shall see. Margot nods her head, agrees with her own words, shows by lifting one shoulder that the subject could be further refined, that there are other ways of thinking about things, she goes a little closer to the mirror and plop the black flap drops back down between the eyepiece and the tube of the telescope. Jacques digs around in his pocket, no more coins, anyhow not enough, and besides he shouldn't carry this little tactic too far. He looks at the sea with an empty stare in which no sea is visible, suddenly he's feeling an inexplicable sadness descend on his shoulders, is it because he's seen Margot being so autonomous, so self-sufficient in her room where, as she conversed with herself, she seemed to do just fine without him, is it because he's figured out Margot's gesture of We shall see and doesn't know the best way to fill the coming hours? Jacques decides to go back to the hotel, Oh, but no, he's walking the wrong way, down into the wet pebbles, all the way to the next seawall, up in the direction of the café that's next to the reading room.

The reading room is set up in a corner building, so half its windows look out on the road, letting you make out the episodes (some of which are really quite shocking) playing out behind the opposing façade, framed by a casing, or, when the weather's nice, in plain sight on a balcony (consequently, the theater rather than TV version, switching from miniseries to stage play), or else, if you go out on the small patio there, you can distract yourself from your book and watch the action, the entrances and exits and the pantomimes in between, you can rewrite the dialogue, or even, if the reading-room windows are open, just put up with them all, why not, listening with a knowing ear, or on the contrary, plugging it, that ear, sinking it deep in your hand, like so, and leaning on your elbow, too bad for the other ear left out there in the open, though you can always plug that one too, both elbows on the table, face staring stubbornly down at the page, while the other half, to continue what I was saying, frame portions of the sea and spread lots of different, more or less blue, monochrome tones across the wall, and then, we shouldn't ignore them, half-sea half-sky colors at the top.

The idle and vaguely disenchanted moments that Jacques is presently spending in this reading room will give me a chance to describe a few of the pictures, prints, watercolors, oils, and photographs sprinkled all over the two other walls, which are full of them and oppose the rectangles of the windows across from them with the rectangles of their plastic representations, competing in a way for one's eyes.

So first (listing them in the order in which they appear to a reader seated at the one long conference table when the panorama it creates is read from left to right, and sometimes downward when necessary, as in reading Japanese, because of their arrangement; anyway, that's the principle, for what it's worth) comes a rustic, somewhat rural landscape crossed by a flat river that's obviously low if you look at the horse apparently stopped and standing in it, carrying a rather indistinct man on its back who's wearing a cap and has something on his shoulder, maybe a stake so he can measure the depth of the water here, or is it a bundle, it doesn't look like a spear in any case, there's nothing warlike here, just the peaceful cool of unruffled water reflecting a few fragments of nature without distortion, the horse seeming to drink from the river, head down, with the same lazy serenity as its master's; there's no good explanation for their presence in the middle of the river given that there's a wooden bridge nearby, no more than a few yards away, that they could have crossed on perfectly well but everybody has his own reasons for things, remaining in this unexplainable pause while on both sides of the stream the landscape stretches out in its immensity, mountains, hills, and clearly in the distance some very blue mountains, in a blue that indicates how far away they are, connecting in this way the remarkable peacefulness of this figure on horseback with the idea of the vast space spread out behind him. It's a very good connection to make if you're into grandiloquent monologues, except that our man has his back turned to the mountains and is looking at what, something outside the picture, right where we are, that we'll just have to imagine. But then the nearby hills suggest conversely the

165

notion of being circumscribed; very dark fence lines ripple and pour across them, defining irregular-shaped, not at all quadrilateral properties as they no doubt follow the convexities and concavities of hills and valleys one after the other. What is contained inside these fences is itself curiously disparate, because sometimes they enclose only a few trees, other times a whole forest around a central estate, other times entire villages, two or three of them, dispersed in the intermediate band between the river where we're wading and the mountains that, in all their perfect blueness, play the role of all that's out of reach. Within this same band, inside this same half, in which things are certainly across the river but still on this side of the sapphire hills, inside all this circumscribed area there's another minuscule man on horseback who, unlike the one still stuck in the river, is certainly not at a standstill but obviously galloping, all four of his horse's feet off the ground and preparing to run right through the picture from right to left ignoring the little villages. In the foreground, on our side of the stream, a rather large farm is laid out on the right, with a haystack, a water trough, a quickly sketched rooster, a similar hen slightly farther away, a few boards left lying around, and perhaps, yes, inside the darkness of the stable door, in charcoal gray against the black background of the room, the silhouette of a man who's stopped and is looking in the same direction as the calm, wading man on horseback, toward the same thing as he, in the end it makes you wonder. You check your information and it turns out the farm is a wire factory, but then why the rooster and the hen, anyhow the wire-factory-farm occupies two thirds of the foreground, while the remaining left-hand third represents the end of an enclosure where a man on foot is about to leave a stretch of trees and a low, light-colored stone wall, carrying a stick in his left hand and a sack on his back, legs wide apart like dividers, calipers to measure out the landscape with his long stride on this bucolic morning.

I move on to the prominent fir tree, in watercolor #2, central and isolated, coming out of the picture at the top, rather lacking in branches so what's there is mostly trunk, with a device attached to its side that must be used to collect sap, don't ask me exactly how, just imagine resin, gum, and at the foot of it there's a man sitting who has a long, untrimmed beard, sort of a Robinson Crusoe with his legs crossed and back turned slightly away from us, he's holding a knife in his hand and has a pot in front of him, at least that's what the things look like to Jacques who is slightly too far away to know for sure, they must be used to cut into the trunk and get the resin out some other way. This huge, central trunk divides a small bit of green from the corner of a microscopic village and mountains that are only slightly larger, and as for the background, it's four-fifths sky, the artist obviously had squatted down to compose his picture.

Continuing, I see two men from the back who are walking along a river. On the left a pasture where a horse is grazing. In the river several small boats, almost obliterated, one of them looks like a raft. Buildings in the distance. The man on the left is wearing a wig, he raises his cane, you can tell he's talking on and on. There's a dog going their way.

Next a pile of rocks, with trees that seem to be growing right out of them. A shepherd standing, one hand on his heart under his open, thick, blue jacket, the other around a stick. Lower down is a shelter with its two very realistic fir trees.

Bleak landscape. Just two birds in the sky.

Then comes a crowded table, red noses, shiny round faces, a card game, laundry drying, an arbor, pitchers and pipes, Jacques blinks his eyes, altogether it's pretty hard to bear.

Plains with cattle. Four cows parallel and from the side, like the same one repeated four times. The whole thing in pen and ink with brown and light gray washes.

Next. Men smoking pipes in a guardhouse. Beautiful moldings on the ceiling but a number of cracks on the walls. It could all use some paint. Work to be done.

Washerwomen. Splashes of light on the white sheets. A feeling of work. Against a vast landscape dark vaults of a washhouse cover the laundry basins.

Jacques's eyes return to the guardhouse (moving not according to plan but that's the way it goes), where the very long, white pipes register as three white lines, one diagonal descending to the left, one diagonal descending to the right, a third one parallel to the second. A paunchy man is sitting and reading some official document; five others are listening to him, three seated (one of them has his left hand on his hip with the palm turned out brings the first diagonal pipe in from the right; another, holding the divergent pipe in his right hand, has settled his left on his knees; the third, pipeless, rests his hand on the table while the other hand holds his cheek), two standing, one in the shadow on the other side of the table with his eyes looking down at the missive, the other in front leaning on the back of the reader's chair wears a blue frock coat catching all the light. Farther off, the third smoker sits beside the fireplace and lights his pipe with a bit of burning wood. A soldier opposite this smoker has his back turned to the flames, sword at his side and wearing a hat, well, you'd think it was certainly warm enough in there, he must be cooking like that, he's forgetting his discomfort looking somewhere else, off to the right, toward a man in a cocked hat who's reading a map hung on the wall beneath a shelf where there's a single book, a mirror, and a compass. An empty chair is pushed up against the wall. You can't see what country or region is depicted on the map. Between the soldier in his warm hat and the man in his cocked hat is a second table where two men are playing cards, one wearing a wig and the other another cocked hat, you can clearly see the cards this man in this cocked hat is holding. Four cards, the fifth that he's setting down on the table is a red ace. All the way off to the left, framed in a doorway, is another man in another cocked hat, from behind. Toward the center, adjoining this door, a doorframe leading to the entrance, opening onto a tiny elongated rectangle of the town.

Then there are the washerwomen we've already mentioned.

Then an art collector's room, unfinished (large areas just sketched in, others empty). From this distance the paintings are too small for Jacques to decipher them easily.

The port of Dieppe. Sailboat masts, hulls in three-quarter view, some of them swinging to the left others to the right, a messy, disorganized feeling to it. On the dock three seated men and a fourth almost lying down. A few standing figures. Nothing worth mentioning.

Beach with dunes.

Vegetable garden. Little lettuces starting to sprout. Ground carefully hoed, neat and tidy.

Chalk cliff, in the middle of which we see the sea. Three boats in profile, in the distance, identical, with their numerous white sails forming successive panels on each. One light-colored boat shown frontally like a single square sail. In the foreground, grass, tree roots sticking up. The boat seen head-on and coming toward us, toward the inlet at the bottom, gives a sense of returning. It's a feeling, Jacques thinks, that makes this watercolor peaceful.

A group of fishermen with a skiff. The skiff is upside down, it's drying on the beach, the fishers are four in number, one standing, the other seated on the hull, a third squatting in front, the fourth sitting directly on the pebbles.

Two paintings by Albert Cuyp bring the series to a close.

The first, a chateau half in ruins, mainly on the left-hand side— really destroyed, whereas the right-hand side still has its whole donjon, peaked roof and all, with its spire rising as tall against the contemporary sky as it did in earlier days when the lord of the manor lived there. A thin tree, almost dead, scratches the front wall and is topped off with some leafy branches, a sure sign of rebirth.

The whole ruin sits imposingly in the middle of a lake where the water is so clear, so calm that there's a perfect reflection of it, without a flicker to the lines, in a clarity that contrasts sharply with the notion of time passing and destroying the edifice as the days go by. In this line-for-line reflection, it represents the idea of something that's intact, as opposed to the stones eroding and the windows of rooms open to the sky where you can see straight through to the mountain lying beyond.

In the foreground, two men, backs to us, one on horseback the other a shepherd on foot, are looking at the chateau in ruins, or rather it's the man on horseback who's doing the looking and the one on foot has his face turned toward that of the rider, as if to study his feelings, his melancholy, how much he admires the motionless waters and the perfect reflection. The horse, croup toward us, twists its neck; it's pretty clearly looking at us. Across the lake there's a couple in conversation, perhaps discussing the rider on the other side, and three cows with their backs to us as well, vaguely studying the background to the right and something outside the picture, leaving us to imagine that there are other places where one might gaze.

In the second painting, a shepherd is flopped down and lying almost flat on the rock emerging from a grassy surface, leaning on his elbow; another shepherd, standing, holds a large cane cutting a line across him at the level of his calves, his back is to us and he's wearing a bag at his waist, or maybe it's a leather flask, and he's looking at the shepherd lying down, obviously talking to him. The shepherd who's lounging there has raised his head toward the other. There's a sort of peacefulness emanating from this conversation, we don't think that they're making any particular revelations to each other, certainly nothing sensational, and yet at the same time it's an intimate moment of confidences, they're saying what's on their minds, what they feel, it's nothing lying heavy on their hearts, no, just the weight of a day in the mountains and the pure air that swells your lungs and makes you sing better. In the distance, a herd of cows, with other human figures, three men actually, two who are half showing above and behind the cows' backs and feet, facing each other, wearing hats, talking but about things less personal than those our foreground shepherds are discussing. A third, seen almost whole except for the bottom of his legs, in a medium-close shot let's say, mid knee-level, but in profile, watches them from a few steps away. He's too distant for us to understand what his stare means, so we don't know if he's feeling excluded from this conversation or just watching some social event from a distance, one in which he might very well participate but feels a little too lazy to do so.

To get back to the foreground, on the left of our two men and apparently forming a group with them, two cows. Their positions are symmetrical with those of the two men, one lying down and the other standing and in both cases face to face: the standing cow stands facing the standing man, and she's looking at him, the one lying down forms a right angle with the man lying down, and she's gazing at him (whereas he, remember, is looking up at the standing man). It's as if the four of them are at a bridge table, as if they marked the four points of the compass, and as if the conversation included them all. The participation by the cows makes the scene even more peaceful, in a sense. The words exchanged are so simple that even the cows understand them. Which in return makes them sort of storybook cows, slightly anthropomorphic, less outsiders. The sky takes up two thirds of the painting and when you've stared good and long at this scene of the foursome, you can raise your eyes to its clear blue, where a few bright clouds function not to obstruct the blueness but, on the contrary, to form little islands of increased light, reflected, archipelagos of light in an almost transparent landscape.

Jacques's gaze, escaping the pictures, goes off toward the window; faced with this moment that would have been better spent in thinking about his situation but that he's wasted in lazy contemplation of the sea and the sky and these pictures getting you nowhere, he's feeling sad again. He regrets being incapable of successfully following through on this love story with Margot, regrets his escapes, his way of going off to walk alone and then staying away like this, overwhelmed by his own ineptitude. It must also be said that the narrator is obviously playing a part by relaying our character's avoidance, lingering over descriptions, describing the postcards one after the other, the one for André and the one for Constantin, then the pictures! That took the cake! Completely foreign to Jacques's story! Rather than facing up to writing romantic sequences and simply on the pretext that they turned out to be where he could see them, that was no help, Jacques thinks, chin in hand and feeling all over again the extent of his abandonment, there, in that reading room where he doesn't know anybody, where, in fact, there isn't anybody except this narrator who's not doing her job, and Margot's come back down to the lobby perhaps and is waiting for him just a hundred yards away, deep in a sadness equal to his, except for her the sadness is passive, one she suffers largely owing to Jacques, who only has to get his little butt out of the armchair and go join her, so, Jacques, what are you waiting for?

With his retreating forehead, cheekbones creating two round cones high up on either side of his face, and rather sturdy mandible, *Homo erectus*, endowed with the bipedality that is completely human, agrees to get up on his compact feet graced with arches and journey across the savannas, steppes, forests, the way it will have to be done.

They spent several invigorating days together. Jacques and Margot, I mean. Sometimes walking together in the acid winter light along the edge of the sea, their feet twisting in the large pebbles, with Jacques, as we've said, occasionally stopping to pick up one of the flatter stones and trying to make it bounce a few times on the surface of the water. Margot behind would be watching him do it then her gaze would be distracted, perhaps by a gull flying past; she'd lean down, pick up a pebble, and weigh it as if weighing her love, apparently spending a long time in reflection while thinking at the same time that it wasn't very important. Sometimes walking more inland and usually confining themselves to a few streets of the town, they'd read out the names of the villas they passed, which provided them with all sorts of subject matter, some for commentary, others for personal reverie (deep in highly charged and pleasant silence).

We can't exclude the possibility, moreover, that they took, and several times perhaps, the street that will be named for Jacques, a pretty street at right angles to the promenade, so that you can see the ocean at the end of it, which creates a lovely opening, it gives an idea of distant locales, adventures, great projects, a place where you hope to emerge, feeling in advance just how dazzling it will be, all those photons reflected by the sea, you walk happily toward the pure sublimity of this opening onto the light of the sea.

It could have been a nice coincidence if Jacques kissed Margot for the first time on this very street, a way of winking at History, so that when passersby in future generations stop in front of the sign painted in white letters on a blue background and attached to the corner house, at the height where the ground floor stops and the floor above begins, to read Jacques's name, they would also be unknowingly commemorating this first kiss, but in the first place it's not at all certain that Jacques will manage to kiss Margot by the end of this section, and secondly our man, restricted by his times, trapped in the winter of 1862–1863 and absolutely contemporaneous with himself, has no way of getting the information that we have about the street name. What's more, the building with the sign on it doesn't even correspond to the biographical facts as we know them about the type of house he will live in for a while on this street by and by (and you too might just happen, parenthetically, to survey with absolutely no success all the streets that will almost arbitrarily bear your name, where you've never lived, or maybe not even kissed anybody, and that a zealous mayor will baptize with your last name anyhow, as well as your first, your professional title, your date of birth, and, this is sadder, the date of your death, let's skip that). Jacques must have let his eyes wander across the façades here in the same way as he did on other streets, and what with the sound of Margot's feet trotting along beside him to provide the soundtrack that this solitary hero, unused to walks of such acoustic complexity, had never dared hope for, music composed of two lines, his and that of another person, his broad stride's quarter notes combining with the staccato eighth notes of Margot's heels, which, because of her more rapid pace, made a double rhythm, taptaptaptap, while Jacques just produced a tap tap, the result of it all was clearly rewarding.

On some days the names of villas would stand in for conversation, they would send phrases back and forth between them as if they were engaged in energetic stichomythias, Babillage, L'hirondelle, Les Lilas, Tatiana (no no, it's Margot), nameless, illegible, Esmeralda (no, it's Margot I say), nameless, Le Bleuet, reading them faster and faster, almost running, Brise légère (frankly that villa's more wind than breeze), La Côtière, nameless, nameless, Les Tilleuls (ah, lindens, lime-flower trees, the good old-fashioned infusions, the lime-flower teas of my childhood, Jacques saw the closed shutters hiding the town, saw the bed where he used to lie, the nightly infusion they'd bring him to lower his fever, my brother used to call it *un bon dilleul*), Coup de vent, La Vague, it was like they were exchanging insults, compliments, advice, sometimes the word would be straightforward, explicit, clear in the white, wintertime light, sometimes obviously a code of some sort, then they'd talk to each other using a code made up of the terms that had to be deciphered, Aigue-marine, Les Coccinelles, Chateau (some chateau!), La Rafale, L'Horizon, nameless designed by H. Ravon, architect, and built by A. Thiessard, contractor, Margharita (you're beginning to get on my nerves, Jacques), Picardie (that being where we are, though apparently this is debatable, apparently the junction that is Mers is a bone of contention between two opposing regions, Really?), nameless, Les Manillons (what are *manillons*? Margot asks), Les Goélands (a lot to talk about here, *goélands* or gulls being the subject of much literary verbiage, still we mustn't forget they love garbage; anyhow they do provide a suitable soundtrack for this walk), Petit tout (that's what it looks like to me, anyway, Me too), Le Poussin, and that's it.

Once, taking advantage of the possibility of being in a seaside landscape that was a rural one at the same time, they climbed up into the hills where the fields stretched out before them.

They saw cows with big round udders who must have been waiting impatiently to be milked. In the afternoon all the cattle would crowd into the sparse shade of a single apple tree that in the summer must have given some protection but now, completely leafless, was no help, just an old habit they must have gotten into.

They walked over the hills of Mers. You could easily see the rooftops cascading down toward the ocean and the vegetation already smelled like the country, with the smells revived by the recent rains, as were the colors, the entire landscape had an air of exaltation, like the heart of our humble hero, breathing the fresh, country breeze, less violent than the wind on the beaches.

They went past a garden where they saw some hydrangeas that had turned white, as if the rains had washed them clean, as if the storm that night had washed away their color.

It was a happier walk than the others. Jacques said something to that effect. Margot replied, Maybe, the way someone speaking to Socrates in one of Plato's dialogues might say it when the final proof has not yet been provided.

VI

So now our two characters are sitting under the roof of the train station in Mers, in the almost nocturnal cool of the kind of morning that has a hard time getting started. Margot is asleep, yes, Margot does readily remove herself from the scene, we remember the first time she dozed off in the train taking her to Mers—when the situation seems merely transitory she lets reality make do without her, dropping her light and lifeless envelope beside Jacques and taking off to unconstructed realms where identities roam freely, Wake me up if anything's happening, whereas this, in fact, these final moments in Mers, could well be the something happening: our hero could be spurred on by the notion that his kissing scene has still not taken place. The fact that it had been floating overhead for the entire length of the visit makes its execution nevertheless easier on the station platform, after all, than it will be when they are back again in the familiar spaces of Abbeville and their, let's say, firmly fixed platonic habits, but here we are, it's early, night is not yet over, they're just going on a train trip, plenty of reasons for Margot's sleeping peacefully and as if this were a perfectly natural thing to do, I don't think we can do anything to prevent it.

Jacques watches the day slowly emerge. He sits facing the sea's dark and steady blue, with just a few abstract forms silhouetted against its monochrome, nothing identifiable yet. At first they're just variations in the monochromatic shades. Nothing really figurative, volumes barely distinguished from everything else, a cube seen from the front, a few triangles up high, that's about all you can say. There's something in this visual confusion that's analogous to the state of a man dragged out of bed and sitting there in the cold before his usual faculties have gotten under way. By no means an unpleasant analogy. On the one hand, you're feeling somewhat stunned, not at all certain you'll be able to respond properly to whatever situations come up, you haven't, how to put it, quite reached the level of intelligence, you're kind of down, just floating there, and as a result rather incapacitated and just about the only thing that you're conscious of is your disability; it's a strain, for example, to think about standing up when the train comes into the station, getting on it seems not at all simple, you know you could perfectly well just stay sitting there, hunched up and in a stupor on the bench, with your hands between your thighs, staring emptily at what, the train cars going by make no impression, and whereas the noise of the machine rushes into your eardrums you're not giving it any name, not identifying it as the train you're waiting for and now let go right past you just like that, just because of your ineptitude. And at the same time, there's a harmony you feel between your indistinct thoughts and this lack of any visual distinctness to the world around you, which is a small saving grace, you tell yourself, look, I'm exhausted, I'm unfit for anything, I'm afraid of not doing things right, but the way everything seems blurred fits right in, at least, with this buried station and the landscape across from me that I only know is an urban landscape, moreover, because I knew it before, it's knowledge from my past, even if I'm actually incapable now of recognizing that that's what it is, because there's nothing but one dense color, with an occasional edge that may stick out, some geometric excrescence, something vaguely cubist.

Then the outlines naturally become sharper, colors change and separate, details come to light within volumes that first you took to be uniform, and bit by bit, why yes, at the same time that, watching the scene move toward increased sharpness, you begin to recover your faculties, the idea of naming things starts to take on more legitimacy. In the railway landscape now becoming visible, you can start to give things names, begin calling the aforementioned triangles roofs, start to make out the shutters closed over windows behind which people are launching into their final sleep cycle, some of them already tossing and turning under their comforters, aware of the imminent sunrise and reviewing, reviewing with more or less confusion the obligations that await them. In cases where two are sleeping together, the one who's awake knows he runs the risk of annoying the other and usually holds unnaturally still under the sheets, but it may well happen in the course of a thought that he'll forget that he's part of a duo and roll over too vigorously, taking with him a disproportionate amount of comforter so that the other person, now deprived and feeling the tug of cloth as it's pulled away, opens his eyes to see a room still in shades of dark gray and lets fly some more or less veiled insult. It's also possible, in the best cases, that a bit of coitus ensues, sweetly cocoonish in the respite provided by morning's lazy arrival.

Just as developer in a photographer's solution makes an image slowly appear, the dawning day makes the station earlier drenched in darkness and the buildings surrounding it more and more legible. The fence separating the platform on the right-hand side of the building from the esplanade that runs behind it becomes more and more assertive with its white hatching. And it's possible, yes, that ten minutes from now, when the stationmaster comes out to announce the train's arrival, his pants will already show as blue and his hat will be rather clearly red.

How can one not be delighted with the manner in which the morning world suddenly appears to stereoscopic man, because we have to realize, if you'll excuse this didactic parenthesis, that in the savannas a long time ago, there came to be a difference between those who had only monochromatic vision and those who could distinguish colors.

In the evolution of primates the exact same operation occurred as the one at play in this seaside dawn where Jacques can see the landscape more and more distinctly. The primate endowed with stereoscopic vision and the ability to grasp the world no longer in a confusing monochrome could evaluate distances, which, when a lion is pouncing on you, is mighty convenient, and it's the same when the stationmaster, no doubt drawn by the fact that the two of you, Jacques and Margot, are the sole individuals on this platform, and wishing, since he has nobody to talk to, to engage you in conversation, heads in your direction, first a distant silhouette, predatory, you can tell that in an instant, squinting your eyes to watch his steps come progressively closer and, plop, you close your eyes so it'll look like you're asleep when he gets to you. That same primate also found ledges and overhangs in landscapes that his ancestors saw as having no relief, grasping the world as if it were on a video screen, flattened as on a page so they were always afraid of bumping into things. That primate must have been extremely happy when he finally saw clearly the berries against the background of leaves, which, up until that point, had merged chromatically, a lucky moment for a gourmet also one for a thinker, because he could then grasp notions of difference and similarity, and he learned to count. Every day he would count the number of berries he ate the same way that Jacques counted the number of posts on the fence that was becoming clearer from one moment to the next. He identified the berries' names and triumphantly shouted these out onto the savanna, like Jacques who is now saying roof, beam, corner post, scaffolding, to himself as they begin appearing.

Margot's head is definitely moving more and more in the direction of Jacques's shoulder, at first just on a diagonal that's grown out of the earlier vertical when it was tilted back, but pretty soon it's brushing against it; a strand of her hair, bolder than the others, has gone out to scout around and comes to lie in a curve there on his frock coat, coiling rather ornamentally, then it's followed by several more strands, a whole bunch of them that, by dint of brushing over cloth, could easily leave a hair behind, caught in the wool, one that our hero would find the next day in the solitude of his house in Abbeville, where his life would, all things considered, be back to normal and he'd be putting on his frock coat so he could go to the river for his daily swim and then look, what's that, he catches the suspicious object between his thumb and index finger, a hair, much too long to be mine, a hair, obviously Margot's, and our Jacques, dangling the hair at face level in the hallway as he's preparing to leave, would experience a real dilemma, not daring to throw it away, considering its owner, considering the vague (because the visit to the shore had done nothing for it) bond connecting him to her, yet not daring to keep it either, how and where could he, really, on this table it would be in danger of flying away on the least breeze, a tiny trophy, a flimsy cast-off flying to the base of the mantel where, one way or another, it would disappear, carried off on the sole of a shoe, crushed like some poor insect hidden in the grass or dispersed along with the dust and fluff swept out two or three times a week. Wavering between these two equally impossible solutions, our hero would hold the aporetic hair pinched between his fingers for a long time until he came up with the best solution, the least interventionist way of doing it, the one that would provide chance and the natural order of things the most access, which is to put the hair back where it was on the cloth of his frock coat and let the wind and vigorous walking, the ambulatory rubbing of cloth in the air do as they please on this cool morning in which the hair would certainly find some way of getting away on its own, without any help, the way things come and go.

So, a generous amount of Margot's hair is now brushing Jacques's shoulder, enough that its weight begins to be felt, the combined weight of a few butterflies, just to give you some idea, something light, volatile, and the only thing worrying Jacques is that the feeling may stop, that the head may go back to its vertical position, or even topple over in the other direction, against the bench, but no, the head remains hanging for a while and then, continuing its motion, ends up completely on his shoulder where it rests from that moment on, finding a perfect way to arrange itself into the hollow between his collarbone and his neck, like continents that were formerly connected, each having kept the shape of how it first fit with the other and ready to receive it again, if a geological shift should occur, easy as pie, or like puzzle pieces finally put together, there, make yourself comfortable, here then are our two Siamese lovers joined together in the station at Mers, forming one and the same creature, fifty percent asleep and the other fifty percent watching the dawning day, as we said.

Jacques's dear Margot. She'll certainly have to be left at the station in Abbeville, or else on her doorstep, to go back to her former life, and she's going to leave a large empty spot in Jacques's hours, because, what can I say, we get used to someone else's presence and afterward it leaves something like a holographic extension of itself that even turns up in places where we went before, without that person, for instance his house in Abbeville, which had never been filled by her actual presence and yet will seem empty without her, so that it's no exaggeration to say that you'll have to learn how to live there again, I mean in the everyday sense of the word, in the unfolding of the simplest activities; and faced with this new absence, just to ensure, even if artificially, throughout this transition between days shared and days alone, I'm not going

to worry about it, you'll regain the earlier configuration by incre-
ments until you'll once again, let me reassure you here and now,
feel like yourself again at home, it'll take no time at all, getting
back together with yourself, something you don't want to have
happen immediately mind you, and put off so you'll have at least
some slight sense, almost an illusion that Margot, a fragile, ghostly
Margot is still present and now moving through the house like a
delicate double exposure that the least bit of additional thought is
likely to pfouf debunk, you'll definitely have to develop all sorts of
stratagems, which will consist, for example, of reproducing certain things you did with her, ways of doing them, you might delay
mealtimes perhaps so that you eat some ingredient or other that
you ate with her on Mers time and not the regular-as-clockwork
Abbeville time, who knows. You'll willfully repeat things you did
together like that, especially eating habits, usually pretty effective,
while underneath and less consciously, you'll begin casually imitating the other's gestures, facial expressions, and tone of voice, as
if, yes, ever so slightly you were turning into her.

In the way he spends his time in Abbeville, Jacques therefore
will be making a few changes, but temporary changes, because
the trip, within Jacques's grand project, is only a parenthesis. Our
hero, let me remind you, has a task to fulfill.

III
THE DISCOVERY

I

We're almost there. Today is D-day minus something—this morning we're approaching the event, you can tell because the room
just feels a certain way, it looks, see, with its bed almost on the
diagonal, almost like a room seen through a wide-angle lens, its
slight deformation itself exciting and making us think that something is about to happen. Yet simultaneously it's still a room in
the morning with its shutters closed, so, this something, rather
than being in a hurry, is brooding, that's what we sense, this something brooding, needing a little more time yet but not very much
and we feel, as they say about gestation, that it's due soon, you
could tap on the imaginary belly containing the thing that's getting ready, look at Jacques and say, Coming soon, eh? But hoping to get Jacques's attention at this particular moment is just pie
in the sky, because right now while we're discussing possibilities,

Jacques's gaze, buried deep behind his eyelids, is turned toward the fantasies that make up our dreams, and since even his face is under the comforter, Jacques's body is nothing more than an ill-defined, slumbering form beneath the covers. What's more, it's so motionless that it could be a fake, some trick, like when a character wants to make someone (his enemies, for example) think he's lying there and puts a decoy in his bed, a big lump of thick clothes, pillows, who knows what, so that if the enemy comes in and gives a quick look around, he'll think the other person is there, whereas, no, not at all, the other person is getting away, gaining time for every moment the decoy works, though it will certainly end up being discovered, but meanwhile he's taking to his heels, escaping into the countryside, well really you never know, maybe Jacques, tired of being the hero, embarrassed at being always looked at, has said to himself, Okay, I'm going to take advantage of going from Part II to Part III, the ellipsis there, the page being turned, and stuff some pillows in here to take the place of my body under the covers, and when the scene opens on my bedroom in the morning they won't be able to tell the difference in the half light, they'll think it's me sleeping there, naturally, because it's my room, but as for me I'll be safe from being looked at for a little while, I'll be off doing as I please or not doing anything at all if it suits me, I also like not doing anything a lot, no longer subjected to the pressure of whatever it looks like I'm doing, but in the secrecy of hours going by without a thought; I won't have to behave either well or not well because being somewhat sloppy suits me fine, released from performance I'll just peacefully smoke my cigarette on the doorstep while I wait for the reader to notice my stratagem and come back down from the bedroom, saying Well, hey, that's where you were (because by this time, after so many pages, the reader would be justified in addressing me in such a familiar tone, so long as he doesn't give me a friendly nudge too, that would really be going too far, Jacques says to himself the same way he would say anything else), and remaining there on the doorstep for a minute, looking off in the distance with a gloomy expression, Jacques would answer, Yes, you can see that, but without irony, more with a sigh, the sentence and breath both vaguely directed at the garden, he wouldn't laugh over his trick, but rather feel dejected because it didn't last a little longer. But, of course, you don't believe a word of this, though it probably did cross your mind to wonder about this motionless shape, slightly too motionless on a morning that's really well under way, a bit too well advanced, you're easily fooled, you'd suddenly feared this possibility, but just in passing, hardly formulated, like a fleeting sense of physical discomfort rather than a phrase in your interior monologue, and just to get rid of this anxiety, which could always return, insidiously pretending to be extinguished and then reviving, But seriously! That shape is really pretty motionless! you could even persuade yourself to such an extent and get so angry at the idea that we might catch you having been fooled that you'd stomp over to the bed your fists on your hips, then both fists would leave your hips, your hands would open, grab hold of the comforter and the blankets, and then, holding them tight, with great determination, you'd pull the whole thing off, convinced that you'd find a decoy underneath: pillows, coat rolled up in a ball, but no, there's our hero's defenseless body, not well covered by pajamas because they always twist around in the night and get crumpled and ride up here or there and gape open in other spots, and our hero, suddenly dragged from sleep and not at all understanding why you're being so violent, starts to shiver, wrapping his arms around his body and then noticing just how sloppy he looks, tugs here and there on the cloth so he'll seem more presentable; consequently, to make you less anxious and at the same time keep this scene from taking place, because after all I'm Jacques's protector, that's certainly my role, I wouldn't want you to see him like this, with his hair disheveled and vexing strips of flesh showing through the rumpled pajamas no longer doing their job of politely covering a body and behaving, if you will, like something you'd throw on at night just in case you might run into somebody in the hall (even though wearing a bathrobe over your pajamas is to be recommended when you leave your room, a nice tight waistline and your body well disguised beneath the checked wool cloth you don't have to worry), we're going to have Jacques, not necessarily awake, turn over in bed, oops, the body's alive, you still haven't had enough time to make sure that it's really Jacques, his face, hidden under the comforter, hasn't yet appeared, but at any rate, it's a person and though someone might cheerfully put pillows or folded up clothing in a bed in his place to fool us, he'd be a lot less willing to put a person there, no, anyhow, that's my opinion, and it's yours too, so now your mind is completely at rest; very unlikely that that's Constantin, for example (really, you're extremely suspicious, your mind keeps racing even when it all seems settled), in on the conspiracy, You'll take my place in the bed, be careful that the comforter covers your face well, meanwhile I'm off to dillydally a bit where the reader can't see me, we have a hard time imagining Jacques explaining this to Constantin and then getting him to agree and then offering him his bed, which, after all, is his last refuge, eh, his little cave, all his own, hard to imagine that, you get rid of that notion and think you vaguely recognize the color of that clump of hair emerging, a sort of tuft straying outside the comforter, at first just a bristle but then a great mass of capillary anarchy, that's not Constantin's mousy gray, but then of course you don't know everybody else in Abbeville, Jacques could have chosen a man who looks more like him than good old Constantin with his easy talk and cap always screwed down tight on his head, except, most likely, when he's asleep, a man with brown hair like his, one who would make a better impression, who would drag the joke out so Jacques would get to smoke not just one cigarette on his doorstep but several, he might even have the time to take a little walk, now you see him now you don't, off toward the river where, among the birds and rocks there he can stop deploying the monologues of a hero in a novel and just think whatever comes to mind, unimportant things the way you do in real life where it's completely natural and very restful to have thoughts of no particular magnitude or charm and you're perfectly content with being such a dull person, it's good for your blood pressure and improves your heart rate.

Anyhow, you should have more confidence in yourself, why would Jacques play jokes on you when you've come along with him so nicely up to this point and he's happy to have you with him, discreet and attentive as you are, warming his heart in his humble bachelorhood where, precisely, he has no one to accompany him and he hopes you're single as well (I really mean: maybe you have affairs, but at heart see, you're single) because you'll take better care of him, he thinks, you'll be more touched by his trials and tribulations and you'll be better, more sincerely able to hope for and concentrate on his happiness, and this is why it's certainly Jacques who's asleep there, what were you thinking, it's Jacques, trustful and sleeping the sleep of the just, even, listen, snoring, isn't that Jacques's snoring, the rhythm, the breathing, isn't that the snoring of a man who dreams about caves, and in his dream holds a club and wears the skins of animals, isn't that snoring right out of prehistory? You sit down on the chair, you rub your forehead, you've been through a lot of excitement with all this anxiety, you relax a bit, you stretch, you're comfortable there with Jacques snoring, which, come to think about it, could cause you some annoyance, those snores, not a charming sound, they could make you nervous (it's like there really is some huge animal ready to leap out of its cave specifically for the purpose of pouncing on you and ripping you to shreds in no time at all, you, running across the savanna, tripping over roots, breathing hard in a countryside that's too dry—your throat burns—or too damp—you're suffocating, so much water in the air—and it, the animal, in three leaps having caught up with you now beginning its carnage), but, well, actually they've always had the power to calm you instead, so there you are, waiting in Jacques's snores the way when you were little and safe inside your grandfather's snores as he napped sitting on the coarse cloth of the sofa, you were waiting for the nap to be over but you weren't impatient, understanding what the nap was and experiencing it and taking advantage of it to develop thoughts of your own, thoughts that knew they were unfolding in the shade of this nap, as if they were under some great plane tree that was protecting them.

You stay sitting there, in our hero's noisy breathing, in the room's half-light, in the hatching made by the outside light coming in (as opposed to the naps you were talking about just now, when bright daylight came in from the side and onto the sleeping man, all the light from the garden was pouring in through the glass door and landed there while the sleeper made a screen for the light, a sort of huge mountain in blue wool sheltering you on his left in the shadow he cast, your eyes wide, you were counting on his waking up because then you'd have somebody to play with and you could go out in the garden to play Indians, because it was always Indians you used to play together, parading and dancing around imaginary fires), counting on his waking up and speculating on the event that must be coming, that is obviously brewing in this wonderfully lit bedroom where light and shadow are so skillfully and prettily arranged that it just has to be in preparation for said event, there you are, deleted by the light a bit as in one of Man Ray's photos, as if the merging light and shadow have thrown a veil over you, with its design, its hatching, its subtle geometry hugging the contours of your body, and at the mercy of your volume breaking its lines. And in the same way, in the rest of the room the conflict is replayed between the projection of shadows, rays of light, and the volume of objects making the lines wavy, or breaking them into segments depending on how they meet, and, looking at this damask, you sometimes fix your attention on following the trajectory of one particular ray, but other times, treating it like a piece of cloth, you stare at a whole area, and make some observations to yourself concerning its design. The minutes spent in contemplation go by and meanwhile the light changes, so that the task of observation, which probably hadn't exhausted every area of the room or studied each ray of light in detail anyhow, is endless, and what you're watching in short are the minutiae of infinitely mobile light in the room: the ray just now striking the foot of the bed and what's more rather strongly, bright no doubt because of the varnish on the wood it's made of, lifts imperceptibly and comes to bury itself in the flat flesh of the comforter where it stays for a bit, though still continuing to make some progress, and suddenly plink splashes onto the eyelid of our hero who feels it through the musculomembranous veil and consequently opens an amazed eye, instantly closing it because the shaft of light on his naked eye actually hurts, groaning, moving around a bit in bed, opening both eyes this time and then closing them the same way, fluttering his lids in the variously distributed morning light that we've been watching, he's making some progress toward keeping both eyes open, gradually reducing the amount of time they're shut until they take on a daytime rhythm, lids only blinking to keep out dust or moisturize, but that's all, and now our man's well awake though still horizontal with his gaze meandering across the ceiling, following the sinuous line of the moldings, going slightly down toward the wall and the cross-hatched and trapezoidal figure on it now, continues sideways toward the door, moving over a picture frame where the light reflecting in the glass conceals the portrait it covers, then onto a bare, opaque fragment of wall, and then all of a sudden, Leaping Lizards, catches sight of you, our man jumps, he mustn't look like he's vegetating, How long have you been there, good lord, he sits on the edge of the bed, a hand on each thigh, his heart beating fast, his pajamas approximately the way you'd expect, higher on the left ankle than on the right, actually riding up slightly on the right calf too, while the line of his shirt buttons isn't straight at all, really not the least bit straight, we could go on for a long time on the subject of the sinuous line that's almost riverlike except for the fact that it's vertical. Our man rubs the nape of his neck, starts vaguely to rearrange his tousled—that's the only way it could be—hair between his index, first, and ring fingers while his thumb and little finger, totally uncooperative, still point straight into the air, and he wonders regretfully, Why did I say Leaping Lizards, sorry for the not-very-epic lexical register of his first interjection, And besides, who thought up that leaping lizard business anyway, the way you try to get your thoughts rolling when you wake up, loosening them up on unimportant subjects, It wasn't the best choice given my morning toilette, some men call their penises the lizard, he's done with rubbing his neck and using his hand as a comb, he scratches a thigh with his index finger and concludes, Must remember to look it up in the dictionary (he'll probably forget. And don't let it bug you, leaping lizards comes from—well, just go look it up for yourself).

Despite the lexicological interest of these reflections it would be in good taste to change the subject of his monologue, or so our hero tells himself as he puts on a large, periwinkle-blue dressing gown with a hood (or else, if you prefer, a navy-blue, corduroy bathrobe with a chamois-colored shawl), always taking pains to be up to what lies ahead, and at the same time looking at the room rather happily, his hand on the doorknob and casting a final glance around it before opening the door to go down to the kitchen, and covering up the nighttime puffiness as well as the layer of uncertainty and lack of self-confidence setting his features in a way that's hard to explain but visible and easily interpreted by just about anybody, with the image of tranquil happiness that would make for a worthwhile day, a softening of the facial muscles that competes with that first image (uncertainty) and ends up prevailing because not everybody gets to be a character in a story with lighting by Henri Alekan.

So, his mood given a bit of a boost by that observation, happy over the honor paid him and at any rate rather enjoying the light himself as well as the graphic nature of the play of shadows when seen in conjunction with it, our hero goes down to his kitchen with an unaccustomed optimism that he manages to be surprised by, Hey, how about that, Jacques! Well, I'll say, Jacques! His twisting staircase though not an outright spiral is set into the white masonry (test: if you feel like stretching your legs, put this book down for a couple of minutes—but come back, okay?—and go into the adjoining room and ask whoever's there what a spiral staircase is. Leaning on the doorframe for example, or possibly further into the room, say "Just what is a spiral staircase?" The other person, it's almost guaranteed, will answer literally "It's a staircase that twists like this" and make an upward spiraling gesture. If I'm right then come back), okay the staircase is set into the white masonry so that when you go down you can let yourself slide against the walls in a centrifugal motion, see, and sort of, stay with me now, as if you were on a toboggan and all that white around you were snow, and so our man voom, in his staircase, voom voom moves as if tobogganing all the way to the bottom of the descent, where the toboggan vanishes with its snowy walls, and he finds himself on the tiled floor of the hallway which is cool enough to make him notice that he forgot his slippers, Tarnation, my slippers.

So all right, one of two things, either our hero goes back up to get his slippers, struggling up the snowy ascent then coming back down but not quite as fast as just now, because you wouldn't necessarily toboggan all day long, or else he keeps on going to the kitchen, which he enters barefoot, pretty uncomfortable, his entire breakfast with a draft on his instep and around his arches so he'll catch a cold (and then be wiping his nose throughout the next chapters, you're not enthusiastic about that prospect); or else it's a joke (you like that better), he was holding them in his hand while he slid his shoulder along the white masonry, and when he touches the tile floor he remembers to put them on, sits down on the next to next to last step (the next to last, or worse, the last, would really be a bit low, legs way too bent for it to be pleasant, almost insect legs no that wouldn't do), here we go, left one then right, boyohboy I never expected to have my hero in his slippers, but he's completely at ease, comfortable in the clothes he wears around the house (the full array) and is getting ready to go fix himself a cup of coffee.

Don't believe for an instant that the impending event is forgotten, that our hero is thinking Being a hero would have been nice but making oneself a cup of coffee isn't bad either, no, not at all, the wonderful thing about coffee in the morning, in the fact of sitting there in front of your coffee and drinking it, no rush, little sips, and fully conscious of the fact that it's one of the first sensations of the day, is precisely the whole enormous reservoir of possibilities that the morning holds and that is crystallizing in that first coffee.

There are two perfectly correlated reasons for drinking slowly. First, there's your drowsiness, the body's memory of how cozy it was in bed and of how it was almost immobile before, but now must be present for its own very slowly forming present. As if, and Jacques doesn't consider this much of an exaggeration, you're reborn every day. Births are never a matter of indifference, especially when they're your own. Birth is always marvelous. So you savor it. Going slowly gives one both the time it takes to happen and time to appreciate the incredible value of coming into the world like this every time you start afresh.

The second reason is that this is precisely the time when you're weighing all the possibilities before you. This weighing yes is manageable and can be deliberate, how you'll use your time foments inside, listing what's to be done, working out a plan with only a few empty spots, assigning some to your obligations, leaving others open, getting your daily calendar straight, and then oh look here you've transposed two or three things and this goes before that yes that makes the day come out right. But there's also a weighing taking place that's more evanescent, one where you're content just feeling this potentiality while you sit right there contentedly, aimed toward upcoming events but relaxed, perfectly content, and that's enough right there.

Remember your breakfasts in the country, the oilcloth softening sounds with the very thin pieces of flannel glued on its reverse, the bowl between your two hands, the warmth, the steam, the china against your lips, the caffeinated vapor begins to wake you up even before you've started drinking, it's like you're breathing in sulfur fumes that are moving across your face to purify your skin, your mind is like a sandy beach in the morning landscape where a thousand people in their sleeping bags are just starting to move, those are your ideas getting started, dragging themselves out, oh no hurry, you're there watching them as they wake up and you find this a source of wonderment. Jacques goes about things the right way, every move he makes involves his complete concentration, he composes his still life with the blue bowl and the butter dish upside down in cool water, the knife in the right-hand corner serves as a foil to direct the eye toward the grouping as a whole, the loaf of bread is perfect, the color of the jam something to admire. Standing with his back to us, waiting for the water to boil and glancing distractedly toward the lawn through the net curtain, just to make these minutes count, he puts the finishing touches on his little philosophy concerning mornings, this thing about rebirth seems to him a relatively serious matter, how every time one goes through the motions of relearning it's like replaying a miniature version of the progress of humanity, Saint-Simon was already thinking that. Jacques pours the water into the coffeepot bearing his family's coat of arms. Yes, mornings are major events, and you move softly and gently into the beginnings they imply. You keep in mind the memory of the night still numbing your body rather comfortably, and inside this cocooning body, thought is aquiver with the idea that this is only the beginning.

II

Here's our hero having his daily swim, taking a few mostly under-water breaststrokes now you see them now you don't, then lifting his head out of the water plouft spouting like a fountain, a rather pretty curve. Our man occupies on the surface no more than the volume of a duck, from a distance his head could represent a palmiped swimming calmly along, if it weren't for his chaotic wake, something quite different from the impeccable V opening out behind an unruffled bird; no doubt you've occasionally con-templated this phenomenon on Sundays when you were out walk-ing the town park and stopped at the lake like everybody else, watching a swan on the bank busily nibbling an itch in the flurry of its feathers and farther off the orderly Vs of ducks seeming to glide along as if pulled by invisible cords (or like Japanese women in traditional dress on the silent floors of paper houses).

For the swimmer, this duck analogy is not without risk and you can see there's an anecdote coming: One morning when the river was almost frozen, old man Nadaud—but keep your lips sealed because our man knows nothing about this distressing matter—loaded his gun and aimed it at that dark ball that looked so good to eat (already envisioning the cherry glaze or the honey sauce and at the very least the scene of its being plucked at the big table where he deposited game whenever he came back from hunting) and, thanks to his clumsiness, missed his first shot, reloading his weapon and grumbling (with that one shot he saw both his skill diminish, yesterday's few evening drinks possibly having something to do with this, and the possibility arise that his imaginings of the rustic scene in which, proud as a peacock, he hovered over the table while Madame, wearing an apron over her long skirt, pulled feathers out in a great flurry as when you tear apart a pillow, would come to naught) as he moved closer to take better aim, upon which it suddenly seemed possible that the object in question had no relation with the anatine he originally thought he had identified. Bloody hell! It's . . . he took to his heels and were this another story they'd tell you he's still running.

Unaware of this danger our swimmer keeps swimming along the varied river banks to his right and left that offer two contrasting sights at the moment, on the left the tidy vegetable gardens that border the Somme and on the right the unkempt meadow grasses, that, seen like this from ground level, form a variously fringed edging that intrudes slightly on the changing sky and our man makes the diorama stream past him peacefully all the way to the moment when he'll see the chestnut tree appear.

You shouldn't imagine this as one of those sturdy trunks rising so uneventfully toward the low sky that it can even be seen as representing a certain idea of republican order (municipalities are only too happy to plant them along promenades and you frequently see them in schoolyards), no, this tree had been the victim of who knows what incident with the result that its trunk, which grew at an angle on the river bank, almost lying down, almost right on the ground, was split wide open in a deep canyon from which emerged a great many thin trunks, like those of birches, under the circumstances you perhaps should call them branches, tangling and untangling in broad tentacles that reached out into the river so that, from the viewpoint of a passing swimmer, this tree looked a lot like an octopus, a huge octopus frozen in a Pompeian pose, which didn't bode well. I refer to it as a chestnut tree because I had the opportunity to go there and observe it from the riverbank one day when spring was imminent and saw some leaf buds that were a sufficient indication of the emerging digitate leaf by which I could identify it (I'm saying "I" just to get on with things), but it certainly must be acknowledged that it didn't look like a chestnut tree, didn't even remind me of one, especially since, like today, it had been stripped of leaves and was letting its naked tentacles wave over the surface of the water, a monstrous trap and one that anybody would be concerned with outsmarting, swimming off to the side, gazing at the horizon, acting as if it were nothing at all. But our hero, for his part, always valiantly faces the ordeal and willingly swims over to bug the monster, and after he's cast a panoramic glance to make sure no one's around, addresses a few provocative remarks to it that the other takes in stoically, though deep inside there's a sort of I'll get you, you just wait, that we can tell the thing is thinking from the way it remains there in its supernaturally steadfast posture.

With a rather woeful expression on his face, two or three emphatic wrinkles on his receding forehead the torus of which is divided into two arches, *Homo neanderthalensis* stares from the opposite bank at our hero without really giving him much thought. The hairy mass on his barrel-shaped rib cage keeps the pendant formed from a bear's canine tooth from hanging quite vertically. He reaches toward the sky with his arm; the elbow doesn't lock very well, the hand on the end of it is short and broad, and stretching like this in simulated nonchalance it looks like a fan—for reasons of which we know nothing (you can't know everything) his companions have gone off with their javelins on a horse hunt without him, and he's having a hard time getting over this—then he sticks a finger in his retromolar gap, a handy position for thinking.

Our hero launches into his usual matinal verbal provocation under the white sky, blank as a page on which the chestnut-octopus is sketching an excellent likeness of inky tentacles, Jacques gives it a fine dressing down, then, having finished his tirade, does a few more peaceful breaststrokes as he starts to think about his day.

Today, after his swim, our man gets it into his head to go for a jog in the countryside, nothing very ambitious, just around the adjacent meadows, swimming has his breath under control so getting started is easier, breathing the outdoors air in and out rather deeply is one way like any other, though rather intensified and in the end quite effusive, eh, to make an exchange with the environment as drops of water begin beading his body from the exertion and making his clothes stick to his skin, his internal temperature going up he's pretty sure and his head spinning because the air is so bracing, after a moment you don't know whether it's pleasant or unpleasant, look, let's focus on this question, Jacques says to himself, breathing like an ox into the baby-blue sky and apple-green meadows, and it seems to him that the Gaussian curve that might explain all this would develop in three stages, the pleasant moment when you set the machine in motion and are showing off your body in harmony with the countryside, breathing eas-ily, moving fast enough to get some pleasure from it (this is me, me taking these panoramic shots of hell in the fields of Abbeville, moving like a supple horse, *that's me*, hmmm), then comes the stage of obvious displeasure, you're too hot, the blood beats in your veins, and you wonder if maybe you're not about to faint, you don't know if you'll be able to anticipate your limits and stop in time but you keep on going resolutely despite this uncertainty, and then, third phase, you transform this displeasure into plea-sure, you transcend it, and suddenly the effort that's never a good thing to Jacques's mind and I agree becomes, how should I put it, a sort of great soft field where you roll wildly along.

On the morning of this second chapter, Jacques notices one of the workmen busy drinking coffee at the bar of the Café des Voyageurs. The work wasn't going as fast as Jacques would have liked. Night put a halt to their research and the workmen were often busy somewhere else during the day. And now here's Nicolas Halattre, seen from the back, drinking coffee, he's a new man who's been working for a short time at the Moulin-Quignon quarry. So, Halattre, says Jacques, putting a hand on his shoulder,

Do you like it at Moulin-Quignon? The other man, without taking the cup from his lips, having just barely avoided being splashed by his coffee when Jacques delivered this paternalistic backslap, motions vaguely to indicate that it's okay. Jacques orders a coffee for himself and they drink like this, parallel, in a community of gesture that dispenses with dialogue and takes the place of it. Finally Jacques says, Even so, it's irksome for it to drag on so long, when are you going back to the quarry, Nicolas Halattre wipes his lips on the back of his heavy blue sleeve and replies Tomorrow. He leaves the café.

An interior. Daylight. Jacques is still at the Café des Voyageurs. He's sitting next to the bay window and watching the silhouette of Nicolas Halattre grow smaller and disappear like on a magic lantern. Nicolas Halattre has his hands in his pockets and looks like somebody who knows where he's going. Is that why our man keeps staring there, his face turned toward the street for a long time, well after Halattre has vanished from the field, and now at the façade that's hiding him, and behind which there are roads, mountains, and valleys, you could draw them, with the quarry on the right (you can hear the sound of picks and shovels in the open air), and here, take your colored pencils, a gray one, a yellow, a brown, and a black, that ought to be enough, and beneath the topsoil, from top to bottom, fill in a gray band (you can put in the tiny shapes of broken flints mixed in with this first layer of sand), then a yellow, clayish color (you can begin drawing flints again, larger than in the preceding band), a small layer of gray then once again a yellow band, ferruginous this time (there, your turn, you put in a few teeth from an *Elephas primigenius*), then a band of black or dark brown (you use both pencils, brown and black, putting the two colors on top of each other) argillo-ferruginous sand, and there, well now, the remains of a small prehistoric man, if it were possible to find it now it would be a godsend but this is only the 26th of March and you have to learn to wait.

In fact, Jacques says to Constantin, who, carrying his morning coffee spiked with calvados, has come over to sit down next to him, tomorrow I have a meeting with a scientist from England. Constantin doesn't find this particularly important, but it was important above all to find some way of informing the reader so he won't be surprised when he turns the page.

III

Sky that you'd like to call blue but really more stormy, more a muddy sky if that makes any sense, as if you'd just stirred it up, bringing up silt and deposits from the bottom that would soon disappear, at least that's what the sharp wind seemed to promise, spinning and gathering speed before chasing it all away for us, piles of clouds at the moment still stuck together in a gray-brown conglomeration that you can only hope will dissipate. The third chapter of the third part begins by describing the English scientist on his boat, because there's no reason, after all, for us to see things only from Jacques's viewpoint. The scientist casts a glance at the sky, which is by no means inspiring, then, in a vertical rotation of his eyes, toward the sea reflecting it exactly, and takes his pocket watch out, double checking, departure would be imminent. The gold watch picks up a gray-white reflection as he does so and then goes back into the shadow of his pocket.

Boats are rather romantic, the scientist thinks to himself. That's understandable. He's only seen boats on the line of the horizon, gliding horizontally like paper models moved by cords. Or else ones returning to port when he'd be on the dock waiting for a visitor, moving his head like a bird's to try and see over the shoulders of this or that person if the visitor was indeed leaning on the rail and looking for him as well on the dock, every time it was the same suspense, until clink, in accordance with magnetic dynamics the eyes of the two meet (of course, it occasionally happened that only one of the two would catch sight of the other's silhouette, or else that one would do so after the other, because I really am aware that these are things that don't necessarily happen at the same time). Or else ones that are leaving and he'd be on the dock like before, surrounded by people waving their white handkerchiefs like doves. He'd be stoic in the midst of this aviary but his body torn in two because departures are terrible. *Nevertheless*, you could also go down to the docks when there was nothing better to do (or even after a full day's work) and watch the boats depart with no one you knew on board. As for those moments, they were rather more agreeable and in the eyes of our scientist contained a kind of poetic essence, he'd sit on some old forgotten trunk and listen to the sound of the water, the wonderful engine, the huge creature maneuvering awkwardly in order to get out of the harbor, and think ahead to its incredible destinations, imagining guess what, yes of course palm trees hundreds of them beneath which people must be smoking pipes and thinking about home. It didn't last. He stood up suddenly, his body not torn exactly the same way as in the earlier instance, but run through by a little arrow, and what if, what if on the boat that I'm peacefully looking at while producing my little exotic poem, what if just by chance, you never know, it's possible nobody warned me, but then why would they have, in this big city and all, statistically it's not at all impossible, in reality someone I knew were on this boat.

The idea is absolutely petrifying and our scientist watched the craft growing more remote with his hands out to the sea and arms slightly away from his body, a stance denoting complete destitution, an allegory of powerlessness placed like a statue on the paving stones of the port, as if playing the part of everyone you've ever left this way, taking a boat, a sort of symbol yes it might very well have been sculpted, the town council might very well have commissioned a statue and chosen from among all the proposals this allegory of powerlessness when confronted by another's departure, in this exact position, hands out to the sea. Then in his mind he went over a few people it could possibly have been, which calmed him a bit, because thoughts about something sad are always better than vague and unpersonified anxiety, after which he reflected, individual by individual, on all the reasons each would have for not leaving. Head down, he started on the road back, while still crossing off the components of his inventory, one by one, occasionally casting a glance at some shop just to supplement his list with one more man still there, and he'd arrive home somewhat dejected but still thinking this through, push the wrought-iron gate open and, gravel underfoot, go down his short lane to, come on now, go make himself a nice grog and forget all that.

But this time, HE was on the boat, that's me, on the boat, he said to himself, while behind him the boarding process came to an end and overhead the wind had far from completed its job of cleaning the sky, *As far as I can see, it's still very very cloudy*, and wrapping his arms around his frock coat, *It's so windy*, he did the best he could to fulfill his function as a passenger, presenting his silhouette to the eyes of the people quayside, a distant profile, meaning he was heading off to adventure, *that's mystery*.

Meanwhile, our Jacques is in his house preparing for this meeting, devoting himself to a few projects of classification, organizing flints and other things, then, pacing up and down his dining room, he goes back over a number of arguments that he mustn't forget to make, reformulating them, reciting them, striding counterclockwise through the room, finally stopping next to the window, close to the velvet curtain with its border of frolicking butterflies along the bottom, and watches the rain come down, all that rain.

Which isn't falling on the boat, despite the constant threat, from the rain I mean, the rain in the garden in Abbeville stays in Abbeville, while the boat sets off and our scientist remains outside offering himself to the four winds so he won't miss any of the sensations that arise, feeling a sort of tingling in his heart.

He stands there focused on the way the boat leaves shore, gives some thought to the tiny people in their scarcely larger houses, reflects on why it's reasonable to stay at home, then on traveling in general, what's difficult about it (you're leaving) and what's exciting (you're going somewhere you know nothing about) and again what's difficult about it (you're going somewhere you know nothing about) and what's exciting (you're leaving), in short everything he's feeling seems to him extremely perplexing, reversible, whirling, exchangeable, typologically like a thousand compartments where everything is both opposite and similar. He leans against the iron wall that is painted white, on his right a rectangular window makes the room inside look like an aquarium, where several passengers you can't hear from here are going bla bla bla with their mouths, which reinforces that first illusion, yes because on the one hand leaving is *the most terrible thing*, and because on the other leaving is necessary, how invigorating it is to go capering off on your way, how light you feel relieved of the great weight of affection, and because on the other hand going somewhere you know nothing about *is quite entertaining* and moreover going somewhere you know nothing about scares you, so then what, *a* minus *a* plus *b* minus *b*, the result is not much the scientist is thinking as he attempts to solve the equation of his departure, you hope he's better at paleontology than he is in the math of feelings, since he doesn't exactly excel in that field.

Calm down, says the scientist to himself—like our Jacques he doesn't hesitate to talk to himself—and he looks around here and there just for distraction, stopping for a minute on the smokestack, against the gray sky, a geometric shape with thick clouds of smoke coming out of it, he studies the clouds, the way they arrive, not continually, the way they go off into the distance, stretch out, merge with the air, he counts them, this goes on for a while, then the flag comes into his view, he's turned his head slightly and the flag he hadn't seen at first is there, lively, flying happily in the wind, it flaps and wrinkles, almost straightens out, and then folds back on itself all over again.

The English scientist watches the flag for a very long time, he monitors its every metamorphosis, or almost all of them because

sometimes one does escape him, some passing thought makes his
gaze opaque, blinds him for a full second during which the flag
takes some specific shape before moving on to the next which has
been deprived of that specificity, but let's say that even so, in the
end he'll have seen a good percentage of the shapes the flag has
taken. He closes his eyes and reviews those shapes, at first they
appear spontaneously behind his closed lids, and then he grabs
hold of them, makes an inventory, tells himself it's something to
ponder just like any other and concentrates on the matter, then his
focus softens and the shapes of the flapping flag continue to flash
behind his lids but now seem to do this completely on their own,
while other, unrelated images insert themselves between their
shapes, the ivy-covered house he's leaving behind, what he expects
Jacques's abode to be like, two or three minor events from the day
before, and then you have no idea why there's the recurrent image of an old servant carrying tea, the fat old servant wearing her
dark apron, the tin tray radiant with painted fruit, which strikes
him as odd, because when the teapot, saucer, cup, and the plate of
cookies are on it you can't see anything else, you can't make out
any part of the bunch of grapes or the orange or the cherries, the
consummate tray with all those dishes on it and him in the armchair drinking tea, as if in homage to his mother who drank her
tea that way and his grandmother as well and to his nation of great
tea-drinkers, thinks Jacques who likes to contribute uncalled-for
remarks, and so he contemplates this familial and national activity that represents for him the ultimate act, which makes him, as
an individual, fit perfectly into both his society and his genealogy,
with this thought the English scientist goes to sleep, the height of

consent, willingly adhering to the rites through which one professes I'm a member of your great group and ever so delighted that I am, reproducing from one descendant to the next the gesture of the ancestors, as if they were all the same, dozes there on the deck in spite of the wind, in spite of the noise made by the slapping flag, while over his shoulders, behind him, the English coast grows distant, softens, blurs and, there you go, completely disappears.

An old *Homo sapiens*, with his short and powerful hand, which is no doubt aided by the muscular lateral articulation of his shoulder, takes advantage of the scientist's drowsiness to paint a bestiary for us, daubing it on a vertical rocky surface that happens to be out in the open in a wind just about as strong as the one blowing onto the deck of the boat, giving us a series of caprines, bovidae, a red antelope, a large, brown elephant, *and so on.*

The English scientist is still seated on the deck, it's his first voyage, with not a bit of his national coast over his shoulder and no sign of the French shores before him, lost in the middle of the sea and not knowing what to think of it, kind of in no man's land, in French we might say he's *entre deux eaux* but it just so happens that instead of between two waters he's between two lands, a semantic void of water and sky so far from shore that it's even abandoned by the seagulls who'd followed the wake for a while and permitted themselves a few nose dives after fish stirred up by the propellers and, either in panic or physically sucked up by the whirlpool I don't know which, come to the surface, showing here a tail there a head, a fin, a bit of belly, so they (the gulls) could snatch them up and take them back to land to eat comfortably on the beach with their families who were waiting for them,

Look what I brought you isn't this a beautiful whiting Oh yes really good crunch crunch terrific terrific, and while presently the seagulls must be on shore chewing on the results of their hunt our English scientist is experiencing a sense of geographical absence that he finds very troubling because of how closely the question of where am I is linked to the question of who am I.

Luckily, in the distance before him a block of gray shadow begins to emerge and he doesn't take long to identify it as a coastline, *the French one this time,* a coast where the natives must be busily preparing to receive the boat and all the stuff it's bringing and setting up the gangway so when the passengers debark they can run one hand along the ropes and hold their baggage in the other, some of them coming back home *happy fellows* while others are setting their feet down in a strange land and confronted by the unknown and suddenly submerged in its surprising babble, *this is Calais I presume* where they make fun of your question and keep right on sounding like a barnyard and there you are Mister Scientist with your bag, which you've put in the other hand so it will take its turn sharing the strain you feel there, all but treading the red soil among the Martians, making your way in the midst of all these *little froggies,* looking for water lilies. Our scientist has now stood up and leans against the rail watching the progress of the shore as it approaches, wondering, *this Jack, did he really find something,* chin in hand, suddenly rather calm, while at the same time he's also thinking about the moving landscape, the land coming closer and the birds now back again, *French birds all right,* and engaged in the same sort of fishing as those others earlier, as if there's been some exchange of techniques from one shore to the other, common strategies (possibly they had also migrated to Africa, *the English birds and the French ones*, and met each other over there where winters are less harsh and just to pass the time of day, taught each other what they knew), and thinking too at the same time about science in general and paleontology in particular, and meditating concentrically from the larger to the smaller, about the question of flint tools, and more specifically (pursuing his subject methodically) bifaces, flint stones that have been shaped and tell us what, that's what must be established more narrowly, chin in hand still and looking off into the distance, staring at the double horizon, the material one of the coast and the intellectual horizon of the scientific task to be performed, and having a sense of being to some extent like this boat, yes, in motion.

IV

Okeydokey, says the scientist from England, holding a shaped flint stone up to his eyes, *Very interesting indeed*, he turns it in the light coming in from the garden and between two velvet curtains to splash across its sides as he offers them alternatively like this and reflects, giving a good deal of thought to the flint and everything else. On the docks there'd been the expected brouhaha and our English scientist's body had been pushed and shoved a number of times before he could escape the crowd's imbroglio, there you go there you go, using his elbows and even occasionally his suitcase with no hesitation—its bulky size came in handy for bumping people in the calf, *Sorry Sir*, anyhow it took him an awful lot of time to get through all that mess where he didn't know the rules, that crowd of actual *Homo sapiens* with their knees locked in hyperextension, their short, arched feet with the big toe adducted, its fifth toe much reduced, all striding across the paving stones in the harbor following various obviously improvised choreographies, indeed he'd missed his train *Because of all that* and our Jacques had caught cold for nothing (See, I'm coughing) on the station platform in Abbeville, I'm not going to get too worked up on the subject because the fact remains that our English scientist ended up reaching his destination, which is what's important. And it's what makes it possible now for him to be turning the biface around in the light, asking himself questions out loud and coming down hard on Jacques. *Do you really think this was done by a human being*, he runs the edge of the flint along the pad of his thumb, *and that this human being lived millions of years ago, I mean it might have been your neighbor or anybody else, that man who said he found it, those workers they might have a financial interest*, and our man sitting on the sofa (or rather on the edge of it and barely touching it with his buttocks) stiff-backed and used to hearing such talk but for once he'd hoped, telling himself that this man, because of the way he entered the room, and also something about his tie, its large bow so perfectly tied and certainly in the sort of knot a man of keen judgment would have, this man will surely see that I'm right, and his validation will give my research a new lease on life, these sharpened flints accumulating day after day, that my workmen find constantly and that are evidence of their having been here, our prehistoric ancestors, faces lowered to the task and skillfully carving their tools for you, done! and after that using them to cut animals up and feast on them, but this current *Homo sapiens* seems puzzled, all sorts of hypotheses pass beneath his vertical, convex forehead, such a graceful zygomatic arch, high cheekbones, the profile of his vertical mandibular symphysis, the base of which is in relief, and when he speaks you can clearly see his well-developed incisive, reduced canines and much diminished molars, with two cuspids and a root and a tendency to lose M3. *I can't tell, my goodness I cannot tell*, he keeps turning the flint around in the light to no avail, looking for what, for some proof to the claimed contemporaneousness of its carving, I'm used to seeing Jacques disappointed but maybe this is new to you, and looking at it from your point of view our man is in a state of collapse, our hero bringing in the remains and the others think it suspicious, did you really kill him yourself and is this really the enemy we're looking for, and the warrior holding the remains as far away as possible feeling the fool and having no proof and when he'd exposed himself to danger in combat it certainly wasn't with this sort of suspicion in mind, no, It's unimportant, says Jacques, he reaches his hand out so the other will return it to him, that incredible object, carved by Prehistoric people, *Can you imagine*, all these years of this and here's this English scientist just as suspicious as the others, makes you believe they really don't want to acknowledge those ancient times when people didn't pour first the tea and then the milk no the flint would cut right through animal hide and the flesh would appear and then there'd be feasting and not on cookies, Jacques gets a bit wrapped up in his monologue, suddenly he finds something crooked about his guest's neck tie, something unacceptable, hard to describe but it makes it, no, that bow, not quite right. The scientist sits down across from Jacques, he's placed the flint on his thigh and continues studying it there, on the dark blue background where it looks already museumized, already resting in its glass case against a background of cloth where soon there'll be the label beside it Found by the men working for Jacques Boucher de Crèvecoeur de Perthes on the Abbeville site, others will then join it in different cases, and in the end they'd be writing Collection of J.B.D.C.D.P. and everybody will understand, oh yes, we owe him so much concerning the subject of our origins, but instead, the Englishman with his leg completely motionless now calmly studies the biface against the serge of his trousers, *No proof, no way to prove it, we really are rather anxious about the mistakes we could make,* he's no longer moving, his eyes fixed on the stone but as if he didn't see it anymore, as if his gaze went right through it, not onto it to imagine the prehistoric epochs of which, to Jacques's mind, it's exciting evidence, but thinking instead about his return, the train and boat schedules awaiting him before he's back with his spinach-green wallpaper and the side table where he'll put his tea, his only feeling that of physical fatigue from the voyage and nothing more.

The Englishman projects *coming back home,* his old governess still in residence, her slow footsteps as she waits on him, the portraits of members of his family on the wall, the recent and secure genealogy that he inhabits.

He imagines them overall at first but then pictures what he remembers of the portraits one by one, his mother hanging onto her hat against a stormy background in which tree branches are twirling like the ribs of an umbrella, and her opposing this cataclysm with a smile that contains every motherhood in the world; his father dressed for the hunt and carrying a gun, with an equally tumultuous sky behind him and some partridges running by at ground level, *unfortunately* for him, however, he has his back to them, looking at the painter makes him miss a lot of prey, and, caught in the dilemma of whether to have his portrait painted or to stuff the open bag at his side full of game, he's creating a number of wavy lines across his forehead, though his wife's smile on the adjacent portrait ought to make them disappear; his grandmother seated next to a lamp, a checked blanket over her legs on which she's set down her book, on its spine golden brushstrokes the size of rice grains spell out a title you can't make out and everyone, whether guest or family member, who looks at the picture must have come up with their own reading on rainy days (*when you can get so bored*), while, staring off at the invisible horizon she imagines what comes next in the novel she's just started; his grandfather is a man you'd say is a thinker, seated at his table with a pile of books beside him and holding his forehead while, through the window, you can see hills, their bright green next to the clear blue of the sky above making a sharp and pleasant contrast with the darkness of the interior; his great grandmother as a young, rosy cheeked girl reading a letter is it from her fiancé, his great grandfather off at war (there's no picture of him in uniform) at the time writing amazing words to her that make her tremble in the hope of actually hearing them aloud some day.

They didn't go back any farther. As you went along the living-room walls there weren't any ancestors who'd come before that shy little brand-new fiancée, and nothing that became huge and hairy and apelike in the end as you went along—imagine at the end of the hallway, once past the courtier with his enormous medal and a red velvet curtain in the background, and then the behelmeted medieval character, and then the Breton warrior on his Percheron, white as the lone cloud overhead, imagine at the very end of them all, in its gilded frame like the others and decorated like them with more or less edible vegetation, apples, cherries, and an oak leaf all in painted wood, imagine the monkey smack in the middle of that frame, the last in the series and hence the first, surrounded by some scraps of food, chewing on something the other half of which he holds in, ought you call it his hand, plus what he's planning to eat next in, ought you just come out and say it's his foot, right there, and just as beloved as the others, and you'd study him with the same ignorant affection, the same puzzlement as you had for the great grandmother reading her letter with the contents you'll never know, the medieval individual whose character you have no way of ascertaining, and, having reached the end of the gallery, you'd look at him with the same benevolent gaze as you bestowed upon the others before going upstairs and back to your bedroom.

V

A hero can also feel discouraged. It's an uphill battle and though success is closer than it seems, suddenly there's such a violent setback that he doubts he'll ever succeed. Then he plops down right where he is, right on the spot, no matter what the landscape, on a big stone, on the ground itself, in the middle of a field, under a tree in the forest, and in the case of our man on his stone doorstep, while the Englishman goes off in his frockcoat and suitcase in hand toward his *English destiny,* pushing open the garden gate and vanishing, *Thank you very much you don't have to take me to the station I'll enjoy a little walk on my own*, he'd said as they shook hands, dumping our host there and leaving him to his sad monologue.

To him all the cold in Russia seems a minor matter relative to this further disappointment, which is reviving all the others to dance hand and hand around our man in a sort of sacrificial dance, closing in concentrically then moving away, eccentric, then returning to perform incomprehensible figures with their legs in a manner that in itself is so abstruse that it increases his torment.

The tree branches wave sympathetically but their gesture is perfectly useless, because our hero, his eyes misted over, sees none of these expressions of nature's kindness. Even a bird (here's an example) could alight close by and begin exuding a few comforting words and he wouldn't even see this miracle because he's so completely occupied with his disappointment and it's a disappointment that how shall I put it is closed off, impermeable to outside influences, not seeking out the similarity between this sadness and the gray of the sky, between his broken heart, right, causing him to burst into tears and the cloud that soon, as if deflated, as if pierced by something sharp, will spill the water it contains, anyhow everything you imagine he might be saying to himself and that he's not saying to himself, no, because actually he's not saying anything at all to himself, he's absolutely shattered, simply sitting there, *little froggy*, with the ruins of his collapsed hope scattered all around him.

And yet this stage, which might make us worry and think *oh*, not making any judgment but nevertheless somewhat bitterly because he's not going to succeed, this stage in which our confidence collapses with that of our hero and we share his feeling of moral fatigue at the thought of all this time invested for nothing, as far as he's concerned all those years of paleontological investigation and for us all this reading at the end of which surely we had the right to hope for a somewhat triumphant dénouement, well, in reality this stage, like the trough between waves, might itself constitute the moment necessary to success, the moment signaling its imminence, in short the breakthrough of reality itself.

I'm trying to convince Jacques of this by suddenly appearing beside him on his doorstep like a sort of Wim Wenders angel, feeling so sad as I listen closely to his monologue because his sorrow is really unfounded, so trying to use some unauthorized means—magnetic, supernatural—to force germination of the idea of imminent success inside him, Come on Jacques really you can't collapse like this, you know perfectly well that it's not rare to have a moment of discouragement before success and it gets things going again because what comes next can easily prove it was unfounded, Listen Christine, you can surely see that it's down the drain nobody wants to believe in my flints, Jacques sniffles, whimpers, it's not a pretty sight, he pulls out a large checkered handkerchief and blows his nose in it like a rhinoceros in the savanna (hearing people blow their noses I often think of rhinoceroses, I have no idea where that comes from).

Anyhow I keep on trying, that's what I'm here for in some sense, Come on my dear Jacques, tomorrow, I can feel it, what am I saying feel it, I know it, tomorrow is *the big day*, the big day Jacques, the one you've been waiting for since you were a child, wounded by others' disbelief, their hasty judgment of you, remember when you used to come home from school having once again failed to recite the lesson the way they expected you to, in the expected manner, word for word, why did they expect that, and then later, how the idea had formed, how it came to you, this hypothesis about antediluvian man, and your research, these flint tools, you know perfectly well what they're worth, you have no doubt as to their authenticity, keep at it, Jacques, tomorrow, you'll see, you're not going to believe your eyes, nor will we, we'll be utterly astonished at what you've done, Jacques, do you hear me—he's getting on my nerves, he won't budge, he's still in a state of collapse on his doorstep, with the rubble of his hope around him—Jacques, quit being so spineless (it's true you know), stop (I give his shoulder a shake, it has no effect).

After a while I give up trying to convince him (I too can get discouraged), I sit down beside him, I look at the garden, a garden rather gone to seed, I think, with the grassy parts too high to look like a lawn and with no real flowers, which I'm not sorry about, I prefer greenery, plants, and trees all right but flowers, I don't know, their colors don't always match, the little splotches they make in the landscape draw your eyes and keep you from considering the whole, I'd rather look at the whole, look at things synthetically, like that, gauge the lines of force, to the extent that I can, the perspectives, the general organization, not to mention the fact that there's a certain silliness connected with flowers, and a certain consensus on the subject that makes me not like them, same with stars, maybe because of that short story by Daudet that I read as a child, that story about a shepherd, about the couple contemplating the stars, the way the young man explains things to the girl, and the way this discussion about stars is an oblique way of declaring his love, something to decipher, to translate in the bright night, on this hillside where, side by side, the two of them are studying the constellations, starry skies bore me and the way you look up, the way you duplicate the story, Oh look there, that's the Great Bear's chariot, the onomastics involved with it all bores me too, in short, same with flowers, It's nice, Jacques, I congratulate him, that you didn't plant any, our shoulders touch, and we look at the flowerless garden, if there aren't any flowers we don't have to figure out their names and that's really nice. Really, I'm the only one actually looking—at the grass, the fence, the branches; Jacques's just inside his thoughts, no doubt remembering the scene with the English scientist, continuing his inner litany, still deeply disconsolate.

This goes on for a while, this silent contemplation, Jacques's despair, his circular monologue in which there's no progress at all. And then the narrator advises Jacques to go find some distraction, See, go to the café and talk about whatever comes up, play cards if you have a chance, act like a man who's at the café and very happy to be there, one who moves around in there naturally, with all the ease of a fish in an aquarium, the fish being flexible, see the way it can get around so well despite how closed-up the place is, zip zip, avoiding that plastic rock there with a quick movement of its hindquarters or fin (for you it would be the corner of a table), a fake plant (for you a dangling jacket), a tiny jar that pretends to be ancient (for you a pitcher on the edge of a table), a miniature pirate's chest, half-open, inside it a treasure that's starting to spill out (and for you a leather sack that's stuffed so full that it almost seems to have blisters on its surface, peaks, an unevenly stretched out barrier making you think something might finally pop right out, piercing the leather and emerging Here's *Me* grrr grrr and I'm going to eat you all alive why not); zip zip between the tables, between the people, around everything people have put in your way, the clients, the owner, the waiter, and everybody appreciates your dexterity, Oh here's Jacques, they call you over, invite you to their tables, people are proud to have you sit with them, He's got real class, this Jacques, we'd like to be able to weave through obstacles as easily as he, not running into every table and getting bruised, not cursing, remaining erect and supple, twisting and turning like the aforesaid fish, like you, Jacques, who are becoming the principal character in this group scene, see, that's something, and not simply because of your name, not simply as a notable, but because you're as handsome as a hero in a novel and because everything seems to be smiling upon you.

Fine, says Jacques.

I'm by nature pretty calm in society. My anger only erupts in private, though there are exceptions, I can certainly fight, it can happen, I get started, I zap, make some searing, stinging remark. But now here, even with you watching me, I'm finding it hard to contain myself. I'm seething inside. Usually I find my own rejoinders ridiculous, but really, what did I do to deserve this? I concoct a nice provincial notable who's not at all bad looking and dreams of being a hero, I help him realize his dream, I make myself his eulogist, his bard, his rhapsodist, and now, just at the moment he's getting hot, getting closer, really close, he sits down on his stone doorstep and refuses to get up.

I persist stubbornly. I describe the café more realistically. I quit with my fish story. I just tell him much more simply, Here, just go, you shake hands with a few people and say a little something to each one, you focus on their lives, listen sympathetically to what they say, maybe you tell a few jokes to cheer them up if need be, and you laugh at theirs, at first you have to force yourself a bit, but then it will come more easily, the heart to laugh in the warmth of the café, with the windows misted over, that's reassuring, condensation on windows, it means you're alive, you look at the condensation on the windows and then you laugh with them, you talk, loudly, too loudly, you're part of this recording turned way up high, building to a level like the hygrometric pressure in the air, it all runs together, everything is saturated, and in the noise and the convivial humidity you forget, just a bit: tomorrow is another day.

Jacques grumbles. I take that to be progress. Grumbling means he's no longer flat-out refusing, it represents some headway toward agreement, his unwillingness still obvious but now as his only refuge deep inside acceptance. Imagine (here's my coup de grâce), if this were the end and it stopped with your defeat, your giving up, we'd have come all this way with you and then here's this blockade in front of us, a hero gone soft on his doorstep, not looking at all like a hero any more, up to now he might have found it slightly difficult to fulfill his function but he did it courageously, best he could, and now he's a thousand miles from what he wanted to be, a thousand million kilometers, and here we are, stuck, not so much disappointed as slightly embarrassed, and scuffing our feet in the gravel just to make the minutes pass, and our disappointment.

Jacques says Fine, okay, right, he gets up, oh not quickly at all, to put it mildly, but as if he were lifting a stone block that weighed tons, in stages, slowly straightening his back, leaning on his arm, and then, once standing, still hunched over a little, not completely stretched out, using one hand to get the dust from the doorsill off his pants, he tugs on his jacket, rubs his cheeks, puts both cheeks in one hand, like this, as if checking the progress of his facial hair, as if wondering whether he needed a shave now or not yet, crumpling his face in his hand in short, and turning his gaze to the distance, letting his eyes wander across all sorts of landscapes, real or invented, catching the reflection of a tree, a hill over the fence, making the road that he knows by heart unwind all the way to the café, taking in a few abstract entities as well, still visibly hanging around, for example sorrow, melancholy, vague considerations, two or three opinions, some leftover resistance, a few words against me, then against himself, and the decision to go after all, rather than stay there in the coolness of his doorsill, among the rustling branches, their long lines drawn in Chinese ink against the Abbeville sky, the vision of the inside of the café, the condensation, the condensation, okay here we go, I'm on my way.

So off he goes. Now Jacques is at the Café des Voyageurs, teleported because there's no apparent necessity to describe his itinerary, always the same, and as for today pretty uneventful, no knight in rattling armor crossing the road, no iron clinking, no flashes of cling! reflected light on the silver metal, nor is Margot's silhouette passing by, nor any flowerpot falling right at Jacques's feet oof any closer and it would have been his shoulder, or worse his head, eh, You should be more careful, and the fat, clumsy woman at the window would say Oh dear Oh dear, but no, a road known by heart on which Jacques always retraces his steps, in the palimpsest town of Abbeville, where he is continually deleting his journeys, look, highlighting them, forever starting all over on the same ten sentences, and really ten is stretching it, from his house to the river, from his house to the café, and returning to the customhouse, from time to time stopping on the esplanade of linden trees so as to stay in the sweep of fragile, shimmering light through bright foliage and to exchange a few remarks with Constantin who may very well be there in this sort of pointillistic air.

But who, at this time of day, is at the café, which is a good thing, welcoming Jacques enthusiastically, Well, so, just between you and me, that was a good idea, sometimes it's so simple to please someone. At the café, okay, so it takes a bit of time, Jacques is still grumpy, bad tempered, it's perfectly clear that his mind goes blank from time to time, that he's allowing his own solitude into their interaction and not his usual little islands but outright peninsulas, not to say continents, Plaf, Plaaf, great gray zones in which he becomes absorbed, practically disappearing, and having nothing to do with the bucolic excursions he's accustomed to allowing himself, straying off the common path with microscopic flights into the underbrush where he's perfectly happy whistling to himself amid the greenery, no, instead he's sort of enshrouded in a vast gray monochrome but with none of the pleasures of a monochrome, for example being made to think, being shown a certain image of perfection, of the greatest accuracy, of a demanding aesthetic, that's how I see it, geometries excite me, but rather just dissolving into this monochrome's obvious grayness, wearing a gray look on his face as if in imitation, more and more resembling a gray monochrome himself, a character in black and white in the midst of all these people who were already colorized ages ago, and then from time to time reaching a hand out Eh oh get me out of this, and Constantin unfailingly grabs him by this hand, dear indispensable Constantin, Yes, Jacques, here, asking some simple question that Jacques can answer and thus reintegrate himself into the conversational chain, then quickly a second question at the same level of difficulty before he sinks away again, Constantin's intuition tells him it's still too early so he stays at the beginner level, and Jacques recites his faltering replies nicely, gaining in confidence as he sees a measure of success.

And then those continents shrink and grow farther apart, Jacques is more and more up to the task, just as I predicted, his cheeks growing pink and brightening, back to his old color, his own voice, and sometimes even taking the initiative, setting off on some subject of his own, off we go, and the company at large happily picks it up, jostling each other, arms uplifted and clamoring after it and then, wait, Firmin has it, he's answering, his voice is stronger than the others and this time he's the one who takes off with it, then passes it again, avoiding his contradictor and sending it underhand to Justin who catches it perfectly, takes it further, laughing heartily, then Justin rolls his eyes looking all around, anxiously deciding which member of the group he should give it to, maybe . . . but he's a little far away, or then maybe . . . you can see him hesitating, Constantin takes advantage of this and steps into the breach with a phrase that concludes the game, getting the upper hand, a witty victory, Justin just sits there, empty-handed, stunned, his subject snatched away, Jacques gives him a little pat on the back to make him feel better, now he can be concerned about somebody else, it's all going well.

The group makes a unanimous decision to play a round of cards and they go sit at the largest table, Sir, something to drink, the owner serves them all, they are wonderfully distributed around the table, each has his own way of sitting, the dealer with a cigarette stub at the corner of his mouth shuffles the cards, bending

two piles (the cards' shiny backs up to show their mark) then forcing them to face off so that the two beasts absorb each other until
there's only one, this battle takes place several times, each time
with the same result, Jacques watches this (if I may say so) as if he
were making a nature documentary, showing a ritual struggle in
the savanna, in the clearing represented by the table and marked
off by the players' hands, some of them crossed, really tightly engaged, in a knot, fingers so mixed together that you think pulling
them apart might pose a serious problem, others with one hand
placed on top of the other, waiting more calmly, or else lurking
in that position, sometimes one hand on a forearm and the other
hand, as a result, all alone and held out against the wood, while
in the center the two whale-toothed combatants go at it merci-
lessly, still in their reciprocal absorption but finessing the element
of suspense, because it can happen, ah yes, that one card escapes,
one part of the animal becoming autonomous to wander off, oh
not very far, before the dealer's hand, ringmaster in the skirmish,
none too proud of having failed in its duty, recaptures it like a
lion-tamer, Jacques, a good spectator, observes the scene. I think
we're out of the woods.

They start the game, each man surrounds himself with an invisible bubble that no other person can enter, their bubbles bump
without bursting, you'd say the walls were elastic, I pass. At a certain moment Jacques gives me a little sign, with his hand or head,
meaning, See Christine, I've perked back up, ready for the on-
slaught, here with all these people, Constantin and his friends, I'm
fooling everybody, I seem plenty jolly, I don't think they suspect
anything, I'm doing what you told me, and insha'Allah, eh, I'll get

my recognition if God wants me to, he goes back to his game, draws from the pile, studies the card carefully, plays the best he can, assuming the same gangster face as the others, because that's the way it is, a gangster veneer comes easily to faces in card games, don't ask me why.

Then, a great stroke of luck, Margot pushes open the glass door of the Café des Voyageurs. Jacques hasn't seen her this whole week, not since they came back from their trip, finger to lips (Margot's finger, Margot's lips) she tells him shh and goes straight to the bar where she orders 1) milk with grenadine, 2) a lager shandy, 3) coffee with lots of milk, 4) a little glass of noisette, 5) a Rivesaltes (cross out any choice you don't like).

Seen from the back, waiting for her order, she's wearing a flowered dress that peeks out from under a blue wool coat, her chignon came slightly undone while she was walking and Jacques's eyes become lost in her chignon, her blue wool, So are you playing or what. Yes yes, he plays, badly, his mind somewhere else, in the jumble of Margot's hair, and begins to lose, it's delicious, Margot brings her drink over to sit down at the adjoining table, facing the group of card players, Ah, no cheating, says Justin, who's always afraid of cheating, and that his cards will be squandered in some reflection where Margot could read them, No no replies Margot, sipping her milk with grenadine (her lager shandy, her coffee with lots of milk, her little glass of noisette, her Rivesaltes, whichever you prefer, but preferably the same as before, required for realism).

Jacques is sort of floating in happiness, surrounded by his village friends, wearing his gangster face and with his ladylove close by, playing cards, a kind of regressive game, recalling for him his prenatal state, we'll take it further, he's swimming, the water is 30°C, 86°F, transparent, he's floating on his back beneath a peaceful sky, he lets himself go, just moving his hands from time to time, that's all.

At a certain moment they pause, the dealer again begins his animal struggle in the center of the table, Jacques turns toward Margot, puts a strand of her hair back onto her chignon, he holds the brown strand between his fingers like a nugget in the fingers of a gold digger who's spent his years in the presence of this river and suddenly picks up in his sieve the means to make his days more beautiful, Jacques has a sweetness to his nature, sweetness that's only evident when Margot is there.

At the end of the chapter maybe he'll walk back with Margot, in the darkness that always comes early in the winter, in all the sky's dark blue, down muddy paths.

Beneath their feet you hear the crackling of twigs, and all sorts of insects and little animals going about their business in the thickets not far away, creating an audible notion of danger in your minds, constructing a threat that is all the more effective because it has no specific content, or maybe just the vague notion that it all might come out and pounce on you and that's why Jacques is protecting Margot with his presence, his protection being just as vague as the danger he'd be keeping away, but felt in the same irrational manner in the nighttime countryside, and Margot walks along in the shadow of her protector, even if there's no shadow, or nothing but shadow, or possibly one thrown by the moon, there you go, in the shadow projected by the moon: Jacques's silhouette in his frock coat, taller than she, and providing her with an immense shield, a mobile tower, against any attackers, so that she's calm, with just enough of a shiver to heighten the flavor of it all, just the slight resistance of a fear that refuses to go away entirely, just the tiniest, not-especially-unpleasant pangs, you know, as they make their way through the country night.

There's a moment when a puddle maybe, a minuscule ditch, anyhow when something would make Margot lean on Jacques who'd give her his hand, helping her over it, the way he did on the pebble beach in Mers, and we can't be absolutely certain how much semantic depth to assign to this gesture, what it might hold, offered and accepted, other than aid, nor what the darkness adds to it or the flashes of milky light enlivening fragments of the scene, or the muddy splashes on Margot's ankles.

Is it the violent interaction of the dark blue and the lunar light, this muddy disorder, the solitude of the two of them in the midst of shifting scenery, surrounded by bitter cold, you'd certainly like for Jacques to take advantage of this moment to rip off Margot's cloak, her flowery dress, her underwear, Margot all very pink in the winter night, all trembling in the moonlight, with her hundred thousand little hills of goose bumps, so he'd wrap her in his own frock coat while still wearing it, giving her very little room to move, and for example a backside might stick out, a thigh, the skin would catch the moonlight suddenly, you'd certainly like for him, foaming with emotion, to kiss her on the neck, and squeeze a breast while we're at it, holding it tightly in his hand, there, the whole breast, then the nipple oh oh oh erect with cold and desire, the other hand holds her waist, the first hand, what would you like the most, going down down oh god and still going down to hmmm it's sweet it's delicious it's all warm, Jacques, finally touching it, would be weeping, our hero in tears in the country, I've waited so long, just plain sobbing, falling to his knees, overcome with happiness, and actually his mouth right at the level of how you go about it, whereas they're just walking side by side, each with his or her own thoughts, which, mind you, may not be all that different from yours, but anyhow, from there to . . .

Safe and sound and Jacques is on the threshold, you know what thresholds are like, Good-bye Margot, see you soon, just barely touching her hand, See you soon Jacques, and Margot's body whoosh vanishes into the house and bang is hidden by the door.

VI

The next morning, as we catch our hero with one arm in his frock coat and the other still exposed, groping around to find the sleeve's opening (never something easy, remember your own problems tangling with linings that are too slippery, jackets all in a twist, so hard to make your arm slide into the armholes that you'd think they're almost hopelessly blocked, and even worse when someone holds the piece of clothing behind your back and the first arm went in just fine but the second one, well there's nothing to be done and you're twisting it awkwardly in every direction trying to find the opening, you'd think the sleeve had been sewn shut on purpose and that this is a trick, a practical joke, until the other person, who's now a little tired of holding the coat, guides you, takes hold of your arm, If I may take the liberty, and sends it in the right direction, well anyhow), so this morning when he puts his overcoat on the way he ordinarily does, no more or less skill-fully than usual, there's a special breath of air in the room, a sort of quiver emanates from Jacques's body, as if conditions inside him were causing minute changes in the flow of molecules compos-ing the air outside or in the dust sparkling in the shafts of light entering through chinks in a shutter, and now moving around in a completely different manner, as if driven by this inner condi-tion, as if pushed and shoved, not merely by the ordinary action of getting dressed, which necessarily does cause some disorder in the arrangement of the dust (corpuscles hanging there—some of them going their merry way while others laze around phlegmati-cally in the air at almost zero velocity before the action throws them into confusion) and molecules of oxygen, nitrogen, and ar-gon ordinarily orbiting tranquilly through the room if one were not there, just going along at their own tempo without changing their itineraries, not just that, not just this spurt of photons shifted around by arms, by cloth, like a sail gathering them up and forcing them to flow around in all sorts of ways, but like there's a subtler, more secret impetus radiating, in short, thanks to a kind of inner excitement, thus chemically changing what lies outside, making this ordinary scene of getting dressed before going to town, where no doubt all sorts of social obligations await him, take a particu-lar turn, and you can easily see, no need to add a musical score, something we'd have to call suspense beginning to appear.

Because what is this thing that's getting ready to happen, some-thing our hero can sense with a premonition strong enough to change the atmosphere of the room, that's the question you're gradually formulating to yourself, beginning to feel some turmoil

yourself, rather like our hero's, simultaneously pleasant and unpleasant, but the unpleasantness, how shall I put it, is part of the
pleasure, because look, it seems more and more clear to you that
there's about to be some event and will the nature of this peripeteia
be happy or unhappy and will our hero be able to survive it he
who of course has conducted battles in the past, lurched skillfully
around on the wooden decks of boats under the threat of pirates,
yes waged war unwaveringly but who also is such a dreamer by
temperament (at this point you're feeling somewhat condescend-
ing), so introverted, so absentminded, perhaps because he talks
to himself so much that the event could turn into a comedy, a
burlesque pratfall, his foot uh-oh in a hunter's trap and the body
of our hero plop into the underground pit where he stays two or
three days in the shade of the leafy branches concealing it and
that apart from the main hole are still all around it and he can't
get back out because of his badly twisted ankle and maybe even
· a broken leg, three days later our hero, emaciated with hunger
and exhausted from the sleepless hours and his body thoroughly
caked with mud, is finally discovered by some poachers who
make crude jokes at first but then suddenly get nervous Oh but
look it's our Customs Officer, taking off head over heels before
he recognizes their faces, and so on, with him rotting there a few
more days before some good, decent fellow out for a walk comes
along, that does the trick, our hero saved, bathed, rubbed down,
put back on his feet in clean clothes and fed, It's okay, Are you sure
I'll walk home with you if you'd like, and our man, still weak and
still slightly wild-eyed on the arm of his savior, nodding—Well,
since you're going that way.

Or maybe even worse (you haven't run out of possibilities yet), no passerby out for a walk and our man stuck in his muddy cache and seeing no way out, and his fingers grasping at the crumbly walls in vain, and his fingernails all black, and finally tearing out some roots for sustenance, and weeping with rage yes weeping because he's so powerless, and when night falls and the sky is dark blue and the moon clearly delineates its crescent, thinking about his life and saying all that for this and weeping twice as hard yes because in the nineteenth century men aren't afraid of crying, and you have to admit he has good reason, Jacques Boucher de Crèvecoeur de Perthes, this is too ludicrous he wails, what a miserable dénouement in the chronicle of my life if one day there's someone who wants to write it, what a pitiful outcome, and he's expecting one of you, dear readers, to finally make up your mind, take the train to Abbeville, come on, you can certainly find a slot in your schedule, you get off at Abbeville, first you go to the tourist office and reserve a hotel room for the night and then you set off to comb every inch of the Eu forest in search of the trap, and there they are, the uncalled-for leafy branches, the opening to the trap, you bend down over it, There you are poor friend, he can't get over it, is already overflowing with gratitude, how are you going to go about this, you've forgotten your climbing equipment or even any sort of equipment at all and you're not very good at improvising, Grab hold of my arm, there, he hangs on, you almost fall in there with him, Watch out, you start over, you brace yourself better, Come on come on, you're sweating, this is serious, a delicate operation, because to have both of you in there wouldn't get us very far, you're imagining endless days and nights with your hero within real reach yes what happiness, but stuck in there and risking your life too, how dangerous reading is eh if you start believing in it a little bit, Come on that's better, he holds tight to your wrist, falls back, grabs it again, uses the walls that in the end can be something to brace against even though they're crumbling, Come on, a few more inches and there we go, I'd be proud of you, reader, if there were a shred of truth in all this.

The truth, far more modest, (but what comes next, ah, what's coming next, you'll see, it's going to be really something), is that when our man has managed to put on his frock coat, whew, routinely dusting it off with the flat of his hand and taking the opportunity to get rid of a few wrinkles, because one should always be impeccable (a subliminal image of his mother waggling her finger as she uttered these words), and trembling vaguely because of the premonition inspiring him, putting on his hat but without aiming it just right at first (the hat is on sideways and balanced in a way that it's bound to fall off, and in the end it falls off, our hero catches it midair now you see it now you don't, and puts it back on his head, having performed a *chassé* to the right putting him directly in front of the face-level mirror, which allows him considerably more precision in his action, and second time around it's good), presently completely well-dressed and wearing his good hat, he engages the handle of the front door and somewhat apprehensively finds himself again on the threshold, breathes the outdoors air, air rather like any morning's air but in it you can nonetheless detect that who knows what has changed, just a few unidentified particles imperceptibly modifying its texture and giving you a sort of lump in your throat, our man in the cool of the morning breathes more quickly and the clouds created by his breath are those of a steam engine tearing along; he closes the door behind him with the vague sense that when he opens it again he'll be a different man (here his chest swells), goes down the path where the crunch of the gravel rolling underfoot seems more obvious than usual and joins him in the impersonation of a steam engine—cut to a childhood memory, the classroom's divided into two groups, we're going to make the sound of a steam engine, one group whispers Jo-sé-phin'-qu'est-c'-que-tu-fais, and at the same time the other whispers chfais-c'que-j'peux, chfais-c'que-j'peux, give it a try if there are several of you or even just two, you'll get some idea 1) of the experience I had a long time ago, which is of secondary importance, but 2) and primarily, of the acoustic sensations on this morning when our man, breathing heavily, pushes open the gate, add to this the gravel rolling around (crunch crunch crunch) and the squeaking of the gate (creak creak creak) and there you are, a few birds if you'd like (peep peep peep), rustling leaves (shshsh), a flapping wing (whoosh), and here he is, taking his first steps of the day in his street, but wait, guess what else, Constantin.

This encounter is a little upsetting for our hero, because unless the miracle is going to come via Constantin, which Jacques doubts, as do we, it's going to put off the great moment in question, but with a quick glance you estimate how few pages still remain and tell yourself come on, this is probably the last time we're going to hear tell of Constantin, you feel a vague (very vague) sadness about that, like you do when you leave people you've spent some time with, on a cruise for example, or during a semester abroad, or some such brief professional assignment when you know it's pretty unlikely you'll see them again afterward, once the thing is over, and it's a strange fact that even if there were no obvious affinities, there's something about the prospect that's almost heartbreaking because of the threat of never again that it contains, shocking just in itself before you've even examined its contents, and usually you manage to shift this abstract threat (having to do with how time passes and life goes on) onto the personalities of the individuals concerned, really very nice after all, you tell yourself, and this is why, in place of your first reaction of annoyance when confronted this ill-advised diversion, you substitute a sense of indulgence, good old Constantin and his bagful of stories, he too has kept Jacques company so we're somewhat in his debt, and if you could give him a hug right this very minute you would, Oh hello Constantin, says Jacques but he doesn't recognize his own voice.

Wow, look at you, says Constantin, nothing ever escapes him, wow look at you, what's the matter, he thinks Jacques looks pale not to mention that his voice is changed in a way Constantin could never have imagined, you'd think he was a girl, eh, big wink, in order to relax the atmosphere just in case there's been some crisis, Nothing at all, our hero makes a real effort to get his voice back, really nothing I assure you, So then, let's go have a drink together, and our man decides to put up with it and just enjoy a drink with Constantin while he savors the imminence of the *big* scene that's bound to happen. The poppy-red awning at the Café des Voyageurs is flapping as usual and you feel a certain familiarity as you enter, they sit right where you expected them to sit, on the same bench on either side of the table and over the top of the cozy curtain Jacques watches the heads go by like flyers advertising a hairdresser or a hatter.

Well really, Constantin tries this tack, he likes to force secrets into the open, well really, you seem pretty dazed, No no says the other, anyhow what would there be to confide when he doesn't himself know exactly what it's all about. As for you, mum's the word, and besides you don't know any more than they (unless . . . ?).

So then Constantin proceeds with his counter-attack, still wondering about Jacques and what could possibly be worrying him so much but generously brushing over the matter to make it less obvious, he adopts his big good old Constantin voice and tells two or three anecdotes in no particular order, accompanying them with reassuring maxims, just in case, playing out several scenarios, heartaches, money troubles, how cold the winter is, one more lover lost, money isn't everything, summer will be back, Let's have another little toddy okay, our man no more knows how to say no than he knows how to reassure Constantin about what's going on, he sits up straighter than usual, his movements are slow and he hardly says anything at all, Constantin courageously fills in all the acoustics, he almost deserves a medal for taking on our man's absent gaze and using words as if he were wiggling his fingers in front of his eyes looklook how many do you see, wiping his forehead (he's put his cap on the table where it looks so soft, almost like a cat with its paws tucked under its body, nothing but an oval mass, waiting for this to be over yet not unhappy right where it is—you might almost pat it absentmindedly, the cap, paying no more attention than that and all the while continuing to talk, you'd go tickletickle on the top of its head, and in fact Constantin does rub it with his finger, the palm of his hand, is that to mark it as his property, checking that it's really there, that it hasn't fallen to the floor, isn't crumpled under the table how dreadful and obviously unable to get back up on its own, or else because of the unavoidable confusion between the cap sitting there and an animal accompanying you everywhere you go and waiting the way it should, its expectation merging with its presence, what I mean is that you detect no sign of impatience on its part but rather on the contrary a kind of quiet satisfaction, also of interest because it passively authorizes anything you do; and obviously this is not the place, when our hero would like to get back on track toward the heroic moment that will definitely confirm him as the hero, he hopes, to start some sort of little essay on this question, but rather when you have a bit of time, for example you've closed the book, and for example you're visiting some friends who have a domestic animal and spending the evening with them, you'll be able to contemplate in greater detail how the animal usually installed nearby (even if, occasionally, it may—basically taking off like a shot—suddenly race into the living room, putting it into immediate danger of becoming a battlefield) establishes a different temporality, one belonging to it alone, essentially placid, and this flaunted placidity and the different temporality brought into the room by its body will, and this will become clearer and clearer to you, have an impact on your own temporality, some repercussion yet to be defined but we're not there yet) despite being able to see the extent to which he's failing, constantly reflected back to him by Jacques's flat, empty expression, Constantin plies his oars with renewed velocity making thousands of swirls on the surface of the water, you'd think he was dragging an entire boatful of convicts along all by himself, slaving away for sure and, by dint of so much activity, spluttering spume, sprinkles of light, splatters right in his face, but so stubbornly and with so much obvious altruism that it finally gets through to our indifferent Jacques who suddenly returns to real life, sees (taking stock of the situation once again) Constantin yelling, sweating, getting completely exhausted and clearly dangerously close to overturning his narrative boat.

Jacques puts his hand on Constantin's arm the way he'd give him a hand on the helm, let's get back on course okay you're way off I'm not grief-stricken this is a great day for me and that's why I look slightly stunned, that and, combined with it, the fear that in the end this isn't a great day at all, but a little nothing sort of day, rather paler than the others and one which, because I expected something, I'll have particularly neglected to fill and, between the fear that it's not going to happen and the fear of what it will be, I'm struck dumb, does that summarize the situation sufficiently? That's roughly what Jacques's gesture means but nothing comes out of his mouth yet and then, look, it's twisting into a smile (his eyes haven't entirely caught up, but gradually they come along and in a moment their gaze takes on a gleam and a look of mischief as his lips start to move), finally ending with We'll meet tomorrow, I'll have something amazing to tell you, the most incredible news, more amazing than any story you've ever spread around.

But as for us, we're sure we're not going to be there tomorrow, you know by feeling with your fingertips how few pages remain, not very likely that we'll be present for the scene, with Constantin literally flabbergasted and slapping his thighs and stuffing the most incredible story of the decade into his bag, let's take a good last look at his sweet face, how nice it looks, full of friendship for

Jacques, and visibly a bit worried, is this a good thing for Jacques, is he maybe going too far, but one's word is one's word so see you tomorrow, Constantin gets to his feet and stands there in a formal manner, proof that he believes Jacques, that this doesn't seem improbable, this promise of some event surpassing all those recorded so far in the fine town of Abbeville where he's worn out the soles of so many shoes, he puts his cap back on, wrong, does it again, it's looking sort of like a hot-water bottle on his head, It's not on quite right, your cap, says Jacques and for the first time in all these years, he's the one who fixes something, sets it right, checks the effect, okay that's good, they go outside and with the poppy-red awning flapping overhead they shake hands, their bodies diverge, one to the right the other straight ahead.

You look back one last time at Constantin, his cap is impeccably positioned from behind as well, you're satisfied with his looks, he has one hand in his pocket and the cloth there trembles, the hand, rather than staying nice and limp, moves around, showing how anxious he is and the scratching of his fingers on the cloth saturates the soundtrack with an element of suspense, filling it once again with air and wind, foliage shivering like flesh, and the footsteps of our hero, who, what more can I say, is walking toward his fate.

You pause here and turn the bulk of your thought to walking in general, and your own way of walking, specifically (people frequently tell you it's like you're strutting, cowboy style if cowboys even walk, so they can always tell it's you by the sound, the rhythm you strike as you proceed is like some little song always accompanying your arrival) to how you walk in the city and how you walk in the country, about the undergrowth, about the berries and the achenes (unripe hazelnuts, mulberries you've picked and tossed into baskets and turned into jam in big copper pots, checkered dishtowels, wooden spoons, all the kitchen equipment cementing childhood), about little roof-towers, about tiny town halls, tractor wheels in the paths and the mark they leave behind, about Indians who have no equal as far as reading tracks is concerned, the mud, the rubber boots, the clothes you borrowed, childhood again, the bootjack shaped like a camel at the entrance to the house, how hard it was to pull off your boot, getting your foot into the thing just right, the noise the boot makes when you take it off, the noise your city boots make on the sidewalk, a sharp, swaggering sound as opposed to the soft sound of rubber in the damp soil on a footpath, about the strong grip you keep on yourself when walking in the city, as opposed to the slow country monologues working on principles of depth and suspense, stroke by stroke a self-portrait that's usually unfinished, so much the better, about the trees on boulevards, the splashes of shade they throw on the ground, and onto bodies, about the lindens on the esplanade, about, wait, but that's certainly it, Margot's dress.

Margot's dress, our Jacques sees its royal blue speck in the distance, and makes no move to go toward it, he could run, yoohoo yoohoo, and finally, completely out of breath, get where she is, Hello Margot, that was some run, she would look at how he's panting and maybe holding his side there on the street corner, slightly bent over and his hand on his side demonstrating in one way or another how much effort he's just made and the repercussions on his body, his heart still pounds wildly from running so hard, You see, for once it's because of running he'd say to Margot who never explained anything, standing there in front of him with her mixture of indulgence and irony, caught as always between wanting to accept his arms' embrace (Jacques's silent, repeated request, the repetitious note she can read in his eyes) and wanting to take to her heels, in danger of getting out of breath herself, grabbing her side even sooner than Jacques with her heart beating a thousand miles an hour and the wind making her feel she was running far faster good-bye Jacques good-bye, not knowing whether it's play-acting or the truth, this race, does she want him to catch her, does she just want him to be afraid of losing her forever, is she pretend-ing to flee or going away for good, and what she wants godammit collapsing in the grass, because the countryside comes quickly, and weeping there, getting dirt all mixed in with her hair, chloro-phyll on her clothes, but what do I want godammit, Margot who, Jacques would be thinking, was always afraid of love and who'd loved him like nobody else, that would suddenly seem clear to him yippee and he'd take off after her, would reach the square field in the exact center of which Margot's body would be writhing in grief, twisting and turning on the grass and weeping her heart out Margot my dear little Margot oh Jacques and she would cry harder than ever but, see, in his arms now and they'd end up by kissing through the salty water of her tears, in a close-up her hair stuck together by tears getting in the way of their kisses, tongue, lips, strands of hair and the taste of salt, and here no pause ahead of the zoom out that takes in more and more of the landscape and in its center their two entwined bodies smaller and smaller, and the growing geography gives their story more fullness, the visual expansion is like an organ note, the spatial resonance of their individual love with whatever makes you able to begin to contemplate love in general, into which fit loves of your own that you're calmly projecting onto their two bodies now no larger than two grains of rice, sometimes close together, their hands linked and faces turned up to the incredible sky (you're seeing them from the standpoint of the sky above where you play the role of the gods), and sometimes so clouded over and so unclear, one grain of rice or two, you have to squint, that in the end, geographically, two individuals don't amount to anything.

So leave your Olympian point of view and come back down to earth at the crossroad where Margot walks alone with her back to our hero contemplating her from afar, though moved by the sight he doesn't turn away from his hero's path, tomorrow he'll have so much to tell her.

Once again you latch onto the royal blue silhouette of Margot, this is kind of heartbreaking, what's more she's leaving the book with her back to us, it's a pretty dirty trick to let her do this, but we can't always be together and, what do you want me to say, stories go on without you, who knows how Jacques will tell her about his exploit if there is an exploit, or how she'll take it, if she was waiting all this time for proof that he's a hero or if she doesn't think it important, little Margot still seen from the back trotting along and necessarily growing smaller with distance, the road itself forming an infinite trapezoid ending up God only knows where, the trapdoor where characters disappear with a trampoline right underneath so she won't get hurt, *bye bye* Margot *bye bye* and a reverse shot of our hero, as for him he'll see her tomorrow and confident of this he keeps going where he's going, which, it looks like, is toward the quarry, starting to leave the town, tar giving way to dirt, sparrows to starlings, and so forth, all sorts of changes mark this passage and confirm it, the figure of our Jacques, with his hands in his pockets and looking more and more determined, makes the peripeteia more and more believable, even if there's no hint of it anywhere, merely a growing assumption.

VII

The quarry is visible from a distance because it creates something like a void in the landscape, all around it there are trees, some in lines (plane trees), others in clumps (poplars), and still others marking the hillsides according to some principle it's impossible to figure out because it seems so random, but the quarry itself shows as something lacking, it interrupts the succession of vertical tree trunks and the jumble of foliage, from a distance it seems there's nothing there but suspension, a parenthesis between two fragments of greenery that can be authenticated, it's a display of hollowed-out space, close up you have to lean over right at the edge to see the chalky walls tracing colorless mountains, a sort of lunar earth both so absolutely dry and so powdery that you send thousands of particles flying and messing up your clothes as you go down into it, you're all but turning colorless yourself, and if the layer covering you is too thick you become part of the great white monochrome of the quarry and the chalk dust turns into plaster on your skin as well and soon you're undistinguishable, white against a white background, you can still be walking around, waving your arms, doing a headstand or your very best pirouette, or just sit there like The Thinker, and nobody sees anything, not a damn thing, going to all that trouble isn't worth the effort.

At this point we certainly have to tell what happened, something that slows our happy ending down somewhat: our man walking a little faster than necessary in his enthusiasm and getting especially carried away in his dreams and forgetting to match his breathing to his quickened pace, gets, it was predictable, a stitch in his side. Well, a stitch in one's side, you're going to say, not much to it, but still (remember) it can be very painful and above all it makes it necessary to slow his pace down making it somewhat chaotic, not at all like his earlier route to glory, and our hero holds his hand on this stitch he has in his side and stops (temporarily) walking because suddenly the mere effort is intolerable. Just standing there with his hand on his side, he imagines seeing the indentation in things made by the quarry, the great gap surmounted by a watercolor sky; his breath is loud, making a rapid exchange with the outside air entering his lungs and going out again, he stops thinking for a moment, submerged as he is his mind like an empty plain with nothing but his rapid breathing driving the wind across it. And then as a bit of thought returns *little by little*, our hero feels disheartened and ashamed of this little pain whether in his ribs or assimilated, which is a sign to the reader of how nervous he is when he'd have liked to seem calm and determined, his head held high and silhouetted as if, walking, he's devouring the horizon, seeming to eat away at its line with every step, now that would have made a better impression. Yes but obviously, being the hero of a novel doesn't give one a permanent exemption from stitches in the side thinks Jacques, or else I haven't landed in the right novel, that's quite possible, he's breathing less voraciously than before, he'd better think about starting to walk again but okay easy does it, don't overdo it, this isn't about not being able to walk at all.

And there you see our very unheroic hero the exact opposite of what you were expecting, holding his side like no one of note and breathing like an ox and occasionally twisting his mouth in pain (you'd almost think he was a wounded warrior, with Persians surely not far away and behind him the battlefield is smoking and History is being made), but basically it's all for a good cause since now we'll have a chance to talk some and not leave each other quite so fast, while he drags his feet in the dirt that's beginning to be gray with chalk dust blown there by the wind.

In this brief extra moment we've been given, we could, for example, recall a few episodes of our respective lives that contain this same micro-event, the stitch in your side, obviously there are nicer, more ambitious things you could remember, but we shouldn't hesitate to confide the little things, our weaknesses, our ailments while we're at it, and since we'll be leaving each other soon and won't meet up again when one or the other might blush over some confession and frankly be uncomfortable, there's no danger, it won't be possible for the treacherous person you're talking to, the one who long ago had elicited the confidence to suddenly throw it back in your face some day hahaha when you get stitches in your side like that all the time eh you can't get a word out, and you're all crumpled up and twice as hurt because they're both making fun of you and at the same time betraying your earlier confidence, I don't even have to assure you of my loyalty, which is very real, because in any event you can certainly see the occasion will never present itself, let's sit down together and you whisper in my ear the last time you had a stitch in your side, how long ago was that, were you running or just walking, were you alone or with somebody and the person walking beside you could you tell him Go slower because I've got a stitch in my side or was the situation too formal to allow you to make this confession, describe the scene in detail, ah, I can rest now that you're doing some of the talking, I stretch, I cross my arms behind my head, hmmmm, but here comes our man walking past us nearby, seeing him go by we each remember, both at the same time and without any consultation, the tortoise who just pokes along and still gets there before the hare, we'd better get up from this bench so ideally placed in the corner of the landscape where we'd taken refuge thinking we'd exchange a thousand secrets, hop hop hop in a few leaps we've bounded way past him and hop hop hop soon left him behind, we're laughing together, getting slightly out of breath, do we have time for one more story, you put your hand on my arm, How do you expect anybody to remember stuff like that, you say, I can tell you about my first memory, my first joy, my first sorrow, the color I like best and what I'd do over if given the opportunity but the last time I had a stitch in my side that's a joke no, dear reader, I'm a wee bit disappointed in you *dear reader* but I keep it to myself we're not going to have a falling out in these final yards, let's walk arm in arm instead there that's good I can sort of feel your elbow in my ribs but at least we're united for the final stretch, and our hero dragging his feet and still the wounded warrior, whether Greek or Mede I can't tell, sweating with the effort, hand on his side, scuffing the ground with every step as if he's about to fall, sort of keeping his balance as if suspended just above the earth by his long but slow stride, our Jacques Boucher de Crèvecoeur de Perthes, definitely in bad shape, a sort of marathon runner in the final yards, who miraculously will soon be home free, but we don't know that yet.

Imagine here the crowd of reporters bzzbzzbzz like a swarm, war journalists, their mikes stuck out there on booms, cameramen all running around, So Monsieur de Perthes knowing that any minute now you'll become a hero how does it feel, and there he is still sweating away, unable to answer, his hand still on his side and hoping that a wave from his other hand expressing his annoyance will get rid of the swarm but no, Jacky-boy is coming to you live, and since there's no response, the *voiceover* fills the time by describing the situation in exalted terms, Dear Viewers you are seeing live and direct our hero walking toward his destiny, toward the imminent event in store for him within this very quarry where it lies hidden, preparing to burst forth and bring him nothing less than fame, fame I tell you tadada tah to the tune of Beethoven's Fifth.

Enough now! I wave off the swarm of reporters (I'm far better at this than our man) and here he is again his silhouette somewhat twisted in the deserted countryside with the quarry close at hand and the pain persistent, maybe he'd do better to just plain stop, really sit down, ah, here we are, there's a big rock, what am I saying a huge rock suddenly visible by the side of the road, he leans his back against it, taking deep breaths of the air that's starting to be dusty now, his hand still on his side and see this pause is making me calmer, because I too, you have to realize, find good-byes difficult, we've come a long way together and I've gotten used to it; I look at the bright sky and the flat plain and the gray rock against which our man is leaning and I'm doing my best to tell the truth more precisely and more simply, I'm more than accustomed to it, that's the truth, and Jacques's stopping like this, breathing deeply and better and better, we're not worried, those things hurt but are quick to go away and soon he'll be on his feet again, this pause is an unexpected opportunity for me to thank you, yes, yes, because I know perfectly well that you had a thousand things of a more personal and tangible nature to attend to, I'm very conscious that you have your own things to do, things of the highest importance to you and you're right to consider them that important, which is why I feel truly grateful that you've offered to come along with me like this, that you didn't leave somewhere along the way, or if you did you came back, faithful to your post, seeing Mers-les-Bains with Jacques, bracing Margot in the pebbles, contemplating the forest at the end of the layover at his friend's house, vaguely listening to the rustle of Camille's dress as childhoods paraded past and carp vexing him no end slipped through our Jacky's hands reddened by the cold water with the result that he established a makeshift little philosophy of life that he's never really managed to put out of his mind, his now hard-as-rock conviction that he'd never catch anything at all and Margot the royal blue carp was living proof, he thought, and you, always, going into the Café des

Voyageurs with its comfy curtains and its red awning (incidentally, what design did you see embroidered on those comfy curtains?) and not taking advantage of Constantin's lack of attention to steal his cap, even just for fun (imagine what would happen if by chance we met again and I went to your place for a coffee, Yes, sure, that'd be nice, and what do I see on the coatrack where I'm about to hang my jacket but Constantin's cap, you're embarrassed, you give a little cough, you say It looks like it doesn't it almost the same, What do you mean almost, I look at the tag inside, Constantin marks his clothes and look there it is marked *Const* after that it's rubbed out before the *in* it's bound to be his, Constin oh yes, it's my uncle's name, you try that tack, Constin, nothing to do with Constantin you try to take the cap from my hands but I'm not fooled I keep it and take my jacket then and there and leave in a temper, it would be too bad to leave each other like that, you try to catch up with me on the path and tell me It was just . . . I'm such a fan, I love your Constantin, and you add, For me it's like a cap belonging to one of the Beatles, as for the cap I've got it stuffed away in my pocket and I'm walking fast, as I walk I get less annoyed but I'm not going back and besides there's no question of your keeping this cap, that's clear).

Anyhow your behavior concerning the cap has been exemplary and besides you've been pleasant company and we've laughed and wept, which connects us now yes and will continue to do so even after, I tell myself as a consolation, our imminent separation, while our Jacky has stopped holding his side and has placed the palms of his hands flat on the stone on either side of his body, resting as two or three swallows go flying by why am I telling you that. He keeps his head back, looking up at the baby-blue sky and gathers every last bit of strength for the great moment.

Because this wasn't just a come-on: here comes the great moment. Our hero pulls away from the rock he's used for support, he pulls together his thoughts, his strength, and the parts of his frock coat that had been spread out softly around him on the rock, he sets out again but walking in an entirely different manner than before, his body without pain, the stitch in his side poof is gone and suddenly he weighs less than a feather, he feels he's hardly a body at all just flowing through nature as it loses more and more of its color, yielding more and more to the chalky white, and what he's feeling in these final yards is above all a sense of youth returned, it's exactly what youth feels like—always engrossed in striving for the future, right? And the tension this creates is where its distinctive dynamic comes from because, at the same time that it's worried about failing, it would like the future event to arrive already and be confirmed, though since failure is always possible, even probable, youth seldom has any faith in it, so while living through the present as a still incomplete preparation, it's in possession of a force driving it to completion as well as an enormous, heavy feeling that's weighing it down with fear of failure, standing thus symmetrically divided by the energy generated by this tension, well, I'm undoubtedly simplifying things, but it's this youth in the abstract that suddenly returns to Jacques as his stride becomes lighter and lighter, almost floating, and this abstract youth of the first yards is then quickly replaced for the four or five remaining yards by a sort of existence that becomes more and more ethereal, look, there's almost a halo around it, brighter and brighter in the all-pervading chalk dust, more and more luminous, you're forced to squint, and now our man, almost invisible in the overexposure, reaches the entrance to the quarry.

There's a passage going down between the chalk walls, and one of the workers, wearing white dust like a work shirt and his face ditto as if wearing makeup and his hands looking like they have gloves on and his feet apparently in white gaiters, suddenly emerges from it, and this man (the one I named Nicolas Halattre) is carrying something equally white between the white tips of his white fingers, Monsieur Jacques, he shouts and the quarry echoes, Monsieur Jacques, you were right astounding how right you were, and that's it the thing he's displaying between his fingertips and that Jacques takes with his is the jawbone of an antediluvian ancestor, beads of happy sweat melt the chalk on his temples and their wavy, vertical lines look like pink tears in his skin, our hero's skin, who in a single second is seeing all over again his childhood and the carp slipping away and his sorrowful mother who no longer dared look at her child, making him miserable by turning her back whenever he was around her, tearing (metaphorically, she still had her impeccably neat chignon every hairpin of which drove a reminder of the aristocratic origins of their name into his skull) her hair out over the child's lack of memory, his inability to retain anything literally, even if only to recite the day's lesson, Our Jacky has no memory for anything she would sigh as she turned her back on the family in the room and studied sadly the play of the flames in the fireplace, well here's the memory of humanity itself, okay, in the hand of the aforementioned Jacques what a turnaround you might say, but he doesn't really make this connection, no, he doesn't have any feeling of revenge merely one of accomplishment, just the happiness of being able to call himself something (paleontologist, in point of fact) and to have added his little stone to the collective edifice, leaving there the name of his father (de Perthes) and that of his mother (de Crèvecoeur) in fancy letters brought together in this name he has made for himself, Jacques Boucher de Crèvecoeur de Perthes, signing it with a sort of great flourish at the end just for the sake of prolonging the name a bit farther on the line and making it do arabesques and meaning by this that you don't want it to come to an end, just like everything, and then there inside the hollow of the quarry a sort of interior music rises in our man's heart and in the hearts of the workers looking on as well with the worker who had put the discovery in Jacques's hands still in front of the others who are grouped around behind him in a semicircle like a choir and so deeply content that it's as if they were murmuring a chant come from far far away and being amplified, echoed by the chalky walls absorbing it slightly so that it doesn't come back sharp and dry like a sound bouncing off stone, but shrouded and mellow, and now here's the apotheosis, the consecration of our man as a regional hero in this invented music circulating among them, brilliant, epic in the end, calmly triumphant, please sing some music like this for yourself, there, with your lips shut tight if people are looking at you, if, for instance, you're in the metro don't be afraid, what with the car's jolting plus the conversations, no one will know this nice little music is coming from you and it's not even certain they'll hear it at all, or if you're in the privacy of your own apartment you can just go right at it, the hell with the neighbors who'll be a little surprised if they haven't gone somewhere or if their television doesn't drown out your song, go on, sing, so sing, lalalala, yes, open your mouth wider, lalalala, that's better, but it still isn't anything more than a sound from your throat, make it come from farther away, deeper, from your rib cage a sound that rises and comes out and takes over the room sufficiently, lalalala, lalalala, terrific, you can stand up if that makes it easier, yes, that's good, you're really singing, you're striking birdlike poses, like this, in the room, what a pleasure to see you, you hop around and sing at the same time, you arch your arms up over your head, you're the choir of workers celebrating Jacques, you're Jacques himself in all his excitement, you represent the very idea of apotheosis, thank you thank you, and as for me oh I sing very poorly, really, I'm not going to join in, I have this thin little voice, a little off key, what do you mean this is just among friends, don't shove me around like that, quit tugging my sleeve no really I can't, this old worn-out sweater I work in can take just about anything really but even so, I write in a heavy wool sweater in the fall and the winter and even in the spring I find them necessary, usually one sweater per book (very rarely two), always the same one and only worn for that, I keep it on to take a walk only if it's a short walk to help with concentration, always fragile, you don't realize how fragile it is, how rarely achieved, and that's why you absolutely have to call on little stratagems like this sweater kept specifically for that purpose, don't pull it all out of shape, okay here I come, I don't know how to sing but I'm coming, my voice is too small but I'm coming, there, now here I am, right next to you, I'm joining in with everybody, there, with all of you, with the workers with the leader of their choir, and all of us together, the workers, Jacques, you and me, arm in arm and lined up on stage we strike up the final song, in this scenery composed of finely ridged chalk that looks almost like crumpled paper, we go at it heartily, we resolutely breathe in the dust, what's a little more dust to us, anyone can see we're getting whiter but we keep on singing lalalala the praises of our dear little Jacquot, while in a corner of the quarry's amphitheater we catch sight of Margot's royal blue dress that has resisted the white dust, and she's waving at our man, like that, but she doesn't run off afterward, it looks like she had no intention of getting away, standing right there where he can see her, straight as a blue rod in the surrounding whiteness.

A novelist, playwright, literary critic, and theorist, CHRISTINE MONTALBETTI is also a professor of French literature at the University of Paris VIII. She has written six novels, and her successful theatrical translation/adaptation of Stevenson's *Dr. Jekyll and Mr. Hyde* has toured all over France.

BETSY WING is a writer and translator whose book of short stories and novella, *Look Out for Hydrophobia*, appeared in 1991. In addition to numerous works by Édouard Glissant, she has also translated books by Assia Djebar and Paule Constant.

PETROS ABATZOGLOU, *What Does Mrs. Freeman Want?*
MICHAL AJVAZ, *The Golden Age.*
  The Other City.
PIERRE ALBERT-BIROT, *Grabinoulor.*
YUZ ALESHKOVSKY, *Kangaroo.*
FELIPE ALFAU, *Chromos.*
  Locos.
JOÃO ALMINO, *The Book of Emotions.*
IVAN ÂNGELO, *The Celebration.*
  The Tower of Glass.
DAVID ANTIN, *Talking.*
ANTÓNIO LOBO ANTUNES, *Knowledge of Hell.*
  The Splendor of Portugal.
ALAIN ARIAS-MISSON, *Theatre of Incest.*
IFTIKHAR ARIF AND WAQAS KHWAJA, EDS.,
  Modern Poetry of Pakistan.
JOHN ASHBERY AND JAMES SCHUYLER,
  A Nest of Ninnies.
ROBERT ASHLEY, *Perfect Lives.*
GABRIELA AVIGUR-ROTEM, *Heatwave and Crazy Birds.*
HEIMRAD BÄCKER, *transcript.*
DJUNA BARNES, *Ladies Almanack.*
  Ryder.
JOHN BARTH, *LETTERS.*
  Sabbatical.
DONALD BARTHELME, *The King.*
  Paradise.
SVETISLAV BASARA, *Chinese Letter.*
MIQUEL BAUÇÀ, *The Siege in the Room.*
RENÉ BELLETTO, *Dying.*
MAREK BIEŃCZYK, *Transparency.*
MARK BINELLI, *Sacco and Vanzetti Must Die!*
ANDREI BITOV, *Pushkin House.*
ANDREJ BLATNIK, *You Do Understand.*
LOUIS PAUL BOON, *Chapel Road.*
  My Little War.
  Summer in Termuren.
ROGER BOYLAN, *Killoyle.*
IGNÁCIO DE LOYOLA BRANDÃO,
  Anonymous Celebrity.
  The Good-Bye Angel.
  Teeth under the Sun.
  Zero.
BONNIE BREMSER, *Troia: Mexican Memoirs.*
CHRISTINE BROOKE-ROSE, *Amalgamemnon.*
BRIGID BROPHY, *In Transit.*
MEREDITH BROSNAN, *Mr. Dynamite.*
GERALD L. BRUNS, *Modern Poetry and the Idea of Language.*
EVGENY BUNIMOVICH AND J. KATES, EDS.,
  Contemporary Russian Poetry: An Anthology.
GABRIELLE BURTON, *Heartbreak Hotel.*
MICHEL BUTOR, *Degrees.*
  Mobile.
  Portrait of the Artist as a Young Ape.
G. CABRERA INFANTE, *Infante's Inferno.*
  Three Trapped Tigers.
JULIETA CAMPOS,
  The Fear of Losing Eurydice.
ANNE CARSON, *Eros the Bittersweet.*
ORLY CASTEL-BLOOM, *Dolly City.*
CAMILO JOSÉ CELA, *Christ versus Arizona.*
  The Family of Pascual Duarte.
  The Hive.
LOUIS-FERDINAND CÉLINE, *Castle to Castle.*
  Conversations with Professor Y.
  London Bridge.
  Normance.
  North.
  Rigadoon.
MARIE CHAIX, *The Laurels of Lake Constance.*
HUGO CHARTERIS, *The Tide Is Right.*
JEROME CHARYN, *The Tar Baby.*
ERIC CHEVILLARD, *Demolishing Nisard.*
LUIS CHITARRONI, *The No Variations.*
MARC CHOLODENKO, *Mordechai Schamz.*
JOSHUA COHEN, *Witz.*
EMILY HOLMES COLEMAN, *The Shutter of Snow.*
ROBERT COOVER, *A Night at the Movies.*
STANLEY CRAWFORD, *Log of the S.S. The Mrs Unguentine.*
  Some Instructions to My Wife.
ROBERT CREELEY, *Collected Prose.*
RENÉ CREVEL, *Putting My Foot in It.*
RALPH CUSACK, *Cadenza.*
SUSAN DAITCH, *L.C.*
  Storytown.
NICHOLAS DELBANCO, *The Count of Concord.*
  Sherbrookes.
NIGEL DENNIS, *Cards of Identity.*
PETER DIMOCK, *A Short Rhetoric for Leaving the Family.*
ARIEL DORFMAN, *Konfidenz.*
COLEMAN DOWELL,
  The Houses of Children.
  Island People.
  Too Much Flesh and Jabez.
ARKADII DRAGOMOSHCHENKO, *Dust.*
RIKKI DUCORNET, *The Complete Butcher's Tales.*
  The Fountains of Neptune.
  The Jade Cabinet.
  The One Marvelous Thing.
  Phosphor in Dreamland.
  The Stain.
  The Word "Desire."
WILLIAM EASTLAKE, *The Bamboo Bed.*
  Castle Keep.
  Lyric of the Circle Heart.
JEAN ECHENOZ, *Chopin's Move.*
STANLEY ELKIN, *A Bad Man.*
  Boswell: A Modern Comedy.
  Criers and Kibitzers, Kibitzers and Criers.
  The Dick Gibson Show.
  The Franchiser.
  George Mills.
  The Living End.
  The MacGuffin.
  The Magic Kingdom.
  Mrs. Ted Bliss.
  The Rabbi of Lud.
  Van Gogh's Room at Arles.
FRANÇOIS EMMANUEL, *Invitation to a Voyage.*
ANNIE ERNAUX, *Cleaned Out.*
SALVADOR ESPRIU, *Ariadne in the Grotesque Labyrinth.*
LAUREN FAIRBANKS, *Muzzle Thyself.*
  Sister Carrie.
LESLIE A. FIEDLER, *Love and Death in the American Novel.*
JUAN FILLOY, *Faction.*
  Op Oloop.
ANDY FITCH, *Pop Poetics.*
GUSTAVE FLAUBERT, *Bouvard and Pécuchet.*
KASS FLEISHER, *Talking out of School.*

FOR A FULL LIST OF PUBLICATIONS, VISIT:
www.dalkeyarchive.com

SELECTED DALKEY ARCHIVE TITLES

WALLACE MARKFIELD,
Teitlebaum's Window.
To an Early Grave.
DAVID MARKSON, Reader's Block.
Springer's Progress.
Wittgenstein's Mistress.
CAROLE MASO, AVA.
LADISLAV MATEJKA AND KRYSTYNA
POMORSKA, EDS.,
Readings in Russian Poetics:
Formalist and Structuralist Views.
HARRY MATHEWS,
The Case of the Persevering Maltese:
Collected Essays.
Cigarettes.
The Conversions.
The Human Country: New and
Collected Stories.
The Journalist.
My Life in CIA.
Singular Pleasures.
The Sinking of the Odradek
Stadium.
Tlooth.
20 Lines a Day.
JOSEPH MCELROY,
Night Soul and Other Stories.
THOMAS MCGONIGLE,
Going to Patchogue.
ROBERT L. MCLAUGHLIN, ED., Innovations:
An Anthology of Modern &
Contemporary Fiction.
ABDELWAHAB MEDDEB, Talismano.
GERHARD MEIER, Isle of the Dead.
HERMAN MELVILLE, The Confidence-Man.
AMANDA MICHALOPOULOU, I'd Like.
STEVEN MILLHAUSER, The Barnum Museum.
In the Penny Arcade.
RALPH J. MILLS, JR., Essays on Poetry.
MOMUS, The Book of Jokes.
CHRISTINE MONTALBETTI, The Origin of Man.
Western.
OLIVE MOORE, Spleen.
NICHOLAS MOSLEY, Accident.
Assassins.
Catastrophe Practice.
Children of Darkness and Light.
Experience and Religion.
A Garden of Trees.
God's Hazard.
The Hesperides Tree.
Hopeful Monsters.
Imago Bird.
Impossible Object.
Inventing God.
Judith.
Look at the Dark.
Natalie Natalia.
Paradoxes of Peace.
Serpent.
Time at War.
The Uses of Slime Mould:
Essays of Four Decades.
WARREN MOTTE,
Fables of the Novel: French Fiction
since 1990.
Fiction Now: The French Novel in
the 21st Century.
Oulipo: A Primer of Potential
Literature.
GERALD MURNANE, Barley Patch.
Inland.

YVES NAVARRE, Our Share of Time.
Sweet Tooth.
DOROTHY NELSON, In Night's City.
Tar and Feathers.
ESHKOL NEVO, Homesick.
WILFRIDO D. NOLLEDO, But for the Lovers.
FLANN O'BRIEN, At Swim-Two-Birds.
At War.
The Best of Myles.
The Dalkey Archive.
Further Cuttings.
The Hard Life.
The Poor Mouth.
The Third Policeman.
CLAUDE OLLIER, The Mise-en-Scène.
Wert and the Life Without End.
GIOVANNI ORELLI, Walaschek's Dream.
PATRIK OUŘEDNÍK, Europeana.
The Opportune Moment, 1855.
BORIS PAHOR, Necropolis.
FERNANDO DEL PASO, News from the Empire.
Palinuro of Mexico.
ROBERT PINGET, The Inquisitory.
Mahu or The Material.
Trio.
A. G. PORTA, The No World Concerto.
MANUEL PUIG, Betrayed by Rita Hayworth.
The Buenos Aires Affair.
Heartbreak Tango.
RAYMOND QUENEAU, The Last Days.
Odile.
Pierrot Mon Ami.
Saint Glinglin.
ANN QUIN, Berg.
Passages.
Three.
Tripticks.
ISHMAEL REED, The Free-Lance Pallbearers.
The Last Days of Louisiana Red.
Ishmael Reed: The Plays.
Juice!
Reckless Eyeballing.
The Terrible Threes.
The Terrible Twos.
Yellow Back Radio Broke-Down.
JASIA REICHARDT, 15 Journeys Warsaw
to London.
NOËLLE REVAZ, With the Animals.
JOÃO UBALDO RIBEIRO, House of the
Fortunate Buddhas.
JEAN RICARDOU, Place Names.
RAINER MARIA RILKE, The Notebooks of
Malte Laurids Brigge.
JULIÁN RÍOS, The House of Ulysses.
Larva: A Midsummer Night's Babel.
Poundemonium.
Procession of Shadows.
AUGUSTO ROA BASTOS, I the Supreme.
DANIËL ROBBERECHTS, Arriving in Avignon.
JEAN ROLIN, The Explosion of the
Radiator Hose.
OLIVIER ROLIN, Hotel Crystal.
ALIX CLEO ROUBAUD, Alix's Journal.
JACQUES ROUBAUD, The Form of a
City Changes Faster, Alas, Than
the Human Heart.
The Great Fire of London.
Hortense in Exile.
Hortense Is Abducted.
The Loop.
Mathematics:
The Plurality of Worlds of Lewis.

FOR A FULL LIST OF PUBLICATIONS, VISIT:
www.dalkeyarchive.com

The Princess Hoppy.
Some Thing Black.
LEON S. ROUDIEZ, *French Fiction Revisited.*
RAYMOND ROUSSEL, *Impressions of Africa.*
VEDRANA RUDAN, *Night.*
STIG SÆTERBAKKEN, *Siamese.*
LYDIE SALVAYRE, *The Company of Ghosts.*
Everyday Life.
The Lecture.
*Portrait of the Writer as a
Domesticated Animal.*
The Power of Flies.
LUIS RAFAEL SÁNCHEZ,
Macho Camacho's Beat.
SEVERO SARDUY, *Cobra & Maitreya.*
NATHALIE SARRAUTE,
Do You Hear Them?
Martereau.
The Planetarium.
ARNO SCHMIDT, *Collected Novellas.*
Collected Stories.
Nobodaddy's Children.
Two Novels.
ASAF SCHURR, *Motti.*
CHRISTINE SCHUTT, *Nightwork.*
GAIL SCOTT, *My Paris.*
DAMION SEARLS, *What We Were Doing
and Where We Were Going.*
JUNE AKERS SEESE,
Is This What Other Women Feel Too?
What Waiting Really Means.
BERNARD SHARE, *Inish.*
Transit.
AURELIE SHEEHAN, *Jack Kerouac Is Pregnant.*
VIKTOR SHKLOVSKY, *Bowstring.*
Knight's Move.
*A Sentimental Journey:
Memoirs 1917–1922.*
Energy of Delusion: A Book on Plot.
Literature and Cinematography.
Theory of Prose.
Third Factory.
Zoo, or Letters Not about Love.
CLAUDE SIMON, *The Invitation.*
PIERRE SINIAC, *The Collaborators.*
KJERSTI A. SKOMSVOLD, *The Faster I Walk,
the Smaller I Am.*
JOSEF ŠKVORECKÝ, *The Engineer of
Human Souls.*
GILBERT SORRENTINO,
Aberration of Starlight.
Blue Pastoral.
Crystal Vision.
*Imaginative Qualities of Actual
Things.*
Mulligan Stew.
Pack of Lies.
Red the Fiend.
The Sky Changes.
Something Said.
Splendide-Hôtel.
Steelwork.
Under the Shadow.
W. M. SPACKMAN, *The Complete Fiction.*
ANDRZEJ STASIUK, *Dukla.*
Fado.
GERTRUDE STEIN, *Lucy Church Amiably.*
The Making of Americans.
A Novel of Thank You.
LARS SVENDSEN, *A Philosophy of Evil.*
PIOTR SZEWC, *Annihilation.*
GONÇALO M. TAVARES, *Jerusalem.*

Joseph Walser's Machine.
*Learning to Pray in the Age of
Technique.*
LUCIAN DAN TEODOROVICI,
Our Circus Presents . . .
NIKANOR TERATOLOGEN, *Assisted Living.*
STEFAN THEMERSON, *Hobson's Island.*
The Mystery of the Sardine.
Tom Harris.
TAEKO TOMIOKA, *Building Waves.*
JOHN TOOMEY, *Sleepwalker.*
JEAN-PHILIPPE TOUSSAINT, *The Bathroom.*
Camera.
Monsieur.
Reticence.
Running Away.
Self-Portrait Abroad.
Television.
The Truth about Marie.
DUMITRU TSEPENEAG, *Hotel Europa.*
The Necessary Marriage.
Pigeon Post.
Vain Art of the Fugue.
ESTHER TUSQUETS, *Stranded.*
DUBRAVKA UGRESIC, *Lend Me Your Character.*
Thank You for Not Reading.
TOR ULVEN, *Replacement.*
MATI UNT, *Brecht at Night.*
Diary of a Blood Donor.
Things in the Night.
ÁLVARO URIBE AND OLIVIA SEARS, EDS.,
Best of Contemporary Mexican Fiction.
ELOY URROZ, *Friction.*
The Obstacles.
LUISA VALENZUELA, *Dark Desires and
the Others.*
He Who Searches.
MARJA-LIISA VARTIO, *The Parson's Widow.*
PAUL VERHAEGHEN, *Omega Minor.*
AGLAJA VETERANYI, *Why the Child Is
Cooking in the Polenta.*
BORIS VIAN, *Heartsnatcher.*
LLORENÇ VILLALONGA, *The Dolls' Room.*
TOOMAS VINT, *An Unending Landscape.*
ORNELA VORPSI, *The Country Where No
One Ever Dies.*
AUSTRYN WAINHOUSE, *Hedyphagetica.*
PAUL WEST, *Words for a Deaf Daughter
& Gala.*
CURTIS WHITE, *America's Magic Mountain.*
The Idea of Home.
Memories of My Father Watching TV.
*Monstrous Possibility: An Invitation
to Literary Politics.*
Requiem.
DIANE WILLIAMS, *Excitability:
Selected Stories.*
Romancer Erector.
DOUGLAS WOOLF, *Wall to Wall.*
Ya! & John-Juan.
JAY WRIGHT, *Polynomials and Pollen.*
*The Presentable Art of Reading
Absence.*
PHILIP WYLIE, *Generation of Vipers.*
MARGUERITE YOUNG, *Angel in the Forest.*
Miss MacIntosh, My Darling.
REYOUNG, *Unbabbling.*
VLADO ŽABOT, *The Succubus.*
ZORAN ŽIVKOVIĆ, *Hidden Camera.*
LOUIS ZUKOFSKY, *Collected Fiction.*
VITOMIL ZUPAN, *Minuet for Guitar.*
SCOTT ZWIREN, *God Head.*